Murder in the Antarctic

A how-done it

Michael Warr

Murder in the Antarctic

Published in 2013 by FeedARead Publishing

Copyright © Michael Warr

The author asserts the moral right under the Copyright, Designs and Patents Act 1988 to be identified as the author of this work.

All Rights reserved. No part of this publication may be reproduced, stored in a retrieval system, or transmitted in any form or by any means without the prior written consent of the publisher, nor be otherwise circulated in any form of binding or cover other than that in which it is published and without a similar condition being imposed on the subsequent purchaser.

British Library C.I.P.

ACIP catalogue record for this title is available from the British Library.

PROLOG

The sea ice moved. Dave Bapton tightened his grip on Sven's collar. The cold Antarctic wind tore at his back. Through the swirling snow bloody Boyd and the husky team disappeared south. The surrounding sea ice rippled and cracked. There was a lot of cold water under Dave's feet.

The short spring trip north across Darbel Bay was a break from the cramped wooden hut shared with four other men. The winter had been fine with few disagreements. After the Mid-Antarctic festivities of June 21st the bickering increased. Most was dealt with, but Dave and Bill Barrington snapped at each other several times in the late winter months without resolving anything.

Bill would greet Dave with a: "Morning, Bapsie!" Dave would retort: "You're an idiot. Use my proper name or don't use it at all." Bill would laugh. He had someone to needle. Annoyed, Dave would return to his geological planning sheets until the next provocation. There were several months to go before the relief ship arrived.

Dave thought a short "jolly" or sledge trip might show another side of the younger and annoying Barrington, as well as a chance to examine some late Cretaceous basalt lavas. Eric Sheldon the leader of the expedition agreed. The two sledgers would have to depend on each other. On an Antarctic trip there could be no grandstanding by either Dave or Bill.

Murder in the Antarctic

The rest of the Antarctic Sheldon Expedition needed a break from the exuberant Bill Barrington. Eric's research on Adélie penguins kept him busy as several hundred birds returned to nest in the Antarctic spring. Dan Jones' daily meteorological studies carried on as they had all winter. There was no shortage of glacial ice for Ray Merton to measure.

Bill helped if he felt like it. His cooking, done every fifth day, was slow to improve. He was on the expedition as a general helper. There was a general agreement that Bill was not much help. It wasn't only his age. There was a bit of the "Tigger" in him. His father had given the expedition quite a lot of money. Bill was the downside of this agreement. This also irritated Dave.

The British government in the nineteen seventies was not supportive of private Antarctic expeditions, but had allowed seven less than perfect huskies to be acquired by Eric Sheldon. There were enough seal to feed the dogs. Supporters of non-governmental polar research raised funds for food, fuel and equipment. The Argentineans supplied the expedition with money and supplies. Dave objected to having Argentinean money supporting a British expedition.

But as Eric said: "It helps you complete your geological degree."

The Argentinean military had brought in the expedition's wooden hut sections and supplies the previous February. The site was a small promontory on the southern end of Darbel Bay on the Antarctic Peninsula. The location was deliberately well away from other countries' bases. A three-week non-stop building program raised one small hut, and allowed the five men to winter. The dogs stayed outside keeping an eye on the quickly freezing sea, the surrounding glaciers and the ice-clad mountains.

After a late start - Bill was sure there was more equipment polar explorers should have - the seven dogs pulled the loaded sledge across the gap where the sea ice moved up and down with the tides. Dave skied behind the team. Dan had mentioned a drop in air pressure. There were high clouds moving south across the blue sunlit sky. Dave and Bill reckoned they could cover the twenty or so miles to a refuge hut on the north side of Darbel Bay before the weather set in.

The dogs heaved on their chest harnesses. The sledge piled high with food and camping equipment slid well for the first half mile. A fight between Sven and Max and the two dark colored brothers, Rufus and Brutus, led to a free-for-all. Bill and Dave thumped the main culprits, untangled the pulling traces, and got the team going again. Periodically the sledge jammed in drifting wet snow.

After several hours the two men reckoned they were two-thirds of the way across the bay. Cloud covered the sky, and the mountains around the bay merged into a uniform white as the light thinned with early evening. The wind coming off the Erskine Glacier blew sharp snow into the dogs' faces. They slowed down, and the heavy sledge often stopped. Bill and Dave yelled encouragements, and pushed on the handlebars to lurch the sledge forward.

As the wind picked up the dogs tried turning back home. Dave skied ahead of the team.. Having someone in front helped the huskies for a while. Bill, now the only one pushing, no longer felt he was the tough polar explorer. Wearily he yelled at Dave: "Keep the huskies on course." And then: "We should turn back before our tracks disappear!"

Dave's thoughts were on the hut and the food the Argentineans had left in March:

"If we go for another hour we'll be OK!"

Bill grunted. Both men were soaked from the damp driven snow and the effort of keeping the sledge moving. There was a slight movement under Dave's skis. Nothing showed, but he could feel the spring sea ice starting to move up and down like a live carpet. Perhaps they should turn round. But would conditions be any better over the longer return journey?

He forged on, holding onto Jen the off-white female lead dog. Ahead in the whiteness a black band broke the surface. The sea ice had split across their path. Dave thought of the miles south to the base hut and of being swept out to sea on breaking ice floes. He yelled back at Bill, "Cross!" and pulled Jen and the rest of the team over the water gap.

The team stopped. Bill had had enough.

"Let's turn back!" as the black lead of open water widened.

Dave thought of the three men and the two dog teams that had been lost miles from land on the broken sea ice of Marguerite Bay some years ago. A storm had come up. The ice went out. The men were never found; nine of the fourteen huskies got back to land. Some of the husky traces had been cut so the dogs did not drown.

"We're closer to land if we keep going!"

"That's bullshit!"

It ended there. Sven jumped Rufus. The team fought on the moving sea ice. Dave thumped Sven, and then unhooked him to untangle his trace. Jen who had had enough of polar travel swung round. The team swept behind her, and Bill rode the sledge back across the three-foot wide water barrier. He turned and yelled:

"Come on, damn you!"

As Dave dragged the reluctant Sven to the edge the ice gap rapidly widened. More chunks of ice floated away. Bill did not stop. The wind blew snow across Dave's view to the south. The team disappeared.

"Shit!" said Dave. Holding Sven's collar he turned into the hard wind and trudged on. The refuge hut would have food and an oil stove. He supposed Sven could live on corned beef. Dave would enjoy hot beef stew and rice, followed by tropical canned fruit. After a few days of colder temperatures the sea ice would freeze up again and he could walk back to the base. Dave munched on a Cadbury's Fruit and Nut chocolate bar and for the first time thought seriously of what he was doing here.

His wife Jan had agreed he should go to the Antarctic for a year to finish his masters in geology. Dave had not been interested in his advisor's metamorphized sandstones, preferring volcanic rocks. The two parted company.

Fortunately Dr. Swanson was more amiable to this side of geomorphology, but the only quick way to get the research done without wasting a couple more years was with Sheldon's Antarctic expedition. Dr. Swanson backed Eric Sheldon in having non-governmental Antarctic research. Jan was supportive, but a year old baby girl did not make David Bapton's decision any easier. Jan had some money and her family was close by. "Just do it, Dave. I'll be fine" Dave got his affairs, his fitness and his Sheldon donations in order, and headed south.

*

The dog team with a tired and damp Bill got to the base.

"You're back. How was it? Where are Dave and Sven?" asked Eric Sheldon.

Bill leaned on the wet handle bars of the sledge as the six dogs collapsed by the seal pile. He tried to speak, but felt his words would be misinterpreted. He sat down in the wet snow. Ray unhitched the huskies and fed them. Bill was similarly treated. As he dried off he slowly mentioned the fight, the howling wind and the breaking sea ice.

"And Dave?"

"He took Sven off the team and headed towards the refuge hut. I yelled at him to come back, but he ignored me. The sea ice lead widened. He disappeared into the snow. I shouted some more, waited, but he never returned. The ice was breaking up fast. The team wouldn't cross the water again. I thought it best to head home."

"Christ!" was Dan's only comment. Eric shook his head. Ray suggested radioing for help.

Eric said: "To whom? There's no one close by. We'll wait until the sea ice freezes. Dave can get back then."

*

Bill was an arsehole. It was small comfort to Dave as he lugged Sven towards land. Eric, passionate about penguins, had organized the expedition despite a lack of funds. Dan was a reliable member and tended to keep irritants to a minimum. Ray was quiet unless someone disturbed his glacial movement stakes. Then there would be an explosion. He, too, had academic needs.

And Dave? He had enjoyed the winter despite the isolation from his family. His geology planning for the spring had gone well. He tended to rise to Bill's baits, but generally controlled himself. He just needed to complete his study of the intrusive basalt lava flows, and get home to his two girls.

For a couple of hours Dave dragged the reluctant husky into the snow-filled sharp wind. The further north they went the less the sea ice cracked. Black cliffs rising from glaciers peered through the storm. He sucked on a piece of ice. Dave needed water, food and warmth. Where was the refuge hut?

He headed towards the open side of the bay. The cliffs were too precipitous and the glaciers too broken to leave the sea ice. The only way onto solid land was immediately below the hut. Dave tramped parallel to the land with the wind beating on his right. Dog and man were soaked. A small red hut appeared on the rocks above.

*

The sea ice didn't freeze. A drop in temperature was followed by several days of gale force winds from the warmer north.

Murder in the Antarctic

Dan said: "It's unseasonable. The Antarctic Peninsula weather is brilliant, blizzardy or a bastard."

The ice pack drifted with the winds, neither firming up for travel nor clearing enough to use their small boat. At least Dave would have shelter in the hut even if he had no radio. He would have to wait until the summer relief ship got through. A week or so later Sven, the husky, was found gulping seal meat at the seal pile. There was no sign of Dave.

The expedition carried on with its studies. Eric's Adélie penguins made rock nests, courted, laid eggs, and hatched fluffy grey chicks that peeped incessantly for food. Around the rookery skuas patrolled looking for eggs or unwatched penguin chicks. They too had chicks to feed. Dan tabulated wind charts, cloud cover, and precipitation, as well as the lack of sunshine with the "warm" conditions. Ray tracked the nearby glacier's change in position with more stakes.

When glacier crevasses opened up Bill belayed Ray with a climbing rope. A lot of the time Bill fiddled, made Antarctic souvenirs such as sealskin belts, discarded them, and worked the radio, preferably when others were outside. There seemed to be a correlation between a decrease in his bounciness and the improvement in his cooking.

South-westerlies drove ice further up into Darbel Bay allowing a Chilean vessel to maneuver close to the Sheldon hut in early December.

"Did the "Seldon" Expedition need supplies?"

Eric explained about Dave being stranded at the end of the bay. The *Valparaiso* moved north, but could not get through the mass of packed ice. The Chileans returned, and entertained the four with food from a professional cook and much wine.

Bill spoke with the captain. He mentioned to Eric that he had had a radio transmission from London and needed to leave the expedition early. There were no firm reasons for Bill to stay. The others' research would carry on until the Argentinean supply vessel arrived in January. Dave would be picked up later.

In mid-January some three months after the Dave and Bill fiasco the *Puerto Norte* appeared. Eric radioed they needed to rescue Dave as soon as possible. Where was this man? Eric told them. The radioman said "Oh." The captain came on the air and explained they had not supplied the hut the previous March. There had been a miscommunication with the change over of personnel at the local base.

"We will go in and pick up your friend. He has enough food?"

Eric yelled: "Can you leave now. Dave had no food with him!"

The captain said he would not be returning to their base. The three had to pack up and leave immediately. And Dave, asked Eric?

"We will see when we get there."

Eric, Dan and Ray frantically collected their findings, packed personal possessions, and left most of their equipment as emergency supplies. Within two hours they were on board the *Puerto Norte*.

The coastline showed vertical cliffs and glaciers that dropped off into the cold sea. Any seals lay on ice floes far off shore.

The ship anchored. There was no sign of activity at the refuge hut. The motorboat chugged between ice floes and small icebergs. Eric scrambled up the snow slope to the small weather-beaten wooden hut. There was no noise or footprints. He leaned on the fragile wooden door and pushed it open…

CHAPTER ONE

Josh Fleming had not meant to die. His cruise ship *Queen of the Oceans* with over 1300 passengers left Porto Montt, Chile. It was to sail through the southern fjords to Ushuaia in Argentina and then on up to Rio de Janeiro. Josh on board was moving most of his portable possessions from California to Long Island. He was not going to die in New York. He had a massive coronary, and died somewhere south of Isla de Chiloé, Chile.

His lawyers tore away at his estate though less efficiently than hyenas at a carcass. Like doctors who ignored their own health advice Josh, a lawyer for many years, had not heeded his own legal expertise. His will was not clear. One executor lawyer could see that everything should be in California, another where it was supposed to be, in Long Island. The possessions included several million dollars worth of gold coins: American Eagles, Krugerrands, some old sovereigns, but no Chinese Pandas. Each one ounce gold coin mirrored the day's gold price per ounce.

A judicial decision or rather a compromise for the east and west lawyers left the valuables including the two thousand gold coins in an Argentinean bank in Ushuaia. Neither executor was happy. A later judgment would decide if the Fleming estate was to be cut up like a valuable diamond, or left intact and moved to one of the coasts of the States.

Leon Rosa was competent as a ship's hotel manager, but he was not in the same class as his friend Manuel the hotel manager on the *Queen of the Oceans*.

Murder in the Antarctic

As they drank whisky at the bar in the Hotel Albatros just up from the main pier at Ushuaia Manuel said:

"One trip back an American lawyer died on board my ship. He was transporting several million dollars worth of gold coins to New York. The coins are in a bank here in Ushuaia."

"Why?" asked Leon.

"The lawyers are fighting over the estate. The gold stays here until they can sort it out."

Leon's ships traveled to the Antarctic, and carried a hundred passengers or less. At forty plus, he, nearer fifty to be exact, could not see moving up to more lucrative vessels like the *Queen of the Oceans*.

His family in Mallorca had needs. These never ceased especially as the Spanish economy failed to improve. His son at twenty-three was like many of the young out of work. His daughter needed money to get to university and with no job prospects at the end. Leon's wife's demands he felt in every weekly email.

Leon took some time to think about what Manuel had said. He sent off an email, northwards, but not to Spain. More messages were sent locally.

Mark Springer received the first message. He was a retired and divorced academic who had wants rather than needs. His pension was sufficient, but he preferred wealth. Mark enjoyed traveling in South America. His knowledge of Spanish prevented any designing senioritas from dipping into his monthly allowance.

But having taken the payout from his English community college there was no going back for more. His slim calm demeanor looked at a future of limited financial horizons. There had also been questions about his academic "help" of a certain sixteen-year-old female student. This still hung like an albatross.

Leon and he had shared their needs and wants a year or so back. They were in the bar as their Antarctic bound ship plunged southwards from Ushuaia through a storm. Other passengers kept to their bunks. The two had come to a mutual understanding.

Over a hundred years ago Ushuaia was a prison of last resort for those considered by the Argentinean authorities as incorrigible. Ushuaia at the extreme southern end of Argentina was now a major port. Instead of prisoners taking a slow month's boat journey shackled to other prisoners, there were tourists flocking there in a three-hour flight from Buenos Aires.

Visitors wanted to go to El Fin del Mundo, the end of the world. Unlike much of Argentina's economy travelers and money flowed into the city. The draw was the frozen ice, two days journey south. Ninety percent of the visitors to the Antarctic left from Ushuaia.

On a bright windy morning in mid-November tourists cruised the main street, San Martin. There was Popper S.A., a sports store, Eduardo's for camera needs, La Ultima Bita, for handicrafts such as stuffed penguins, Atlantico Sur, the duty free store, and many other tiendas. The post office was not yet open, but a line of people stood on the stairs leading up from the street. The locals dropped into Tante Sara for a cortado, black coffee with a shot of milk.

The tourists rarely headed up the steep side streets away from the main avenue. Once the cold Museo Presido, the old prison, was checked out and photographed, the visitors moved back to the commercial center of town past gardens of blue lupins and red oriental poppies blazing in the cool wind.

Outside a bank on San Martin a queue a block long stretched along the sidewalk. Like most Argentinean banks there were only three tellers to deal with a lot of customers. Most bank employees toiled away at the back. It was not ten o'clock. The customers could wait.

Two people, by their wool hats, hooded puff jackets, dark glasses and gloves, obviously from elsewhere, stood at the head of the line next to the bank guard. At the opening of the doors an envelope was slipped into the guard's pocket, and the two entered through the shiny doors. The guard raised his hand to stop others from following.

Inside the bank one of the two strangers turned and chained the doors shut. Both put on gas masks, and as a teller squealed two smoke bombs bounced behind the counter. A bank official scrambling to push the alarm button was smashed on the back of the head with the butt of a gun. The rest of the staff lowered themselves to the floor as the sawn off guns waved the employees down to the right position.

A small plump sweating bank manager opened the vault with a gun pushed into the back of his head. His eyes streamed from the gas. Bank bags filled from the vault left for the front door.

The chained doors were unlocked. The guard turned and was knocked down with a blow to the side of the head. He slumped to the sidewalk. Ten loaded bags were carried out to a black Renault that had eased up to the curb. The car roared east along San Martin towards the Naval Base on Avenida Yaganes. Sirens screamed in the distance as the onlookers gasped, pointed and raised their smart phones for that special photograph.

Police cars rushed to the site. Officers fell back from the bank entrance as gas swirled, and bank employees gasped, cried and coughed their way out. The guard remained comatose. One police car headed east to the Barrio General Belgrano in the general direction where the Renault had disappeared.

More police arrived as did a TV crew from Channel 11, a radio crew and a local reporter for El Diario del Fin del Mundo. The police put on gas masks and searched the building. Innumerable interviews were put to the bank employees. The bank guard would be questioned later. He was taken to the hospital at the end of Av. Maipú. Sirens played in the distance as the getaway car was hunted.

Inside the bank a side exit door was open. Where were the two robbers and what else had been taken?

By the Hotel Albatros multiple pieces of luggage were piled for later delivery to an Antarctic cruise ship. Most of a tour group climbed into three buses for the visit to the extensive Parque Nacional that bordered Chile twelve kilometers to the west. The tourists would be back at Ushuaia at four pm to join their Antarctic bound-ship the *Polar Adventurer*. A few preferred to keep their land legs as long as possible, and strolled around Ushuaia until it was time to board the ship.

CHAPTER TWO

"An Antarctic cruise? Isn't that a contradiction even for the twenty-first century?"

"The ship's warm and comfortable and we sail the Antarctic seas."

"So what do you do all day?"

"We look at birds, wild life, the sea, and the scenery"

"You commune with nature?"

"That's right. There's no shopping, no casinos, no dancing, no midnight all-you-can-eat chocolate desserts, no swimming pools, no games, no sing-along piano bar, no wine tasting, no -"

"In other words, it's not my type of cruise. But why would you or anyone else want to go there?"

"It's unlike any other destination. Apart from being vast the Antarctic is isolated. You travel two days by plane just to get to the port where you take a ship that travels another two days to get to the ice. And the weather can make landings uncertain."

"A lot of travel for what?"

"Spectacular glittering icy scenery, majestic mountains and unusual wildlife. It's different."

"Sounds dull."

"No, not dull. Peaceful."

*

The gleaming white *Queen of the Oceans* reared up some fourteen stories high. Well-heeled passengers and crew moved around the weather decks, drinks and canapés in hand.

"Welcome to your Antarctic 'ome! It's not the ship on the left, but the nicer ship on the right! Please take all your handbags with you. Your luggage is already in your cabin."

Felix the local guide on Jim McKinnon's bus waved his arms and himself towards the *Polar Adventurer*, a small mottled one time blue-colored ship. The three tour buses unloaded a hundred passengers. Most people headed up the narrow gangway. Some looked rather wistfully back up at the larger ship.

"What do you think it carries, two thousand?"

Jim and a handful of others went further down the pier to snap a picture of their cruise ship, their home for the next couple of weeks. The city of Ushuaia spread along the Tierra del Fuego coastline in the cool November afternoon. The sharp dark peaks of the Andes loomed over the city. On the mountains the tree line changed to grass then rock powdered with light snow.

By the ship a few heavily built birds flapped slowly off the water into the steady west wind. Distant blue and white Argentinean flags flapped towards the Beagle Channel.

One of the passengers remarked to Jim: "Not a bad place for being the most southerly city in the world. It's been around for over a hundred years."

"Has it? I haven't seen the place. My plane was delayed in Buenos Aires."

"Typical. I always travel via Santiago in Chile. It's the quickest way to get to the southern end of Argentina."

"You've been here before?"

"Several times. My name's Mark." His accent was British and educated.

"I'm Jim."

"Canadian?"

"Yes, though a lot of Brits think I'm American."

"Typical."

"Are all these ships going to the Antarctic?" Jim pointed at four vessels tied up on either side of the concrete pier.

"Yes except for the big one. That came from Rio. It's on it way to Valparaiso, Chile."

"Do a lot of ships head to the Antarctic?"

"More than thirty in a season. They each do several trips from November to March. Thousands of tourists go every year. It's big business getting people to the icy wastes. Especially as the large cruise ships are no longer allowed to go into the Antarctic waters."

"And the reason?" asked Jim.

"Their heavy fuel was too polluting so now only the smaller ships head south. But at least with those you can land in Antarctica. Well, I suppose we should get this show on the road. We don't want to be left behind."

Jim followed Mark up the ribbed gangway to where a smartly dressed officer swept them into the ship.

"Welcome aboard, Mr. Stringer!"

"Leon, let me introduce Jim. He's from Canada."

"Mr. James McKinnon?" as he looked at his check board. "Welcome to the *Polar Adventurer*. Your cabin is down below, 136. Mr. Stringer, your usual cabin is upstairs."

Large pieces of luggage were manhandled along corridors by crewmembers followed by anxious passengers. Downstairs on the port side at the waterline Jim opened the door to a small cabin. The two bottom bunks were already taken.

"First come, first served as they say. We can swap later if you like."

Jim knew by the tone of the large florid man lying on the left bunk that once they were settled in there would be little chance of a change. The second occupant, a slim dark-haired man was neatly packing clothes into a lower drawer.

Jim's one large piece of black luggage took up the middle of the cabin. His bunk was above the red-faced man's. A small ladder led to a narrow bed space above.

Making the best of the situation Jim said: "I'm Jim."

"Pleased to meet you," replied the man in the bunk. "Me name's Martin. I'm Irish, as you can no doubt tell."

"I'm Alec." His accent was mid-Atlantic. He left carrying a large pair of binoculars.

"At least with Alec watching birds all day we'll have more room down here. Once you've unpacked, stuff your bag underneath the porthole table."

Jim asked, "Can't we open that cover?" A large metal cover blocked the light.

"No, we're too close to water. Going to the Falkland Islands the waves would smash through the glass. You need to make sure you turn on the light every time you enter the cabin. The term deadlight is appropriate for that porthole cover." Martin chuckled and turned over.

After two days of flying and waiting around airports, Jim was glad to be in one place though he still felt muzzy. He unpacked. Mostly it was clothes, but he had brought along Shakespeare's *As You Like It* to show he had some culture. Normally he preferred reading thrillers. There was going to be plenty of time to read, especially at sea.

The ship's PA "Bing-bonged" through the ship. "Welcome to your Antarctic adventure! We'll meet in the lounge in ten minutes. It's on the fourth level. See you there!"

Jim shoved his unpacked bag under the table and headed upstairs. Martin stayed. The Antarctic adventurers moved as a herd up through the different levels. On the walls Jim saw photographs of Arctic and Antarctic wildlife; most were professionally taken. He found himself in a large room. Some passengers stood, others found seats, and a few claimed places for latecomers. Large windows overlooked the eastern end of Ushuaia. The gigantic cruise ship blocked the portside view.

The ship's hotel staff handed out slim glasses of Argentinean champagne. Most of the talk among the passengers was muted except for a young blond American who was exclaiming:

"I heard shots from the bank, I smelled tear gas, and then this black car rolled up. Two men dragged lots of loaded bags out of the bank. They threw them in the car. It took off down San Martin."

"Where was it going?" asked one passenger.

"Who knows, but the police were swarming around like crazy. I've got some shots on my camera." He pulled his massive Nikon out of its bag. By then only one or two passengers were interested. Before the epic photographs could be shown a loud voice boomed out from the lounge entrance:

"Hello there! I'm Boyd!" A large British man strode in. "Welcome to my Antarctic trip! I'm glad you could make it!" He looked around at everyone. Most were bemused.

Before he could continue, a sharp English voice broke in behind him:

"Thank you, Boyd! My welcome has been upstaged, but you will enjoy our Antarctic expedition." A medium-sized energetic man stood in front of them.

"I'm Greg, your expedition leader. There has been a slight delay. Some luggage did not arrive. One passenger is up in Ushuaia with the assistant expedition leader, Elsa, buying waterproof clothing. So I'll save the staff introductions for later.

"Each day's great adventure will be posted on your cabin door though like everything else in the Antarctic plans can change. We travel to the Falkland Islands, the island of South Georgia and then on to the great Antarctic continent.

"Remember, the fifth largest continent is the coldest, the highest, the windiest, and unexpectedly, the driest place in the world. And finally, please wear your nametag. Then we'll know who you are, even if you don't.

"Now here is the most important person on board who never needs a name tag, our own captain, Captain Engstrom."

A wide-shouldered uniformed man with grey hair and a Scandinavian accent said:

"Welcome to my ship. I know you will have a good trip to the Antarctic. We have an open bridge policy, but please do not interfere with the officers and crew in their duties." He stopped abruptly.

Of all the cruise ships in all of the world ports to meet like this. Jim recognized the captain from his summer trips up to the Arctic twenty years earlier, when they both were a lot slimmer. They still swapped cards at Christmas.

Greg spoke again: "And another important person on board, our hotel manager, Leon!"

The dark slim officer, who had greeted Mark and Jim, talked about laundry, the open door policy for each cabin, though valuables could be put in a safety box, and of course, no penguins allowed on your bunks.

"On most days Happy Hour is from five until dinner, and then after dinner until our bar tender, Sandy, has had enough of you!"

A voice from the back called out: "How much are the drinks?"

Leon smoothly answered: "Like all voyages there are surprises."

A young American doctor took the floor.

"I understand that you are all fit Antarctic explorers, so my main concern is seasickness. Some people forget there's two days of sea travel before you get to Antarctica. So have your pills, bracelets, ginger ale and ear patches ready before we hit the open sea early tomorrow morning. And if all fails I have an injection guaranteed to put you flat on your back."

Captain Engstrom stepped forward again:

"A mandatory boat drill will be carried out after we leave Ushuaia. When you hear the alarms head to your cabins and bring your life jackets to the muster stations. You will find your station on a sign in your cabin."

Greg followed with: "So until the boat drill, explore the ship and each other, though not too thoroughly."

There were a few groans.

As the captain moved past him, Jim stepped forward and said: "Captain Engstrom, I…"

The captain stepped around him and said sharply:

"Excuse me. I am needed on the bridge."

Affronted, Jim moved past others to the rear of the room and out on to the deck, not quite sure what had happened. Hadn't Second Officer Eric Engstrom and he drunk aquavit together on the Arctic transport *Tromso* from Halifax up to Iqualuit on Baffin Island for two summers? Well, captains had to keep their distance. But what about their exchange of Christmas cards every year? What happened there?

Below, shore men loosened hawsers. Bow thrusters pushed the *Polar Adventurer* away from the pier. The ship moved eastward along the Beagle Channel between Argentinean Tierra del Fuego and Chile. Sea birds flapped along behind.

Jim would take a seasick pill later. Seven short blasts and one long sounded. He fought his way downstairs as others swarmed up. He grabbed the remaining lifejacket, and joined the throng by muster station two. Some passengers nervously asked if their lifejackets were on properly. An officer adjusted one or two errant orange jackets.

Greg, the expedition leader said: "Congratulations everyone, and especially muster station one which was the fastest. Dinner is next up, but do keep one hand on the ship at all times. Some passengers gaily headed downstairs with no hands on the rails. In rough seas they'll find themselves lying battered in the sick bay."

Passengers waited downstairs by the dining room. Some had not paid too much attention to the casual clothing suggestions given on the expedition's website. Two men wore suits and ties. Their wives displayed expensive evening gowns. They were probably the ones with the five oversized suitcases Jim had seen being wrestled through the corridors. Many of the passengers wore clothes by Eddie Bauer, Patagonia and North Face. Jim was satisfied with his cheaper Columbia jacket.

At the "Bing-bong" a Filipino headwaiter opened the doors and the diners surged in. Jim had noticed a slim dark haired woman at the head of the line. Her shoulders looked like a model's, but her figure would have been too full for the fashion industry. As she turned off to a table, Jim followed. He remembered he was no longer married. Jim smiled at her. She nodded. An Australian couple asked if there was room at the table followed by Alec, one of Jim's cabin mates, and a shorthaired woman.

The blunt-looking woman with the short brown hair said: "I'm Kim. I'm from North London. Where are you all from?" as a young waitress, tagged as Rosa, asked: "Soup or salad, please?"

The Australian couple smiled and said:
"Well, we're from Melbourne."
"State of Victoria, OK?"
"Actually, Hawthorne, a nice part of the city."
"It's pretty there."
"I'm John and she's…"
"Marcia."

Kim hurriedly asked Jim, "And where are you from?" The arrival of the soup and salad interrupted his reply. Around them in the dining room there was a murmur as strangers introduced themselves.

Jim said: "I'm from British Columbia."

"Oh, Vancouver!"

"Well, not quite…"

"Been there several times, a great city!"

He did not feel like explaining that he lived several hours' north of Vancouver. He smiled ruefully at the dark haired woman. She looked back at him.

Without getting Jim's name, Kim turned to the dark haired woman: "And you are?"

"I'm Carol, from Portsmouth, England."

Another server asked if anyone wanted something to drink. John and Marcia ordered a bottle of red Argentinean Malbec wine.

Alec had somehow gained his main course of grilled chicken, eaten it, and left before he could be interrogated. Jim said that Alec was probably bird watching.

"That's interesting," said Carol. "I'm keen on birding"

Oh, thought Jim who was not overly interested in flying animals.

"I'm not keen on birds," said Kim. "I prefer mammals. They don't flit around."

Jim ate his Argentinean beef and oven roasted potatoes and looked at Carol's amused face whenever he could. She gave him the odd glance.

Kim suddenly looked up and said, "It's not fair!"

The table searched for the complaint.

"Why do *those* people get to sit with the captain?" Five passengers including Mark Stringer were at a reserved table.

"I thought we were all equal here!"

Jim thought of Mark's upstairs cabin, and started to say: "We're all equal but some are more equal…"

"It's not fair that money talks!"

The group carried on eating.

CHAPTER THREE

Well, that went well. Because the bank robbery could be done it was done. Any problems were academic, and were solved by an academic by the name of Mark Stringer. But shots were fired according to that young man? I heard none. The only glitch was with my companion who almost lost his nerve. I smashed the butt of my AR 15 semi automatic on a metal cabinet to get him refocused on relieving the bank of its wealth. The special pieces from the 4x4 were transferred to another vehicle, and then hidden in my luggage. The four bags were dropped off at the Hotel Albatross.

The luggage remained in my cabin. My companion popped by after dinner and took his two pieces. What he did with them I know not. One of mine was under some academic books guarded by an electronic lock-and-key device. The second one was placed in a hidden recess away from my cabin.

And the two guns used, you ask, what of them? I told my accomplice to lose them with the car. I employ the KISS principle. To mix expressions too many wrinkles in an operation can cause problems.

*

Greg, the expedition leader, stood up in front of the room, and with a microphonic voice, hoped that everyone had had a great meal. He introduced the staff of varying nationalities that included two birders, a historian and a geologist.

"Most of our staff will be driving Zodiac boats for our wet landings. And George, our Australian photographer," a small dark haired man smiled, "will help you get great shots, especially for those who've bought brand new cameras and haven't looked at the manuals!"

One or two passengers shared guilty looks.

"Our staff will be giving you talks on the Antarctic. They're all very knowledgeable."

"I bet!" said an elderly man from a table close to Jim's.

"And over there," said Greg, "we have several ex-Antarctic men who have actually lived down south and will *add* to your Antarctic experience."

Several loud: "Of course!" and "Sure, any time!" were returned.

"The rest of the evening is yours. The bar upstairs is open. We will be in the Beagle Channel until early in the morning. Make sure you take your seasick remedies. Between South America and the Falkland Islands it can be rough, and I'm not just talking about the politics."

Carol slipped away before Jim could make the comment: did they need *two* birders? The elderly Antarctic men rose before Jim like a phalanx. He followed at their heels. They slowly made their way up the stairs to the bar at the side of the lounge. Jim was torn between joining Carol, and learning from those who had lived in the Antarctic. He compromised: Carol first, then the bar.

She stood on the aft deck looking at the seabirds. As smooth as the ship's movement through the sea, Jim asked where Alec was birding.

"I think he prefers the bridge. I like the stern so I can smoke." Seeing Jim's face she said quickly: "Only occasionally. Are you interested in birds?"

"So-so," trying not to be completely out of it.

"OK, so what's this bird?" Carol pointed to a gull-like bird rapidly skimming towards them over the gray-green water.

"A gull?"

"Well, so-so is correct. It's a tern. I see I'm going to have my work cut out for me."

Jim smiled: "I'd like that."

"Of course, if you don't come up to scratch…" She left the rest unsaid.

"I didn't have a chance to explain where I was from."

"I gather it wasn't Vancouver."

"No, several hours north. There are trees, trees and more trees."

"And birds?"

"Yes, though I'm sure we have fewer varieties than you have around Portsmouth."

"The Antarctic is like your area, a small variety of birds, but lots of them." She smiled. They watched the grey albatross like-birds riding the air in the wake of the *Polar Adventurer*.

"Those birds had difficulty in taking off at Ushuaia."

"They're giant petrels. GPs to the initiated. They're scavengers. Sometimes they vomit their food so they can get off the water."

"Nice. Is this your first visit to Antarctica?"

"It is. And you?"

"I worked in the Arctic many years ago, and now I want to see the southern Polar Regions. You traveled all this way to see birds?"

"Yes."

They looked out at the channel as the light dimmed.

"The sea birds will keep searching for food while we sleep." Carol turned to Jim, "I'm not a great sailor so I may sleep in tomorrow morning. I'll see you later." She brushed his arm, and left. For Jim the voyage would be more than just wildlife and scenery. A drink and some Antarctic facts would finish the day off nicely.

*

Peter the passenger who had seen the bank robbery tried to explain where the loot as he called it could have gone.

"There's Chile, just next to that national park. There's the city Rio Grande further north on Tierra del Fuego or even Buenos Aires. And the money might have even been flown out of Argentina all together. What do you think?"

One or two of the bar clients said: "I suppose so." This was an Antarctic cruise not another boring smash and grab like back home.

Boyd was satisfied with his earlier Antarctic welcome to the newcomers. He gazed over the lounge. Not having been back south for a few years he was interested to see how life had changed in the Antarctic. He tucked himself into one end of the curved wooden bar. Multicolored bottles reflected in a wide mirror. A steady stream of passengers asked Sandy, a medium-sized, plump, cheerful young woman, for their favorite drink.

He had already requested a malt whisky. As Boyd willingly exclaimed to anyone who cared to listen or not: "You get a better hangover with malts." Of course, the more expensive and older the malt, the better. He was working on a twelve year old McCallan. The ship didn't carry the eighteen year old. It was too pricey.

"Hello, Frank! Where are the rest?" Boyd called out.

A stocky bald and bearded man limped up to the bar and collapsed on the nearest stool.

"They're coming. We're a little ways down the hall from you."

"You'll have…?"

"My usual, thanks."

Sandy handed over a rum and coke before the next Antarctic adventurer butted in at the bar. The two unmarried ex-Antarctic men gazed over the room as newbies to the Antarctic gathered and chatted.

"Well, it's the quiet before a blizzard of penguin photos pop out of their laptops." Frank mournfully drained his drink and asked Sandy for another, when she could.

Boyd broke in with, "Maybe we should have a trip with only a boat-load of ex-Antarctic types, and no encumbrances."

"What's that, Boyd? You don't love me any more?" A petite, perky woman in a fashionable blue dress led in a short grey-haired man.

"Georgina, my sweet! And Arthur!"

"By the number of grey bearded males we must be back with the old Antarctic hands," said Georgina.

"What do you mean *old*? By encumbrances, I didn't mean you, of course," as Boyd pecked her cheek, "only these uninitiated types hanging around the lounge."

"Oh?" Georgina said: "So, when did I ever live in the Antarctic?"

Boyd was saved a reply by an Australian voice interrupting: "Is this where one can learn about the real Antarctic as opposed to lectures?"

A bluff, chunky man with a few sandy hairs and a red face looked at the group.

"I'm interested in hearing about Antarctica." Doug introduced himself, and suggested buying a round. The offer was refused, and Sandy was told in no uncertain terms by Boyd to get her beautiful body over here so they could all have some more drinks. Jim standing nearby already had a glass of red Malbec wine bought after he had reluctantly parted from his newfound friend, Carol.

Boyd started the ball rolling by explaining that his experiences were not the same as Arthur and Frank's. *His* first Antarctic expedition had been a private one. *They* had been civil servants, part of the British government's study of the Antarctic.

"We at least didn't have to go begging to sponsors for food," was Arthur's contribution for the evening.

Boyd explained that after that Antarctic expedition he had joined the Americans at McMurdo, a government base, but at least it was the real Antarctic. Where cold was cold, not mildly cold as happened along the Antarctic Peninsula. He turned to Doug:

"Do you know that the rest of the Antarctic refers to this peninsula that they were going to as the *Banana Belt*?

"At least we had weather," said Frank. "At McMurdo it's either cold and sunny or cold and cloudy. In the Antarctic Peninsula you can get several weathers in one day. I'm all for change."

Georgina rolled her eyes and said: "I'm going to leave you men to your old battles." She moved down the lounge with her G and T to find less parochial company.

Doug asked about the old days. Had they camped and had they used huskies? The rest of the lounge was content to talk of where they were from and what they did or did not do for jobs.

Boyd told him of ice tide cracks where human waste was dumped, and seeing husky pups coming back from the sea ice with what looked like frozen sausages in their mouths.

Despite his limp Frank demonstrated how he would move from one building to another in a blizzard using guide ropes.

"Jesus Christ!" hissed Boyd. A woman in a pale mauve dress slowly made her way into the lounge. The short dress clung invitingly to her body; her pale straw hair hung to her shoulders. Amethyst earrings dangled invitingly below each ear. The cool bright well made-up face scanned the room. She glided towards the group, and only then did Jim notice her purple high heels and dark magenta fingernails. The crowd at the bar parted like the Red Sea.

"Name your poison!" said Boyd.

Frank interjected: "Very smooth, Boyd!"

Murder in the Antarctic

The mauve clinging figure spoke with a New York accent: "No. It's the best poison around. I'll have a gin and lime. I'm Rachel."

Rachel wore her age and her money well. She beamed at the mature men around her. Her face lingered a little longer on Jim, the youngest one there. The room seemed a little warm. Jim had a mental image – Carol? Rachel? Both?

She gave the men small tokens of herself. Certainly she had acted, and still posed for a few fashion magazines. Yes, she lived in New York. It wouldn't get too cold, here, would it? Reassurances were given. Mind you the wind could get a bit nippy.

Rachel sounded out each male and where they were from. Most of the British men were from the southern counties near London. Doug the Australian was from Adelaide. The interrogator gazed on Jim for some time. He explained he was from Canada.

Further details of jobs, loves, likes and dislikes were cut short by the return of Georgina who said it was time for her to retire. Arthur dutifully followed his wife. Doug who had limited himself to one drink said that he was off too. Jim left with the general exodus. Rachel had another gin, and sauntered around the lounge sizing up females as well as males. Boyd clung to the bar hoping for more polar amateurs to drop by to listen to his Antarctic experiences or at least buy him a drink.

CHAPTER FOUR

Jim's clothes drawer slammed open a few times. He sat up, banged his head on the low ceiling, and fell back. The morning filtered around the deadlight as the room rolled with the waves. From below Martin said:

"I'll fix it. You didn't push the knob in far enough."

Jim gingerly climbed down the ladder. He grabbed a washroom rail, wrapped the plastic curtain around the shower, and had a quick wash. Water sloshed back and forth across his feet as the waves hit the ship's port side. There were no interruptions from the other cabin that shared the washroom. Jim thought they were from Germany.

With bent knees he dressed slowly as the ship moved under him. Alec's bunk was empty. The early birder sees the bird. The walls creaked as Jim gingerly moved up the different levels while hanging on to the wooden banisters. White vomit bags were planted strategically along the way.

On the open weather deck the wind grabbed his jacket. Jim slid open the bridge door. The noise outside stopped abruptly as he closed the door. On the left side of the bridge house Alec stared intently at the waves rolling ahead and at the grey sky.

On the right side an officer with two stripes stood by the chart table. The ship had a steering wheel, but no helmsman. Jim looked around recognizing automatic instruments, the radar, the engine controls, and the wind speed indicator similar to when he had been on a ship twenty years ago. The GPS screen with its yellow line pointing up to the top right hand corner was new to him. A few giant petrels drifted past the windows. In the distance a large white bird with black upper wings grew in size, and glided over the waves, turned on what looked like one wing feather, and sailed away.

"What was that?" asked Jim.

Alec grunted: "A black-browed albatross. There are thousands of them in the Falklands.

"It's very graceful."

Alec didn't answer.

Greg stepped on to the bridge, nodded at the officer, checked the course, smiled at the two passengers, and picked up a microphone. There was "Bing-bong."

"Good morning. It is the first day of day of our voyage to Antarctica. The temperature is 6°C. It's a brisk breezy day, 6 on the Beaufort scale. The wind is westerly at 25 knots. So hang onto the railings. We are heading towards the Falkland Islands. We are at 55° south, 65° west. Breakfast will be from 8 o'clock to 9:30.

"As you saw from your daily program our historian will give a short talk on the Falkland Islands at 10. Lunch is at 12. In the afternoon one of our birders will discuss the birds of the southern oceans. There are several birds flying along with the ship. And as Robert Cushman Murphy said so eloquently: 'I now belong to the higher cult of mortals, for I have seen the albatross.'"

When Greg finished Jim asked him if he could show his Arctic slides sometime. Greg said maybe on the way back across the Drake Passage, and left.

Jim was about to head down to breakfast when the rear door to the bridge swung open and Captain

Engstrom entered. The second officer straightened up, and said good morning. The captain nodded.

He turned to Jim.

"We met many years ago in the Arctic?"

Jim said: "Yes," and waited. Why was the captain still pretending not to really know him too well?

Captain Engstrom went on: "I have some Arctic slides I would like to show you. Come to my cabin at 10 o'clock"

Jim mentioned the talk on the Falkland Islands.

"Do not worry about that. I will tell you all you need to know about the Falklands."

Jim was puzzled at the captain's change in manner, but at least he had been recognized.

Breakfast was buffet style for the few passengers who were up. There was a great selection of cereals, fruit, porridge, yoghurt, toast, several jams, eggs, bacon, sausages, and pancakes. Jim would have to watch his own spread.

He took his plate over to Boyd sitting by a window who looked up and said:

"I'm Boyd. You were with our little bar group last night. And why are we still in the bloody Beagle Channel and not at sea?"

Jim said he had got up early for the washroom. The ship had turned around in the Beagle Channel and returned to Ushuaia during the night. On the lit pier he had seen a man being loaded into a white van. The word "Urgencias" was on the side. Must have been an ambulance.

"Some sort of accident I suppose. He won't be heading south. And you are?"

"I'm Jim from Canada.

"Ah, a colonial who's interested in the Antarctic."

Jim had not heard the word "colonial" for sometime.

"I've spent a couple of summers in the Arctic."

Boyd retorted: "That's nothing. I spent a winter with Eskimos on Ellesmere Island, ran huskies, and gutted and ate seal with the locals. Of course, the real polar stuff is in the south. I've been to the Antarctic several times including spending a frigid winter with the Americans in McMurdo. They're generous, but get a little too bureaucratic for my liking. Yes, real life is the Antarctic." He paused to carve up his fried egg.

"Eskimos?" The Arctic people in Canada were called Inuit. With an effort Jim turned the conversation back to Antarctica:

"What do you think about Scott and Shackleton?"

"Overrated. Shackleton was lucky and Scott was a nincompoop. Neither had much use for dogs. And why is that table rabbiting on in Dutch? Isn't this a British trip?"

Perhaps because they are Dutch Jim said to himself.

"There are too many foreigners here. If you can't speak English, don't come!"

"Most of them speak English."

"Then they should stick to it!"

With an effort Jim brought the conversation back to a neutral area.

"You drove dogs in the Antarctic?"

"Certainly. I tell you all about it at our bar sessions." Boyd wiped egg off his chin, lumbered to his feet, nodded at the headwaiter Daniel, ignored the waitress who had cleaned his dishes away, and headed for the door.

For variety Jim was going to sit at different mealtime tables. Boyd would be avoided.

He wandered up to the lounge which was lined with an odd mixture of mahogany and plastic board. Passengers were opening their journals for the first Antarctic entry. Jim saw some dark colored sea birds trailing the *Polar Adventurer*. Carol would know what they were. Stuffed from breakfast, he made a note to frequent the small gym.

On the bridge Jim joined Alec and Bob, one of the staff birders. A list of birds already seen was posted on a board. Ricardo, the other staff birder, from Chile, joined them. There was a brief argument whether one bird was a juvenile or the female of a similar species. Jim hadn't seen the bird clearly, and hadn't a clue what it was. A P.A. announcement gave a ten-minute heads up for the ten o'clock lecture. All the passengers except Alec left the bridge. Jim took the inside staircase and knocked on the captain's door.

Captain Engstrom rose from his desk:

"God morgon."

Jim remembered his bit of Norwegian: "Godday," (hello).

The captain smiled and shook his hand. The Norwegian's English had not changed in twenty years. Jim's Norwegian had almost disappeared.

"I am sorry about yesterday. You will understand when I explain my problem. But first, a drink to old and new times."

Jim's normal mid-morning drink was over-brewed coffee not Linie aquavit, a strong liquor tasting of coriander. But he didn't argue.

"You remember the Linie story about sending aquavit to Australia and back to make it smoother?"

Jim gasped a "Ja!" as the drink went down, and waited.

"We first met in the Canadian Arctic all those years ago. You were working as a surveyor?"

"A geologist's helper."

"So. We got on well and have kept in contact every Christmas?"

Jim nodded. Captain Engstrom hesitated.

"I need your help with something. It is important, but it will not interfere with your trip."

Jim's vision of a relaxing holiday in an unusual part of the world disappeared like an ice cream left out on a hot day, not one in sitting in the Antarctic. He used to be a policeman, and was now a security consultant. so why wouldn't the captain use Jim?

"It is not difficult. You know about the bank robbery in Ushuaia, the day we left, yes?"

"Er, yes."

"It's a lot of nonsense, but the Argentinean authorities want to make sure the money is not on any ship that's just left port, even one going to the Antarctic."

"Even this one?"

"Yes. The police are scouring Tierra del Fuego and have come up short. You could listen and broach the robbery with the passengers, say at the lounge bar. Maybe you could find something. I will do a search of the ship, but do not talk with my crew. They are not involved. Your inquiry would put my mind at ease as well as those Argentinean minds."

"One passenger saw the robbery," said Jim. "He was outside the bank when the ruckus erupted."

"What?" asked the captain.

"When the robbery took place"

"Oh, well you could start with him. If you need to talk to me ask to copy some of my Arctic flower slides. Only contact me if you have something real."

Jim's pedantic streak surfaced: "Concrete?"

"Quite. You will do this for me?"

They chatted a while about the old Arctic days. Then Jim was dismissed. He would have to discuss this Ushuaia bank holdup. The passengers certainly wouldn't want to be questioned. They were on holiday. And if they were behind the robbery they would say nothing or deny everything. All this before they returned to South America in a couple of weeks.

Jim's annoyance with Captain Engstrom and himself for agreeing to the request increased. Hell! He had taken time off of his security job. He was drained. There had been too many after-hours and weekends watching unrelated spouses making moves on each other. That life had helped break up his marriage with Janet. Jim needed a second wind not more detective work. But he was an ex-policeman. He would do his duty and deal with the situation. Jim toted his burdens down to the aft deck.

CHAPTER FIVE

At the stern of the ship a few passengers attempted to photograph the fast moving birds sailing past. Carol stubbed a cigarette out at the side of the lounge. He smiled at her. Her wide mouth tried a reply, but it looked as if the sea had been working her over.

"How are you feeling?"

"Like your birding, so-so." Her dark hair whipped in front of her pale face. Her eyes looked large and strained.

"Did you want to walk or stay put?"

Carol said, "I'll stay. Everything else is moving. I feel better watching the birds."

Jim asked about the blackish birds he saw earlier. She said that they were sooty shearwaters. Jim was not much further ahead, but at least Carol was talking to him. He mentioned the bird list.

"I'll have to contribute," she said and was silent.

Did he start with the mundane: what do you do in the UK, or should he talk about the Antarctic stories from last night? He had an image of figure in a mauve dress. Jim talked about his job.

"I teach at a secondary school. I've taken time off to recharge my batteries." What does it do to a relationship if you start off with a lie, he wondered? He would have to remember to keep up his teacher persona.

"I'm a post operative nurse. I'm on holiday."

"Have you worked in operating rooms?"

"Been there, done that. You stand around too much. I prefer to move around and deal with people who are at least awake and not comatose."

Questions about relationships, including his own, could wait until later. Jim's separation still rankled after six months, especially as a lot of it was his own fault. He had not spent enough time with Janet, and had ignored her needs. Mind you she had already found someone who worked the regular nine to five hours.

"Did you hear about that bank hold up the day we left Ushuaia?"

"No, should I have done?"

"I don't think so." Jim would bring the topic up again later. His next nondescript question was answered by:

"Maybe soup and crackers."

He mentioned Boyd's belligerence, and suggested they try another lunch table. Jim also wanted to avoid Kim the nosy and demonstrative woman at dinner last night. He hoped there weren't too many more awkward types on board. Jim had already heard Kim complaining to the hotel manager that the cabin she was assigned was too small. She had torn a strip off Leon. Passenger abuse of hotel staff was part of the job, thought Jim.

"Well, you can always sit with me." Her pale face opened up. Carol's blue eyes contrasted with her brunette hair and dark eyebrows. With a wide soft mouth she looked if she was always smiling and happy. As Jim found out later that assumption could be a mistake.

There were more Antarctic travelers at lunch though the conversations were muted. The buffet had several salads, two types of meat, a fish dish, a vegetarian dish of some sort, and several desserts. As the sea was still roughing up the ship, the pea soup was brought to the table by the hotel staff. Jim and Carol joined Mark, grey-haired and slightly pale, who sat alone.

For Carol's benefit Jim asked Mark: "How many times have you sailed south?"

"A few times. The sea parts are the toughest. I must say you look horribly healthy compared to the rest of us."

"I don't get sea sick very often."

Mark and Carol shared a look of disapproval at Jim's lack of discomfort.

"Oh, there you are!" Rachel, attired in a little less glamorous number than the previous night, descended on their table. As she sat down her yellow hair swung across her photogenic features. Jim made the introductions. Carol was interested in how Jim and Rachel had met. He explained about the Antarctic group.

Mark said: "Ah, yes, Boyd and the BAS men."

"BAS men?" Carol asked.

"Ex-British Antarctic Survey men. They lived in the Antarctic, some for several years, but all consider themselves greater Antarctic experts than the expedition staff. Some are even writing books about their polar experience. That experience was often the only important thing that happened in their life."

Rachel was curious about Mark: "Where do you live and what do you do?"

Mark said: "London and I live."

"Live?"

"Retirement and travel if you call that living."

Ignoring Carol, Rachel beamed at the younger of the two men: "I didn't find out what you did."

"I'm a teacher from British Columbia."

"A teacher. So what does a teacher do for excitement in British Columbia?"

"Well, in the winter you might hit a moose with your truck and have it land on your windshield."

The smile stayed on Jim. The interest didn't. Mark had sat with the captain the first night and had his own cabin. He had more potential. Rachel asked Mark where he had traveled. Before he could answer an elderly Australian couple gingerly sat down at their table, and told the waitress:

"We'll just have soup."

*

The bluff chunky Australian, Doug, had missed both meals. It was a sickness, but not the sea type. There was no vomiting this time, only a steady ache in his stomach. The weight loss was OK; he was down to 170 lbs. without any dieting. But there was no way around it. "Pankie" as he called it was here to stay.

Sitting on his bunk Doug rose and fell with the waves. A lecture on sea birds was coming up. Might as well do some learning on the trip. Then there was the ship's store from four to five. Maybe get a couple of prezzies for his two nieces. Happy Hour? Might manage a drink or should he wait until after dinner?

"Boyd at the bar" had a nice ring to it. A pity there was nothing solid about the man. Doug breathed slowly, as his protruding stomach moved with the sea.

He had been hit the hardest. His cousin Ron and their friend Ed had good pensions. Doug had owned a grocery business with several shops, but he had no pension. Fortunately Natalie had died. No, it would have been better if she hadn't.

He was the one short of funds. All his money went into a trust fund – great returns – solid as the Antarctic, and as a salesman himself, he had been sold the goods. He didn't feel good now. The sales representatives all connected to the Antarctic and Australia seemed reliable. Returns were steady, not astronomical so there was nothing to be suspicious about. Then the returns stopped. By then Doug had invested most of his money in the trust fund. Where was the trust?

He could get an old age pension, but he would be joining twenty-five percent of older Australians who lived in poverty in their old age.

And then "Pankie" or pancreatic cancer as the specialist liked to call it, called. The main option was chemotherapy. A drug called gemcitabine was IV'd, but like many drugs had a multitude of side affects.

Count them: fatigue, infections, bruising, skin rash, and swelling, lost of hair (it was too late to worry about that), loss of fertility, (not an issue – he had no issue, ha, ha), and so on and so on. Then the side effects were treated with other drugs, which in turn had side effects.

The woman specialist suggested grief counseling. Doug didn't need bloody counseling. He would keep "Pankie" at bay for as long as possible. Once the Antarctic was done he'd see. He wasn't going to spend the rest of his life IV'd to a hospital.

There was a doctor on board, but he looked a bit young and inexperienced. Doug might see him after South Georgia for more painkillers. Beyond that island there would be no chance of being sent back on another ship if he got ill.

Doug had been a little devious with the trip's mandatory health certificate. A doctor friend in Melbourne gave him a quick once over. A few dollars later he was certified as fit.

He gingerly headed upstairs as the ten-minute warning sounded. Ron, a slight dark-haired man, asked:

"How ya doing?"

"I'm fine. Didn't feel like eating this morning."

When his cousin was ready to talk Ron thought that would be the time to intervene. Ed sitting next to them fiddled with his camera.

Doug looked around the lounge. Most seats were taken, unlike the morning lecture on the Falklands. Most of the people were his age, middle-aged, if sixty-four was middle-aged nowadays. There were a scattering of young ones. Must be computer nerds if they could afford this trip. He had to get off the fairness thing. Life wasn't.

He liked the staff bird expert's slides on the southern sea birds. Doug could never capture the birds with his point-and-shoot like Ron and Ed with their digital SLRs. He hoped to see the light-mantled sooty albatross. It was swallow-like compared to the other heavier albatrosses. It had an eerie cry.

The details of the talk stuck less. Some birds were OK, others were declining. As usual it was humans heating up the planet or taking too much food or accidentally killing the birds off that did it. Several passengers dozed off – a combination of too much lunch, the rolling motion of the sea and the warmth of the room.

*

After the lecture Greg the expedition leader said:
"The Zodiac landings are wet. For those who have forgotten their rubber boots there are a few tucked under the seats at the end of the lounge. Wet landings mean waterproofs. Antarctica despite being a dry continent is wet around the edges."

Jim had brought his own rubber boots. He used them for deer hunting. The moose was the one to bag but you needed a permit. That wasn't so easy to get.

He thought about where the bank money was. Who would be the most likely suspects? You needed money to get money. This would mean the staff probably wouldn't have the loot. Passengers with money could bankroll the robbery, and then hide it on the *Polar Adventurer* till the fuss died down.

Jim decided to talk to the passengers who had suites, the most expensive cabins on board. This trip was expensive enough even for those sharing a three-man cabin. Those suite types must be loaded.

*

Mr. Stringer would like to emphasize that his comments are not written down, recorded, in audio or visually transcribed. They are made *en passant* despite his previous occupation being in media studies. There is a plot, the theft of the gold, (to call the enterprise by its correct name), there is a protagonist, myself, of course, and the scenario is this Antarctic cruise. Have I forgotten anything? We have what is important and that is a story, a never-ending story. I will comment further as the voyage proceeds.

CHAPTER SIX

Carol had Jim spotting birds. It helped solidify some of what he had learned in the afternoon. The bar scene could wait until later. His anal instincts at the lecture had him filling his notebook with names, types, numbers, colors, ranges, foods, sizes, and sexual differences. Carol was amused when he missed some of Bob's close up bird pictures.

She tried to be kind when be brought out his pocket Canon camera with its small lens. He admired her Rebel Canon, a SLR, and the several lens even though he knew he was not that interested in photography. I only want the snaps, was his motto. Creative photography took too much from life. Well that was his excuse for not getting a better camera. His photography was hit or miss even on this big trip with its unusual wildlife.

Carol said she had taken several courses on using a single lens reflex camera. George the expedition's photographer would supply more on Antarctic light, white balances, and catching birds sailing by. Jim nodded in agreement. He wondered if she had money with all this expensive, it seemed to him, camera equipment, and she had a single cabin. Jim was feeling very attracted to Carol. If he was to be the Great Detective he had to be objective. Sure.

At dinner Carol moved to sit down at a window seat. Jim was about to join her when a wide-shouldered man slipped in next to Carol.

"That place was mine," said Jim.

"Sit somewhere else." The reply sounded Irish.

Jim placed his hands on the back of what he considered his chair and was prepared to remove the intruder. Carol got up and said:

"We'll sit over there."

Frustrated in not being able to fight for his territory Jim followed. The other man looked equally disappointed. Carol and Jim joined an American couple at another table.

"He's the architect. I'm the lawyer." The woman spoke precisely. "We've done this trip a few times. Is this your first?"

Jim introduced Carol and himself, and said this was their first trip. Carol asked how they had found the bird talk.

"It was the usual," opined the wife, "though there was no mention of the decline in albatrosses."

Jim asked what that was about. Carol explained about long fishing lines baited with thousands of hooks. Albatrosses ate the bait, got caught and drowned.

"So, where are you from?" was Jim's next question.

A short, "California," from the man.

"It must be lovely there," said Carol, "Even in the winter."

Jim brought up the captain's question. Had they heard of the bank robbery on the day they left.

"Just what that man said. Peter, wasn't it?" she turned to her husband. "He ran on about it. Boring actually."

The couple left not bothering to have the rather succulent German torte.

"Why, the question about that robbery," asked Carol.

Murder in the Antarctic

"I'm curious as to what people know about it."

A pair from Britain late for the meal joined their table. They were middle-aged, the woman dark haired, the man light haired, and both looked very fit. With out introducing themselves they immediately talked about their latest trip when they had dived off their yacht anchored among small islands in eastern Indonesia.

"Superb locales."

"Will you be diving in the Antarctic," Carol asked.

"No. We didn't bring our gear. This ship is not set up for scuba diving. When we've done here we're off to Borneo for more underwater exploring. We love the Far East. This trip is if you'll excuse the phrase is a cooling off period for us. Though we haven't tried diving in the southern continents yet." The couple continued to mention places and dives to Carol. She was especially interested if they mentioned tropical birds.

Jim turned them off. If South America was unknown to them they probably weren't in on the bank job unless they were doing a little fabrication. He looked around and "recognized" several passengers in the room. They looked like people back home. He supposed a lot of people had similar features, so there was a tendency to lump them as people he "knew". Wasn't that man over there his old sergeant? Probably some psychologist would say the idea that he "knew" people here was a need to belong or some such nonsense.

Carol decided to call it a night after a short bar session. She wanted to see the early morning birds as the ship reached West Falkland Island. Jim needed to probe some of the passengers at the bar, though his feelings for Carol were getting in the way of what the captain wanted.

After a last cigarette they joined the bar group. The sea had sobered up; the group less so. There was most of last night's bunch plus Martin, Jim's cabin mate, Colin the staff historian, and Doug's two companions from Australia, Ron and Ed.

"We await Rachel's entrance, and then we'll have two lovely ladies attending our Antarctic get-together." Boyd looked Carol up and down. Her lips tightened slightly, but she came out with:

"You must be an Antarctic expert."

"That's right, girlie!"

Jim was going to step in when Carol retorted:

"I'm not a girlie. I'm Carol."

"Ok Carol, what do you do?"

"I'm a nurse."

"You can nurse me anytime!" Boyd patted his prominent front.

"Sure, but only from the neck up."

Boyd smiled, but he didn't laugh along with the rest.

"You'd better stick with the cold parts of the world rather than the warm parts of your body," said Frank. He drained his rum and coke.

Boyd looked at Jim:

"Aren't you the colonial who was in the Arctic?"

"I've spent a couple of summers in the Arctic."

"You've never wintered?"

"No, I haven't, I…"

Boyd interrupted with:

"Unless you've wintered you've got no polar experience. You're like the rest of these bloody tourists." He looked around at scattered groups of passengers. Some were already talking about car insurance rates back home.

Jim felt like punching Boyd, but enjoyed the slight pressure on his arm from his companion. The captain's investigation would be stymied if he hit Boyd. Jim controlled his fuming by moving closer to Carol.

Doug, nursing his one drink of the evening directed his attention at Frank whose glass was empty.

"What did you drink on the ice in the old days?"

"The British Antarctic Survey supplied us with gin, beer, and navy rum, and we bought extra whisky and wine from our supply ships. The most potent drink we made was moose milk with navy rum at 86% alcohol.

"The rum came in a small woven covered keg. You added condensed milk and cider, heated it and tried to imbibe more than two or three drinks before your legs gave out." That distant Antarctic memory stayed with Frank even if others had faded away.

"I gave a radio operator three Antarctic-sized gins," put in Boyd. "Each one was a triple. The poor sod never got out of his bunk the next morning to do the radio schedules." Boyd continued with:

"Did you hear the one about two Australians leaving a bar?"

Doug from Adelaide groaned: "Please!"

"Well, it could happen!"

Frank said: "There're no original jokes in the world, are there?"

Boyd turned to Carol.

"So, why are you going to the Antarctic?"

She replied: "It's for the birds."

"I make the jokes around here!"

Carol quickly added:

"You are the joke here."

And with a quick grin at Jim, she left.

Boyd's only comeback was: "Well, I'm glad we never had women wintering in the Antarctic even a fine looking one like that."

Ron, Doug's cousin, a slim, fifty-something, asked: "Women weren't allowed to winter?"

"Are you kidding?" Frank got quite animated. "It wasn't until the 1960s that the Russians allowed women to winter. The British held out until the 1990s."

"We always considered them a distraction," said Arthur, wistfully. "Today the British government bends over backwards to get women to winter."

"No way," said Boyd, "they would've been a bloody nuisance. Men were men then and women knew it. You could fart and burp at will and we were free!"

"And skanky!" This came from Georgina as she headed on her way to bed

Jim was about to bring up the bank robbery with Arthur as he and his wife had a suite and must have money, when Colin, the staff historian, thwarted him by asking:

"Seeing as we have such a fund of Antarctic expertise from the good old days how did that man on that old Sheldon Expedition die?"

Frank looked at Boyd: "You were there, weren't you, way back when?"

"I'd left before it happened." Boyd moved purposefully towards Rachel, so that her grand entrance for the others was spoilt. He deliberately led her to a distant corner.

Colin prodded Frank for what he knew.

"I think he was with a dog team," said Frank.

"On his own?"

"No, he had someone else with him. A blizzard came up, the sea ice split, and they got separated. The second sledger turned back with most of the team. The other man continued on to a refuge hut with one husky.

"Arthur, do you remember what happened to the dog?"

Arthur said: "I believe it turned up at the base a few days later."

"And the bloke at the refuge hut?" asked Colin.

Arthur sipped his gin.

Frank answered for him: "They reached him later, didn't they Arthur?"

Arthur nodded.

"And?" asked Colin."

"By the time they got to him he was dead," said Frank. "He didn't have any food."

"Oh," said Colin.

The rest of the group drank, looked at their drinks, and waited.

"That's about it, isn't?" Frank looked at Arthur to finish.

"Yes."

"Would Boyd have any idea who the other man was?" asked Colin..

Arthur said: "Probably," and left the lounge.

Jim knew his question wouldn't be as interesting as what he had just heard.

Martin piped up: "Seeing as there are less of us, anyone for another round?"

CHAPTER SEVEN

"The fair breeze blew, the white foam flew, the furrow followed free; we were the first that ever burst into that silent sea." Greg cheerfully quoted Coleridge as the wind became a near gale. Jim had his second breakfast on the voyage with three Dutch women, one of whom was slim, dark-haired and pretty like Carol.

He avoided most of the glistening fried eggs, plump sausages and crisp bacon, and the gym. The ship was rolling too much.

From Captain Engstrom Jim knew there were six suites on board. Those passengers could have money to plan and pay for the Ushuaia bank robbery. Arthur and Georgina had a suite, as did Boyd, Rachel and someone called Jack. Two elderly sisters shared a suite but as they had difficulty getting down the stairs Jim didn't think they were involved in the robber. One suite was empty. It was expensive so it was locked up. Jim would start with those from the other four suites.

*

During lunch Boyd was trapped by a young American duo who had been down south a couple of times. He was going to remark on Antarctic dilettantes when the sharp-faced woman said:

"Fruit and vegetables from the buffet are better than a hefty protein and fat lunch."

"We exercise in the gym everyday. Did you do that when you lived in the Antarctic?" asked the man, a thin fit-looking type.

"Not bloody likely," Boyd spluttered. Before he could enlighten them on the real Antarctic they left for more birding.

Relieved he gazed around. That old bore Moresby was explaining the politics of the Falklands and Argentina to a Dutch woman. Probably a waste of time. Arthur and Frank joined him. Frank knew a bit about the south. Arthur had more Antarctic experience than anyone else on board. And he had money. The three scoured the dining room remarking on different nationalities. Most of the Yanks were OK. Some Aussies you could talk to, others were a lost cause.

*

Carcass Island, off West Falkland Island, was like most of the islands low lying and wind swept. A few bent trees leaned over, held down by the westerly gales. A brown bird perched on the ship's railing.

"That's a Falkland thrush," said Carol.

"That's for the birds," added Jim. Carol glanced at him. He should keep his thoughts about bbs (brown birds) to himself.

A gangway was dropped down the side of the vessel. Zodiac boats were lowered into the water, and in groups of twelve the passengers, many wearing the same blue colored expedition parkas, were packed into the inflatables.

"I'm going on the earliest boats" said Carol. "I can see and feel the place before its overrun by others."

"OK," said Jim. He gave her his best grin, which was wasted as she trained her binoculars on a turkey vulture sailing high overhead in a blue sky.

The black Zodiacs bumped onto a pale-yellow sandy beach. The visitors waded ashore in their rubber boots, and headed past thick clumps of tussac grass to the penguin rookery. In bright sunlight photographers peered down dark holes. Occasionally a Magellanic penguin face peered back up. A dark skua glided over the rookery looking for penguin eggs or chicks.

Near the main trail fringed with golden blooms of gorse Jim noticed "BOYD NO RIP" written in the sand. He should mention it to Boyd, who like several others, had hurried along to the farmhouse.

Sheltered by a windbreak of trees the farm had three or four tame dark caracaras, hawk-like scavengers, strutting around the garden. Elsa said they were on the world's endangered list. The birds ignored the visitors.

Inside the farmhouse a huge spread of sliced fruitcake, macaroons, chocolate squares, lemon tarts, scones and tea was laid out on a wide table. "I've just had lunch," was a frequent comment. Jim lost count of the variety and number of cakes he gobbled down. Keeping the visitors happy made more money than sheep farming.

Back on board the passengers "chimped" their way through hundreds of digital shots. Carol was more concerned with what fellow twitchers had seen than being with Jim.

He put his mind to the captain's problem. Those with suites meant money, but having South American connections could also be part of the mix.

At the bar Jim asked Rachel what she thought about South America. She burbled on about her wonderful friends near Buenos Aires who played polo. She could be a suspect. Arthur had been to the Antarctic several times. When Jim asked about South America he got:

"Yes, it is an interesting part of the world." Arthur turned away. Before Jim could buttonhole Boyd, Frank said:

"When we went to the Antarctic in the good old days Stanley, our next stop in the Falklands, used to be our last bit of civilization. Then two years later it had to make us civilized again as we came out of the Antarctic." He swallowed his last mouthful of rum and coke and looked at the bar group for a possible refill.

"How big is this city called Stanley?" Doug, the Australian, asked.

"If it's over two thousand I'll buy the next round," said Boyd.

"Two thousand two hundred," said Frank. "I read it in the *Penguin News* I found at the farm."

Boyd counted his friends, the kangaroos and the other colonial. "Sandy, we need liquid here!"

Frank explained about the Falklands War of 1982. "The Argies had home problems so they invaded the Falkland Islands. They always claimed it was theirs. Earlier the British government was even thinking of giving the Falklands away."

"Argies are Argentineans?" asked Ed, Doug's friend.

"Yes. It was 10,000 Argies against 100 British soldiers. The British soldiers surrendered. After a British submarine sank the biggest Argentinean battleship, it was left to the Argentinean warplanes to carry on the fight against the incoming British armada.

"Once the British army landed it was all over bar the shouting. It was professional soldiers against mainly conscripts from the hot parts of Argentina. The Falklands in winter can be bloody raw. The British hung on to the Falklands, and spent millions of pounds modernizing it. The British Antarctic bases benefited as well."

"Didn't some British business types back the Argentineans over the Falklands?" put in Colin, the staff historian.

"They were hoping to be on the winning side," continued Frank. "They lost money by backing the Argies."

"More important in Stanley there's the Globe Tavern," said Boyd as he helped Sandy pass round the drinks.

"No, no!" exclaimed Frank. "It's the Victory Bar or nothing!"

"Anyway," Arthur said, "both have fish and chips and British ale."

"Luke warm, I hope," put in Doug.

"Of course, and they have your Australian lager, Foster's."

"Not that roo piss," said Doug.

*

Greg's cheery morning mentioned the need for lots of sun cream. The ozone level was high. And on the bow there were three Commerson's dolphins.

Daring photographers hung themselves over the rails to catch the black and white shapes slicing through the water. Before them Port Stanley, capital of the Falkland Islands, lay along a narrow harbor. Jim and Carol got on the first tour bus.

Murder in the Antarctic

"I'm Phil," said a rather hairy individual in a plaid shirt. "For safety reasons don't abuse the bus driver, Bill, that's my job. After the tour we meet back at the Jetty Visitors' Centre. There are toilets, stamps, pots of jam and the Internet.

"On the Falklands we have 700,000 penguins, a similar number of black-browed albatrosses, half a million sheep and less than three thousand people.

"We used to heat with peat and raise sheep. Now we use heating oil and sell fishing licenses. You visitors are out second biggest money crop after the licenses. Pounds, dollars and euros are accepted, and the Falkland change is useless off of the islands."

Phil showed them the nineteenth century cathedral with an arch of two pairs of whale jawbones. There were various war memorials including the 1982 one. A wooden hulk, the *Jhelum*, lay rotting in the harbor. When Phil left them he reminded the tourists: "We drive on the right side of the road which is on the left."

Jim and Carol walked back along Ross Road. Carol added a night heron, flightless steamer ducks and two types of gulls to her bird record. She left Jim to go on a nature hike.

He decided to ask people about the robbery. After the first passenger he approached said: "What has that bank robbery to do with this place?" he dropped the subject. There would be more time at sea.

In the Globe a man called Malcolm attached himself to Jim. His promotion of his forthcoming book on different shaped icebergs told Jim why the rest of the Antarctic crowd was in the Victory Bar. He didn't think that the bank heist could rest on the plump shoulders of this monotonous person.

Later Colin the historian said many of the golden beaches were fenced off due to unexploded mines from the Falklands' War. And in the past eight penguins use to be cooked down to produce one gallon of oil.

*

After dinner Peter strode into the bar and with a large whisky in his hand looked around for an audience. A small band of bar regulars including Jim could not stop the explosive explanation:

"Did you know," said Peter, "it was not just several hundred thousand pesos that was stolen?"

"What?" said Frank, the ex-Antarctic worker.

"The bank robbery in Ushuaia!"

"Oh, " said Frank.

"I just found out there was four million dollars worth of gold coins stolen! That lot went out the bank's side door not the front.

"Two men, I presume they were men, drove off in a silver Toyota Hilux."

"What's a Hilux? asked Doug, the Australian.

"A four by four," said Arthur beating Peter to the explanation.

"Isn't that what they used to race a dog team to the Magnetic Arctic Pole?" said Frank.

"Yes," said Peter, "and a Hilux was used to drive 5000 kilometers to and from the South Pole."

"That wouldn't have been a Hilux out of Ushuaia," laughed Arthur.

'They found the Toyota," carried on Peter, "abandoned near the National Park. The gold was gone."

"I suppose the Argentineans are looking for it," said Arthur.

"There's a nation wide search on," Peter said. "Boats, planes and vehicles are being checked. How about a ship leaving Tierra del Fuego for the Antarctic?" He looked expectantly around him. "It would be clever. No one would suspect if the gold coins were stowed aboard."

"Would the captain do a search of the ship?" asked Frank.

Jim said: "He probably has already."

"But why this ship?" said Doug who had not been paying too much attention. "Aren't there several ships heading down to the Antarctic every week?"

"True," said Peter.

"So, why this one?" Doug continued.

"I don't know, but it would give a little panache to our Antarctic cruise," said Peter wistfully.

The rest of the bar's conversation moved onto other more important topics. Frank for one needed a refill.

Jim thought about Peter's comments. Peter had no suite though he had a Nikon camera with a high range of bodies and lenses. And Jim had overheard Peter say he had lived in Columbia for a while. Was Peter bringing up this gold robbery in a sort of reverse psychological move to show that, of course, he couldn't be involved in the bank job?

CHAPTER EIGHT

Jim persisted with the captain's request. At dinner he sat with a British tour group. Being with a group the passengers obviously lacked money, and no one had any South American connections. The main discussion was UK driving conditions. An earlier attempt to sit at an Australian group's table was met with:

"We're saving these places for Harry and Rose!"

Carol worried about putting on some pounds even with an asparagus risotto at dinner, but was strangely comforted by the thought of two days of sea travel. She would not be eating much. She forfeited some bird time by being with Jim on the periphery of the Antarctic bunch. The downside was Boyd the irritant. Unlike the grain in an oyster thinking on or being with Boyd was not going to make a pearl.

Ron, Doug's cousin, asked Boyd: "In the old days was there any limit on how many seals you killed for husky food?"

"The Antarctic in those days was no place for seal huggers," said Boyd.

"I was interested in whether people went overboard in the killing."

"Why?" asked Boyd. "Are you one of those people who reckon humans shouldn't be in the Antarctic only animals?"

"No, but we've tended to kill too many animal in most parts of the world," said Ron.

"No way! There's lots of seal there. I've killed and eaten lots of seal in the Antarctic. I've never had a sick day in my life." said Boyd as he stomped off to his suite.

"Is he always like that?" asked Ron.

"At school he was called Boiling Barrington," said Arthur.

Jim felt his questions on the gold robbery should be done one to one separate from the bar. The bar conversations were generally more interesting. He escorted Carol back to her single cabin. Where did she get the money for this large room, he wondered? She touched his arm and closed the door. He felt rejected but hopeful.

In the shared cabin Alec read a bird book on Peru. Jim described Boyd and his seal killing to Martin.

"He's a certain man," said Martin. "Mind you all those old Antarctic types are a bit different from you and me."

Jim needed to keep thinking about the robbery. Being in a three-man cabin it was unlikely that either Martin or Alec were in on the hold up. Unless one of them was trying to be clever. His thoughts on Carol made his attempt at reading Shakespeare's *As You Like It* difficult.

*

On the two sea days of travel to the island of South Georgia Jim noticed what he called the "captain's dance". As Captain Engstrom moved forward on the bridge the office on watch moved back. The third officer was especially attentive to the needs of the captain and the ship's instruments.

The morning message was: "It is not that life ashore is distasteful to me, but life at sea is better." Supposedly a quote by Sir Francis Drake.

Jim and Carol had a breakfast with two English veterinarians.

"We met in a dissection lab. It was love at first cut," said the wife.

"We've been cutting each other down ever since," her husband replied as his wife ruffled his hair.

Jim's prodding on their South American connections was stopped by them having only been as far south as a Baltimore conference.

Before Carol headed off to a SLR camera discussion Jim mentioned he had a new bird for the bird list.

"Oh, which one?"

"It's the left-winged upper-crusted tern gull."

There was a silence.

"It might cause a bit of a strain in some quarters," said Carol quietly.

"Well, maybe I didn't see it clearly. I'll see you afterwards?"

"I guess so but remember," as she swung her 300mm lens away from him, "size matters."

Getting his laptop Jim headed to the captain's cabin to "copy some Arctic slides". Another unwanted aquavit was downed. Jim said:

"I would like financial information on all the passengers."

Captain Engstrom said it might take a day or so and time was running out. So whose concern was that Jim thought?

The gym looked available, but Jim did not feel like trying it at that moment. On the bridge he said to Alec, his cabin companion:

"Those small prions flitting over the water look like swallows." Alec agreed. Jim had asked him earlier about the bank robbery. Alec said he hadn't heard of it. Probably too busy looking at birds.

A guy with a shaved head who didn't have an accent raised Jim's hopes. He was from Northern Ontario, well that was close enough to sound Canadian. Andrew had been to South America a few years ago, but Jim's query about the bank hold up left a puzzled look on the man's face.

The third officer, Henryk from Gdansk in Poland, told the passengers on the bridge that the air pressure was falling. Tomorrow would be rough. When Jim asked about the ship the third officer said the *Polar Adventurer* used to be a Norwegian ferry.

"Not an icebreaker?"

"They seldom are in this part of the Antarctic. Most of the sea ice melts in the summer. The ships are just strengthened in the bow with some extra steel."

Carol gave Jim a condensed version of the artistic and technical aspects of the SLR world. With computer imaging amateurs could give the professionals a run for their money in the photographic department, and make money as well.

Jim asked: "Do you look at what you see at or are just you making a brand new picture?"

He moved close as Carol showed him some of her birdshots. She tapped him on the arm and said:

"You've had enough!"

"Of what?"

"Of what I can show you. If we have an early lunch there'll be more time for birding. Or do you have something else you'd rather do?"

He grinned and said:

"I can think of a couple of things," but followed her downstairs. They had to keep up with the steady daily eating schedule.

Jim steered Carol to Mark's table. Unpleasant as Boyd might be Jim remembered what his father had once said. You always knew where you were with the difficult ones. The pleasant one you had to watch out for.

When Rachel slipped into the seat next to Mark, Jim started to talk about the Ushuaia robbery. There was little interest. As Rachel pointed out:

"What's that to do with where we are now? What do you think of my outfit?" She showed off her profile and the shimmering green dress to the two men. Unlike Rachel the garment was simple, but like her expensive.

"Rather fetching."

Jim followed with Mark's comment with:

"Very nice."

Carol was ignored so she said:

"Isn't it a bother to have all those fancy clothes?"

Rachel looked at her and asked:

"Is that all you brought?"

"Of course not!"

Rachel switched to Mark and asked which the best hotels in Rome were. She needed an update for next summer. Jim realized that his robbery question would have to wait again. Carol left for a smoke.

At the aft deck he commented:

"Shouldn't you quit smoking?"

"Shouldn't you quit while you're ahead?"

CHAPTER NINE

"Why do we have so many lectures?"

Ron answered: "Well Ed, it fills up the time at sea. Otherwise you might mutiny or worse start up a game of bridge."

Doug joined the other two Australians for the next presentation. The sea mammal specialist from Aberdeen said:

"I hope you're all still wearing your name tags. It makes our job a lot easier when we land at South Georgia."

"Why would we want to do that?" came from one of the old Antarctic guys.

Mike, the sea mammal specialist, plunged on with his talk. Only a small part of whales' bodies were visible so a lot of cameras couldn't do them justice, but elephant and fur seals could be photographed up close. Both seals had large males with harems containing several smaller females.

"Elephant seals like to lie next to each other. In the past some people jumped from the back of one large animal to the next."

From the back of the lounge Frank waved a hand.

"Yes?" asked Mike.

"Been there, done it!"

Mike continued: "The fur seals were almost wiped out for their pelts a hundred years ago. Today there are several million of them.

"The doctor has several interesting antibiotics he can inject into you if a fur seal bites you. So keep you're distance from the furries."

"Why not cull them?" interrupted Boyd. "There're a bloody nuisance."

Rather like you, thought Doug.

"They are part of the natural order."

Arthur from the Antarctic group put in:

"Don't studies show that the increase in fur seals destroys the nesting sites of albatrosses, prions and penguins?"

"Yes," said Mike, "but there're still a natural part of this area."

"Cull 'em!" barked Boyd.

Most of the passengers were not sure what the disagreement was about.

Doug excused himself to lie down. The illness felt worse. But he had a task, mission, quest, assignment, job, undertaking, aim, and purpose, what you will. He nodded off. Later Doug thought of what he had to do about Boyd. But the money lost to those Antarctic Fund shysters would not return.

*

Greg outlined the next day's talks. They were on the old whaling industry of South Georgia and the great Antarctic explorer, Sir Ernest Shackleton. If there was time there would be a session on point and shoot cameras. Carol whispered to Jim:

"Is that necessary?'

The expedition leader added that the weather would be rough the next day. Jim said to Carol:

"Now that is necessary for some of us."

She smiled back at him.

Jim put his (the captain's?) question to a few in the lounge. Carol left for a smoke.

The bar bunch was joined by Peter, the young American. He questioned Boyd:

"How would you cull all those fur seals hogging the coast of South Georgia?"

Boyd blustered:

"I don't know. I'm sure there's a way!"

Arthur suggested sterilization: "I mean I've been done so why not seals."

"And he's been a better man for it," said Georgina.

"I never knew," said Boyd.

"It's not something I broadcast to the world," said Arthur"

Peter broke in with: "Anyone got any thoughts on whether that stolen gold from Ushuaia is hidden on this ship?" There was a silence. They were traveling to Antarctica not concerning themselves with a mundane bank robbery. Boyd concentrated on his drink. Arthur asked Georgina if she was ready for another. The rest decided to ignore the topic. Picking up on the lack of response Peter wandered off.

Jim had observed the reactions around him, and he was taking in Rachel parading another new number. It showed off her body for the men and her brown and gold dress for the women. Her hair shone like the sun shining off of the waves. Georgina remarked on Jim's eyeballing:

"You're quite observant, aren't you?"

Carol and Jim sat at dinner with Arthur and his wife. Georgina asked Carol what she did at home. On being told she was a nurse Georgina said she use to be a hospital administrator, and she had probably given nurses quite a bit of stress.

"I'm sure that wasn't the case," said Carol.

Arthur talked about some of his eight winters in the Antarctic. Then asked Jim:

"What's your town like in British Columbia?"

"It's got lumber mills and paper mills and a newish university."

"A red brick university?" asked Georgina.

"More like grey concrete."

While they waited for two Argentinean trout, one fried chicken and one vegetarian stew, a small vigorous woman in a cuddly pink sweater greeted Georgina. She was introduced as Pamela. Her profile was sharp and her face shone. She did not look huggable. She reminded Jim of a hawk.

Pamela asked Jim where he was from. He told her. And she replied:

"How naice."

Ignoring Carol she turned to Georgina and asked about the Penningtons. They would have liked to have been on the trip as they knew the owners of the *Polar Adventurer*. She chatted to Georgina and Arthur about mutual friends at home.

Carol made a puffing sign to Jim, and left.

"Have you been to the Antarctica?" Pamela asked turning to Jim.

"I've only been to the Arctic."

"No comparison. I've been to both, and I've just been visiting some landed friends of mine near Buenos Aires."

A South American connection and she had money, thought Jim. Before he could ask about what happened in Ushuaia, Pamela turned and said:

"Georgina, I must say that yellow dress looks wonderful on you."

"Thank you. I was not sure what to bring on an expedition cruise. It's a bit common to dress casual all the time."

"True," said Pamela. "Mind you that awful woman who's been showing herself off around the ship is a little over the top."

Arthur and Jim avoided looking at each other. As Jim left Pamela said:

"I'm *so* sorry you are leaving. I hope we can talk again."

*

"It's going to be rough so I'm going to cut short your great company. I going to talk to Alec about a bird sightings then I shall retire"

Miffed at the mention of Alec and pleased at Carol's remark about himself Jim gave her hand a slight squeeze.

An Australian woman ran through a selection from *Cats* and *The Phantom of the Opera* on the lounge piano. Periodically polite applause broke out.

"I notice with my great powers of perception," said Frank to Arthur, "that the Great Boil's not here."

"The Great Boil?" asked Doug.

"Boyd," was Frank's reply. "He generally doesn't miss too many bar sessions."

Doug muttered: "He probably hasn't had enough seal meat." Sandy handed out drinks and wondered why the hotel manager was helping at the bar. A large wave crashed against the side of the hull. A few glasses hit the floor.

"That's a taste of tomorrow," said Elsa, the expedition's deputy leader, as she walked past with a dustpan of glass shards.

In the cabin Alec was making notes from his book on Peruvian birds. Martin asked Jim about the captain's Arctic slides.

"He's got quite a collection of flower shots. I'm interested in the different flora though not in the hordes of stinging insects."

Alec told them that the largest land animal in the Antarctic was an insect, a half inch wingless midge.

"What did you think about the culling of fur seals?" asked Jim.

"We almost wiped them out," Alec said. "We can't seem to leave well enough alone."

*

Mark Stringer calling. I must stress the importance of F.T, which is focused thinking. Because I can focus the right things happen. Most people do not put their minds to a task even those with an active mind. It is why I limit my alcohol intake. F.T. governs my life.

The second point of less importance is what I refer to as cherchez la femme, but not in the traditional sense as used in mystery stories. I have succeeded enumerable times with women. My quiet charm and focused thinking has resulted in seductions before, during and after university. I even retained Isabelle my wife for a few years.

I found several other suitable candidates. Age did not matter to me. Sixteen these days is a woman. What was important was the enthusiasm, a name I gave my last protégé before the unfortunate misunderstanding when the college and I went our separate ways. And now on board there is a blond, buxom, belle from Biloxi. (You do not like the alliteration?). Things are going as focused. Except why was that Canadian talking about the robbery?

CHAPTER TEN

There was no morning quote only a terse: "Keep inside the ship and hang on at all times. The gale force is eight, that's over forty knots."

The ship reared and plunged as if trying to get rid of its occupants. White spume, whipped from the top of racing waves, disappeared into the grey sky. Thick white ropes had been stretched across the dining room. There were few to hang on to them. An occasional dish crashed in the kitchen. Carol arrived pale and shaken. She was not stirred by the storm or Jim. She grabbed a slice of bread and a juice box and left.

"I'll bring you some lunch," Jim called out.

"No!" came the reply.

Jim tripped lightly up the stairs as the ship fell into the waves and fought his way up as it reared back up again. He banged his ankle on a steel coaming across one door, and glanced off several walls in his upward journey.

He sank into a wide tied-down chair in the library. The books banged back and forth behind the glass cupboard doors. Jim thought of Carol then forced his mind towards the missing gold coins. He considered Boyd, Arthur, Rachel, Pamela, Jack, Mark and several others. The old Antarctic types would have South American connections.

Rachel had the life style of money and a suite. A woman could have been one of the robbers. Pamela had Argentinean connections. Jack who had tried to sit with Carol had money. Mark had high end camera equipment as did several others like for instance Carol.

He noticed his mind moved quickly onto others like that California couple.

Jim considered age. Was the age of sixty like some of those old Antarctic types the new middle age? They could have carried the gold coins, or was he trying to avoid thinking about his own advancing years? How much did four million dollars of gold coins weigh, anyway? Peter was interested in the gold, and was young compared to many on board. What had he been doing in Columbia?

Peter had talked to Jim about Canada's national sport, hockey. On reflection Jim thought anyone who could wax enthusiastically about the Toronto Maple Leafs maybe didn't know too much about the sport.

Was Peter being superficial, ignorant or playing a game? He was the right age, had South American contacts, and his Nikon was not the most expensive camera, but with lens, etc, would be worth several thousand dollars. Jim put Peter at the top of his list of suspects. If it was a deck of cards would Peter be the king, the ace, the jack or the joker?

The moving room did not help his lack of progress. Jim was not a mystery novel police inspector, disgruntled, alcoholic, and a jazz enthusiast who with restless drive, criminal contacts plus forensics quickly solved the crime. All he could do was to keep plugging along.

His musings were interrupted by a small grey haired woman who stood over him.

"Are you OK?"

"Oh, yes. I was thinking."

"Cruises are for experiencing not thinking."

"You're right. I'll try not to do too much of that."

Jim entered his cabin and was pitched into the shower stall. He grabbed a rail before there was more than damage to his pride. Strapped into his bunk above a snoring Martin, Jim listened to the pounding weather and the protests of the ship's hull.

After an hour of little rest he got up. Jim caromed of walls, like a good drunk on his way to the bridge. The windshield wiper beat back and forth forcing the water from the glass. Alec and a staff birder peered out as spray hurled itself over the bridge roof. The third officer and the captain braced themselves as the bow plunged into the waves. Frank and Arthur snapped the bigger waves of grey water breaking over the ship.

"Once in a force nine heading south to the Antarctic," said Frank, "the captain had to turn the ship back into the north wind and run all night to keep us afloat. We never did see the end of the film, *The World of Suzie Wong*."

Jim had never heard of the film. He wondered about the bearded types on the ship. Guilt by association with the Antarctic? But several bearded professors on board had never been to South America or the Antarctic.

He ate lunch with the bridge partners. There were only a few others eating.

"It's not a force twelve storm," said Arthur. "There are no penguins flying by."

"Not yet," said Frank.

*

Doug mused that Natalie, his wife, would have preferred this trip to the one they took on a huge cruise ship around Australia You waited for your set dinner time, you dressed up for it and ate, and then left. Being on that ship was like being in an unknown town that moved from one tourist place to another.

The sea would be a great option for dealing with Boyd, especially with this storm, but the Antarctic was where the deed should be done.

He counted off the days. Six maybe? He had to save his strength. If he could hang on until they left South Georgia the ship wouldn't turn back if his cancer got worse. He had enough aches and pains to be able to get more painkillers off the doctor. He wouldn't read up on the stages of "Pankie". He knew the survival rates. Doug had asked Doctor Bob:

"What do you do if someone dies on board?"

The answer: "The rest of the passengers eat a lot of ice cream. It frees up the freezer."

*

Attendance was sparse. Happy Hour was a misnomer. More people heeded the siren song of the dinner bong. They were getting bored strapped in their restless cabins. Jim had dinner with a couple of Americans. Before he could pop the question Rachel slipped in beside him. She beamed all round and said to Jim:

"You seem to be really interested in that Ushuaia bank robbery."

"Er," he said. "Not really. I was wondering whether the money was still back in Argentina or on a ship."

"Like this one?" as braised lamb with white sauce was passed around the table.

"Possibly."

Rachel was more interested in his opinion of her blue dress. The material crossed her breasts and fell to her narrow waist. He received the full benefit of her perfume. He did not recognize it but it smelled expensive.

"It's wonderful. As are you."

"Why thank you, Jim!"

Her hand lay on his arm. Someone must have turned up the heating system. Jim was saved by a voice asking:

"Can I sit here?" Carol lowered herself onto a chair.

Rachel gushed: "Why, of course! I hope you are feeling better. It's been a bit rough for some."

"What were you been talking about?" Carol asked.

"The gold robbery," said Jim briefly.

"Well, I must be off. I want to get ready for tomorrow's adventurer." She nodded at the American couple, who had been trying not to listen too hard, and flowed across the floor.

Carol looked weary. She played with some food. The American couple wondered what came next. Would there be a scene? It would be a break in the boring sea journey.

"That was the roughest storm I've been in." Jim broke the silence.

"I'm sure." Carol got up slowly and left the dining room.

Jim thought of Carol and Rachel, and a beautiful South American woman he and several other men had ogled at the Los Angeles International Airport. She stood unaware among hundreds of milling passengers. He wondered why female beauty was so important to males. Some genetic need? And why was Rachel interested in him? It must be his manly charm.

CHAPTER ELEVEN

"We all survived what Captain Engstrom called the worst storm he has encountered in these seas. Though a few of you forgot to hang onto the rails and got a little bruised."

Greg carried on: "I'm sure you all noticed the sudden drop in sea temperature early this morning. From now on we'll encounter a lot more sea birds and fur seals. Millions of tons of the shrimp-like creatures, krill, sustain life in the southern oceans.

"When we land at South Georgia keep five meters away from birds and at least fifteen meters from fur seals. Unlike regular seals fur seals can move very fast on land.

"Tomorrow morning we cruise Elsehul. You'll find it on the map by the reception centre. Dress for wet."

"What places *will* we land at?"

"It depends on the weather."

"But you have an idea. Don't you have to have this trip planned out ahead of time?"

"You are correct, Boyd. But as you are fully aware things down south are always tentative."

The staff geologist talked about the high glaciated mountains and the deep cut fjords on the island. South Georgia was kept cold by the frozen Weddell Sea to the south. Along a thin congested coastal strip a lot of wildlife came to breed.

Carol had either left early to bird watch or she was still under the weather. Jim glanced around and met Rachel's smiling face. Outside he saw dark black sleeks zipping through the water. Fur seals. They were effortless and miles from land.

Murder in the Antarctic

Jim talked to an Australian doctor couple from Perth. They had been to the Antarctic before, but in the Ross Sea area. The doctors knew of the robbery from Peter, but had never traveled in South America.

"I noticed there's quite a few medical people on board," said Jim.

"They've either got more money than most, or they're interested in the environment. We're for nature," said James.

*

There was much activity in the sea. Prions and terns sailed by. Tiny Wilson's storm petrels, their legs dangling down, "paddled" over the sea. The odd diving petrel crashed straight through the tops of waves. Carol questioned Alec about a dark medium-sized albatross. His reply was"

"A grey-headed albatross."

"Where do you call home?"

"Wherever there are birds."

"I mean which country are you from?"

"I've been all over."

Carol had better luck with the third officer.

"The weather will be better tomorrow," he said.

"I'm glad."

She wondered about Jim and Rachel. Lucky Jim, two women are interested in him. How poetic. And what is my attraction, she thought, a mere cruise fling?

Alec concentrated on a distant bird with his 10 x 40 Zeiss binoculars. They were worth over five hundred pounds. Carol's compact Leica, at half that, did the job but one could always yearn for a better toy.

She smiled at Bob, a staff birder as he entered the bridge. "I'm learning a lot from you."

"Thanks."

She mentioned to Jim that Bob had taught her a lot about the sea birds.

"If you like that sort of thing," slipped out.

"What sort of thing?" she asked.

Jim wasn't too sure.

"It sort of came out."

Carol didn't pursue it.

*

Jim waylaid Frank as he limped to the lounge and asked him if knew about the bank robbery. Frank hesitated, thought a bit and then said: "Very little. It's yesterday's news anyway."

"Have you had much contact with South America? asked Jim.

"What the hell for?" said Frank and headed for the bar.

Once Frank had got down his second rum and coke Doug asked him why he had headed to the Antarctic all those years ago.

"I had no goals in my life at the time," said Frank, "so I joined the British Antarctic Survey. Best adventure I ever had. You missed female company for a year or so, but most of us survived. You don't forget wintering in the Antarctic, especially when you're young."

Jim asked how Boyd had got on that private Antarctic expedition.

Before turning away Frank said: "His father gave Eric Sheldon some money. The elder Barrington ran several businesses in the southern hemisphere."

"Why are you asking about Boyd when he's not here?" asked Doug.

Jim agreed he should wait for Boyd. He wondered why Doug was so concerned about Boyd.

After Carol had had her last cigarette and retired, he hung around the bar trying to catch a few people's attention. The robbery had gone off the radar for most. Their arrival at the island of South Georgia was more important.

As the night lengthened Jim and Peter propped up the bar. (Did the bar need propping up wondered Jim?). Maisie a woman keen on Peter had left for her bed. Jim asked how the search for gold coins was going. Peter feeling slightly "squishy" said:

"Did you know that certain people on board this ship were invited in Ushuaia to an exhibition of gold coins at the Hotel Albatros? The symposium had armed guards waving M16's around the glass cases. I can't tell you who was there, it was a private do, invitation only." Peter paused. "But it might connect to the stolen coins."

He carried on: "Do you know who Julius Popper was?"

"No, I haven't a clue," said Jim.

"End of the nineteenth century, a Romanian engineer and a man of many talents. Single-handedly opened up two gold placer sites in Tierra del Fuego, and ran them like his own armed fifedom."

It probably should have been fiefdom, but Jim didn't think it mattered at that time of night. They had the bar to themselves.

"He made his own gold coins and stamps. And he joined the Argentinean and Chilean extermination of the local Ona Indians. It was one pound sterling for every dead Indian. Ears or skull were needed it you wanted to collect your money.

"At that symposium they showed some of Popper's Tierra del Fuego and Buenos Aires made gold coins, where inshidently…" Peter had difficulty with the last word, "he was later murdered."

Jim looked around the empty bar. A night wind blew outside as the ship plowed on. Was Peter certain that the gold was on board? Jim had seen him searching the decks, or was that to put people off, and did he already have the gold? So why talk about gold coins now?

"So how much would one of those gold coins be worth?" asked Jim.

Peter muttered: "Well, a five gram gold coin is roughly $300, but an original Popper coin would be ten times that or more. There're pretty rare"

"So, what was taken from that Ushuaia bank?" said Jim.

His drinking partner looked at him closely and said: "If I had that four million dollars of gold coins, I'd be happy."

"How many coins were lifted?"

"Don't know," said Peter, "but if a gold ounce is roughly thirty grams that's…" he stopped to use his fingers. "What's five into thirty?"

Jim said: "Six."

"So," again Peter tried to get on top of his alcohol. "One ounce of gold is $1800. Call it $2000. What's two thousand into four million?"

Jim needed a napkin to come up with "2000."

"So," repeated Peter, "some two thousand gold coins went missing."

"What?"

"From Ushuaia. That place is easy to say when you're drunk, right? The coins come in plastic tubes," Peter muttered. "Look for plastic tubes and you will find…" He swept his hand along the bar, and slowly stumbled out through the lounge doors.

Jim slowly followed him. He tried to marshal some thoughts. Was Peter faking it? A curious bystander or what?

CHAPTER TWELVE

Sorry to break into your voyage story but I feel I need to explain a few more things about myself. Yes, it's Mark Stringer again. When I do some navel gazing I come up with another acronym: P.S. No, it does not mean post script as in that lost art, letter writing. It means public school. Yes, I lay all my personal traits at the door of my educational institution. Some will say he was like that before he went to that expensive place. Who knows and who cares. It's my excuse and I'll stick to it.

*

It was a wet and manky morning as the *Polar Adventurer* anchored at the entrance to Elsehul. Greg's quote: "Who would believe in penguins unless he had seen them" was appropriate: three different types swam about the cove.

At breakfast staff members sat with passengers to give them some Antarctic wisdom. There was a tendency to avoid the Antarctic pedants otherwise facetious comments would erupt. The Canadian guy was with an attractive dark haired woman and Rachel. Dubbed the femme fatale, Rachel had already made moves on Colin the oldest staff member. Long painted fingernails had stroked his surprised chest.

At the departure time the staff waited in their wet Zodiacs near the ship. Waterproofed passengers headed down the gangway into the boats helped by a couple of Filipino crewmen. One woman who looked like an aged film star clumped down in bright red rubber boots.

As our sea mammal expert was fond of saying: "Get you' rubbers out!" This always brought a titter from the North Americans.

Jill a Zodiac driver had a few of the older Antarctic types including Boyd.

"You drive like a woman, don't you?"

"Yes," said Jill, "like Danica Patrick, the woman race driver."

With that she gunned her engine plastering Boyd to the side of the boat. Staff always remembered the awkward passengers. The contented ones were forgotten.

In the cove as rain gently fell, black-browed albatrosses took off from the water like slow air force bombers. Slim light-mantled sooty albatrosses screamed eerily as they slipped around the cliffs. Golden plumed macaroni penguins plopped into the sea joining the gentoo and king penguins.

The boats went past narrow beaches packed with breeding fur seals. Dominant males stuck out their chests. Some of the smaller females had tiny dark pups. A giant petrel worked the carcass of a dead young seal. The noise was deafening as competing fur seal bulls roared, defending their harems. Tucked higher up on one beach were rusty try pots used to render down elephant seal blubber a hundred years ago.

The Zodiacs rose and fell as staff loaded the passengers back on to the ship. One large Australian woman had to be yanked quickly onto the gangway by the two Filipino crewmen to prevent her from heading backwards into the sea. As she later said:

"I would have preferred a couple of husky Ukrainians to get me out of the Zodiac. I'm built for comfort not speed."

*

Jim decided that Peter despite his story about Popper and his gold coins was strongly connected to the robbery. Peter was the right age, was used to speaking Spanish, had been part of that gold symposium and was knowledgeable about gold. He seemed to have no steady job, needed money and was keen for an independently wealthy life.

However, Jim did ask others about the gold robbery. Boyd just muttered:

"Who cares?" and pushed himself towards the hot soup tureens for lunch. Here other passengers stuffed themselves after the hardship of sitting in wet Zodiacs for a couple of hours steadily photographing wildlife. The staff photographer reminded them to download their memory cards if they had low giga bytes.

Boyd's voice boomed out on the morning's activity:

"Elsehul or Else's hole. It's not our esteemed Elsa's hole, but it was a good place to kill elephant seal in the old days. And if they needed a sheltered place on the other side of the island the sealers only had to drag their boats some four hundred yard across land."

One French man asked Jim: "What is this Else's hole?"

"I'm not sure but it sounds rude."

Before they reached Salisbury Plain the first landing on South Georgia Jim approached a few more passengers but again with no success. Martin his cabin mate had only heard of the robbery second hand. He had never traveled around South America.

Bob the staff birder told the passengers that the two Salisbury Plain glaciers had receded back a long way. There was plenty of room for over a hundred thousand king penguins. The wind floated the sound and smell of many of them to the ship.

Each shiny Zodiac bumped through the waves and pushed up against the dark sandy beach. The visitors including some crew members slid along wet pontoons and stepped into the sea water. Thousands of yard-high white fronted, black coated, orange splashed king penguins stood along the beach. Jim noticed a youngish long-legged blond woman gingerly stepping ashore. He asked Carol about her.

"Are you interested?"

"No, no, but I haven't seen her during the voyage."

"She gets violently sea sick and spends most of her time in her cabin."

"I guess she won't be around much," said Jim.

Carol didn't reply.

CHAPTER THIRTEEN

Boyd moved past thousands of king penguins. A steady squawking ran through the rookery. There was always a chance for another stunning photograph. Several years ago he had photographed two giant petrels fighting over a dead penguin.

A steady drizzle fell so he kept his Nikon D7000 in its waterproof bag. There might be a good picture from the top of the bluff where like an Old Testament prophet he could look down on his cast of thousands. Not that the penguins were interested in him.

As Boyd reached up to pull his body over a tussac clump on the bluff a large rock from above smashed on a ledge close by. Showered with wet rock chips he pressed himself into the hillside. Blood oozed down his face. He looked up. There was no one there. Below neither penguins nor people noticed what had happened.

Boyd slowly clambered back down. A pair of nesting skuas eyed him, ready to attack. There were some on board who were not too keen on him. But to kill him? He was not a person to be trifled with. The staff would hear of this.

*

Carol photographed rust colored seaweed, seal skeletons, the odd penguin foot and a clump of snorting elephant seals. King penguin shots were continuous: en masse, close ups of wet pelts, off-white eggs, small grey chicks, and older chicks like teenage mall rats standing around in brown fuzzy jackets. She shot through and sometimes without a plastic bag. Jim took the odd snap and left it at that.

Some passengers had returned to the ship for a hot shower and a change of clothes. Jim and Carol waited for the last Zodiac. They turned at a cry from the distance. Maisie, an American woman who had tried to hang around with Peter the last day or so, was waving and yelling. She staggered through the penguins and collapsed by the Zodiac.

"Peter," she wept. "He fell!"

"Where? What happened?" Greg the leader was keen to get his show back on the sea.

"On the side of the bluff! He fell. He's badly hurt!" She held out her hands, pleading for help.

Greg sent Jill, the Zodiac driver and a triathlete back home, loping off to where Maisie had vaguely pointed. He changed channels and radioed the ship for medical help.

Jill on the emergency channel had reported that it was serious.

"Why did he fall?" asked Greg turning to Maisie.

"I don't know," she said impatiently. "Peter was on the bluff above me photographing the whole penguin rookery.

"Peter cried out. He fell right down in front of me on the rocks! Peter's bleeding badly and he can't move." Maisie wept again, now holding her head as if it would stop the image of the crumpled man.

A new Zodiac landed the doctor and a stretcher crew. They hurried through a sea of penguins towards the bluff.

Maisie was given hot tea. As the stretcher party brought their burden down to the beach she started wailing and rushed over to the covered shape. She pulled back the blanket. Blood dripped from Peter's head. There was no sign of life. An eye stared out at nothing. The other was swollen shut. His face was bruised and battered. Bloody mucus seeped from his broken nose. His arms were strapped close to his body. Nylon straps pressed his body tight against the stretcher. Jim noticed Peter's head wounds. They were at the back and front of the skull.

"Is he going to be all right?" Maisie said not registering that Peter had said nothing as the doctor replaced the blanket.

The doctor said: "Yes."

"Why did he fall?" she asked.

"He must have slipped off the cliff," said Greg. This sort of thing did not happen on well run expedition cruises.

"Peter told me he's a rock climber. He surely wouldn't have slipped even in this sort of weather." She looked at the sodden people around her.

Jill said: "The cliff was wet with a lot of loose rock."

"No, he wouldn't have slipped," repeated Maisie.

The doctor led her sobbing to the Zodiac. There was no sound from Peter.

On the ship Peter was taken to the infirmary. Maisie was led by Carol through the disinfectant tray and the water to wash away the penguin poop. Curious passengers about to ask a question were pushed aside as Carol led her patient upstairs. In Maisie's cabin Carol helped her to take off her wet clothes. Maisie looked at the tablets the doctor had given her.

"I hate the idea that pills are the answer"

"The doctor thinks they will help. It's the way they're trained."

"What will happen to Peter?"

"We are meeting a large cruise ship which will take Peter to the Falkland Islands' main hospital." Maisie was not ready to deal with Peter's death. "Do you want me to stay awhile?"

"I guess so." Maisie was silent for a moment. She clutched a blanket on her bed and said: "Just one, mind you." She took a pill and slept.

Carol stayed with her first Antarctic patient.

*

There was a general summons to the lounge. Greg talked about the accident, and that Peter had passed away. Everyone should be vigilant at all times. There would be an inquest. Peter would be transferred to the *Southern Cruiser* at King Edward Cove and then taken to Stanley.

On other matters there would be a three mile hike the next day from Fortuna Bay to Stromness Harbour. This followed the last part of Sir Ernest Shackleton, Wolsey and Crean's twenty-two mile winter trek in 1916 across unexplored mountains and glaciers.

With three others they had sailed earlier in an open boat eight hundred miles from Elephant Island to South Georgia to get help for the twenty-two crew left behind.

"Needless to say," said Greg, "this hike will not be for everyone especially after today's terrible accident. Most of us will stay on board and sail around to Stromness Harbour."

*

"What the heck was he doing over there?" asked Frank as he clutched his usual glass of rum and coke.

"I almost got hit on that bluff by a falling rock. Someone has a grudge against me," said Boyd before anyone could answer Frank's question.

Yes, me, thought Doug.

"But we all love you, Boyd!" put in Frank.

"I mentioned it to the staff," Boyd carried on, "but they didn't seem interested."

"He had climbing experience." Arthur sort of answered Frank's question.

"Obviously not enough," said Frank.

"Most of us don't have enough of anything," grunted Doug.

There were a few nods of: "I could have told you that."

Jim thought about Peter's death. There was the eyeball pecked at by a giant petrel. But why were the wounds on both the front and back of his head? Peter couldn't have landed on the back of his head and then bounced up and hit the other side of his head, or could he? Did someone push him off the cliff? Was Peter getting too close to the gold if it was on board, or did he have it hidden away somewhere?

Later Jim and Carol looked at the passing rocky ridges plunging into the sea as the setting sun light flowed along deep fjords.

"Peter wouldn't have slipped on those rocks. He climbs around Seattle in the rain."

"Was there anyone else up there?" asked Jim.

"Not that I know of. Shaun that young Australian guy took a telephoto picture of Peter on the bluff. It might show something. No one else saw any one. I guess we all make mistakes at some time."

Even with the slight tobacco perfume coming off Carol Jim felt comfortable with her. He had stopped being comfortable with his ex-wife Janet. She was pretty and pretty well organized. He was the carefree part of the relationship. Opposites attract, so they say. Jim later realized Janet was not a fun person. He gave up trying to carry them both. Perhaps he should have tried harder.

High snow capped mountains caught the last of the sun as the ship steamed into King Edward Cove. There were a few lights from the British Antarctic Survey station huddled under dark mountains.

The *Polar Adventurer* anchored close to the fifteen hundred passenger *Southern Cruiser*. A tender arrived with their doctor. The ship's doctor handed the body still in its stretcher over to the new medic. The large cruise ship was anxious to leave. Both ships gave gentle hoots and parted in the dark.

*

Mark, here. Why is it that other people mess things up? Some of Leon's gold is missing. Oh, dear! He left it in plain sight in a life boat. "It's gawn!" as some of the lower class types say. Would he be willing as the Americans express it: "to move in on mine?" We will see. Stay tuned.

I now bring you news, breaking news. Leon assumed that that Tielmann fellow, in nosing around the upper deck, found his gold. Despite the gold not being in Tielmann's cabin, Leon moved on his own initiative and had that Rita person push the said Tielmann off of a cliff. I keep on saying KISS, KISS, (keep it simple stupid), but do they listen?

I, of course, was nowhere near the crime scene. That's my story, anyway. I had hung around with Bob the birder. I added my commiserations to the general clamor of remorse, and managed to bad-mouth Leon at the same time by saying: "Do you know I asked for extra towels and that hotel manager said: 'We have a limited supply. We are environmentally sound.'" One must show that one has no truck with him.

CHAPTER FOURTEEN

Forgetting the unpleasantness of yesterday the adventurers gazed around Fortuna Bay. In a slight rain dark striated mountains rose up either side of the bay, and in front of the ship stretched a low glacier. The visitors hit the beach like a D-Day landing, cameras at the ready to shoot anything that moved or didn't.

Thousands of king penguins stood around. Behind them a few light colored figures moved slowly over new grass. Reindeer. They had been brought to South Georgia by Norwegian whalers for food, more than a hundred years ago.

Jim left Carol, rather reluctantly, as she snapped more birdlife with the staff birder Bob and other avian enthusiasts. He followed four English people from Manchester beside a milky glacial stream.

"Bob's right," said a short woman who had led the way. "Wait ten minutes and you'll get the weather you want."

Jim forced himself to look north as the pale sun broke through low drifting damp clouds.

Avoiding skittish, scraggly reindeer, the group headed over broken mounds of moraine before being stopped by a forceful ice-cold river pouring out of the König Glacier.

Jim broached the captain's concern of the gold heist in Ushuaia.

A round-faced woman looked at Jim and asked: "Why are you interested in that?"

He mumbled about hearing about it and wondered if others had also.

"But why are *you* interested in it?" asked a sandy-haired man.

.Jim had no reasonable answers. He said he needed to look at the elephant seals on the beach. Jim didn't think his tail was between his legs. It just sort of felt like it.

Clusters of passengers snapped the baby weaner elephant seals, careful not to get in each other's camera line. Cute, weighing three hundred pounds, the sleek plump grey sausages with enormous black eyes lay on the shingle. Occasionally one would give a mournful cry. Their mothers had left the pups so they could feed in the sea after a long fast. Jack a thick-necked man from Northern Ireland said you would need big buns for these wieners.

"Talking of big buns," he nodded at a stout woman passing by.

"Oh, Jack," said his wife and turned away. Jim recognized the man as the one who tried to usurp his place next to Carol some five days before.

Nearby a few old smelly male elephant seals, who had failed to acquire a harem, lay side by side like large primeval brown slugs. An occasional red mouth with yellowing teeth would open for a yawn. Snot dripped from bulbous noses. One seal's penis slid out. There was some nervous laughter from the male viewers.

"What envy do they call that?" one woman asked.

A few teenage elephant seals threw their ton or so of body weight at each other like sumo wrestlers. They strove to learn dominance. One or two of them might get lucky in the future and become beach masters with their own group of females.

Jim questioned a few people about the bank hold up, but again came up empty handed. He had asked some of his suspects who was around the bluff where Peter fell at Salisbury Plain. Boyd had been up the bluff but said he retreated when a rock: "Almost killed me." Rachel denied being anywhere near it: "Too much exercise. I don't like to overdo things." Arthur said he had been there several times before and didn't have to do it again. Jack had been near the bluff but on the right hand side. Jim had seen him stalking penguins.

Later the captain informed Jim that Peter Tielmann's cabin had been sealed.

"He could have been a robbery suspect."

There was no gold in the cabin, (was there any gold on this ship thought Jim) but the captain had a list of people who had attended a gold symposium the day before the ship left Ushuaia.

"I presume you didn't know about this symposium?"

"No," said Jim, not sure why he denied it. He remembered Peter's drunken monologue on Tierra del Fuego gold and the limited number of people allowed into the symposium.

The attendees were Boyd, Jack, Frank, Rachel, Arthur, Peter as well as several other non-passenger types.

"I tried to get this list of attendees earlier, but the Argentinean bureaucracy was reluctant to divulge the names even for a gold robbery. So you have a robbery to investigate if that's what happened on this ship and a death. Was it an accident? An autopsy in Stanley may help us.

"Be careful. We are on unsure ground."

What was this "we" business, thought Jim? Who had been asking the leading questions?

*

Doug stayed on board in his cabin. You could only take so many penguin shots. He wondered if Boyd's rock incident was attention getting. When he could get around to it he would give Boyd some attention.

Doug wasn't going to do the hike. The next day at that touristy King Edward Cove Boyd would be safe. Strange how he thought of Boyd as his. Others must have suffered financially as he had.

The deed had to be done in the Antarctic. But would he be well enough to carry it out? Pushing Boyd into the sea would not be real icy justice. Doug needed to rest. Pace yourself. No overdoing the painkillers. Was that what OD meant? The pain in his stomach was steady.

CHAPTER FIFTEEN

Thirty keen hikers landed on the east side of Fortuna Bay in the afternoon. Staff carried "seal bashers", long poles and the odd hockey stick, to make a corridor through nipping fur seals. The visitors hurried over the beach as staff poked back fur seals that wanted to bite the new comers.

From the hillside a rare honey-colored seal was seen further along the beach. Staff told the hikers not to descend. Jack, the man from Northern Ireland, didn't think this applied to him. He cut across the hillside and down through nervous seals to what Mike, the sea animal expert, later called a leucistic fur seal. Mike in turn dodged annoyed seals along the waterline and confronted Jack.

"We keep fifteen meters away from fur seals. Head back up the hill."

Jack gave him the hard man stare, slowly put away his camera, and moved up the slope.

A variety of nationalities and ages pulled their way up the hill using the strong tussac grass. Boyd occasionally glanced up.

"Looking for rocks?" asked Frank.

Jim recognized most of the hikers including the long-legged woman from yesterday. A discreet question to a staff member: "She looks like a dancer, doesn't she?" came up with the name Mandy. The cruise was showing promise.

The group was stretched on the side of the hillside like beads on a necklace. An eighty-one year old Brit, Dan, unlike some of the other beads had no trouble moving up the thousand feet. Below the *Polar Adventurer* moved out of the bay towards the ocean.

The grass turned to shale then old snow. The sun blazed through the cool air. At the col distant broken topped mountains appeared. A group photo shot was taken at a small piece of water called Crean Lake.

On the descent John the staff geologist told the hikers to avoid the cliffs on the right, and the stream on the left. Shackleton, Worsley and Crean had had to slide down through the stream's waterfall. Below along the bay was the defunct rust-brown Stromness Harbour whaling station.

Jim concentrated on Carol. He asked her what music she liked.

"Classical. Is there any other?"

Jim mentioned 1980s pop music.

"Oh, like ABBA?"

"They're so-so. I was thinking of Canadian singers like Colin James and Bryan Adams. How about if I sing a bit of "Never Surrender".

"Only if I can sing an aria from "Carmen".

"Operas are all in Italian, you can't understand them, and they all sound the same."

"Your last two points make them sound like a lot of rock music."

Jim realized he had not listened to any music on the trip. There was too much occupying him.

"What sports are you into?" he asked.

"None. Why should I?"

"For fitness?"

"Being a nurse is being fit enough."

Jim tentatively put forward that quite a few nurses smoked.

"So?"

He stopped being a people-minder and looked at the scenery, though he did ask the question he should have asked some time ago.

"No, I know nothing about that robbery. I have something far more important to be concerned about."

Near the broken down whaling station, people waited for the ship, photographed wildlife and strolled. Carol concentrated on more animal pictures. Jim espied Mandy further down the beach, but she was with the English group from this morning at Fortuna Bay. He did not want to be interrogated again.

By the water a young seal lay bleeding, a flipper almost torn off. The staff photographer took obligatory shots, said the seal would die, but the skuas and giant petrels would benefit.

An Australian woman skirting a cluster of fur seals slipped and scattered some female seals. A heavy-set male seal threw itself forward propelled by its back-turned rear flippers. Boyd dropped a large rock in front of the angry male. The seal paused and renewed his advance. Boyd clapped two rocks together and yelled. The seal stopped, and reluctantly retreated to his harem. He had noticed a young male seal was making advances on one of his females. The Australian woman thanked Boyd.

"It was nothing," and he strode off.

Jim said to Carol: "There's hope for him yet."

"One deed doesn't make a summer. Especially for *him*," as she concentrated on photographing a bleached whale vertebra.

The *Polar Adventurer* arrived, and other passengers disembarked for more photos. At recap time Colin the historian talked about the sixty year long twentieth century whaling industry based on South Georgia. Thousands of whales were killed and their blubber turned into oil. Land-based whaling had now stopped. The whale population was starting to increase, though slow compared to the multitudes of fur seals.

Jim cornered Doug before "Happy Hour" and asked his constant question. Doug denied any knowledge of the robbery or of South American connections. At the bar Doug showed more interest in talking about research that showed that late afternoon was when the human body was most receptive to alcohol.

Frank said: "Any time's good for me."

Ed, Doug's friend, said: "I second that!"

Doug put in:

"You must forgive him, he had a depraved childhood."

"Don't you mean deprived? said Boyd.

"That as well." Doug turned from Boyd to look outside at white-chinned petrels flying back and forth.

While Carol worked on her pictures at dinner Jim forced himself to join Jack and his wife. The aggressiveness might be part of taking part in a bank hold up. Jim asked if there was a space at the table.

"Whatever," said Jack, who did not acknowledge his seating opponent of a few days ago.

"For Jack," said his wife Doreen, "that's polite."

"Keep a civil tongue in your head, woman!"

"Oh, Jack."

Jim introduced himself to the other British couple at the table. They had not been south before. The wife mentioned that one passenger had been bitten by a fur seal and needed antibiotic shots. Jack said a few others needed to be bitten. Jim asked why.

"Too obnoxious and too bossy."

Jim asked Doreen why she had not done the trek.

"She's a bit fragile like a lot of women," butted in her husband.

"Jack!"

Had Jack been to South America?

"Not bloody likely!"

Jack thought the bank robbery at Ushuaia was a good thing:

"It keeps those bloody banks on their toes!"

"A bit tough if you've got money in a bank," said Jim.

"Well, there's always those who fleece and those who need fleecing. I've found in business there's always lots of soft sheep shits around."

"Really, Jack," said his wife.

"That's the way it is, woman!" He looked at Jim. "Why are you interested in that robbery?"

"Curious," said Jim.

He tried the safer topic of music. Jack said outside of Elvis everything else was crap. The husband of the British couple liked Elvis but he also liked brass bands from Yorkshire.

"Christ!" was Doreen's husband's response.

The wife was fond of country and western singers but not the heavy electric-guitar ones, lit up like Christmas trees.

One week had gone. Jim had not narrowed down the doubtfuls for the robbery. Obviously Peter wasn't part of the robbery unless there had been a falling out among thieves. Had he been the joker or an ace of little worth?

That left those with money. What about someone blending in with the less monied tour group crowd? They could have slipped away from their group, dealt with Peter, and then returned to mix again. Jim would keep an open mind or was that an empty mind?

CHAPTER SIXTEEN

On his way to see Carol and her Benson and Hedges there was a light touch on his arm.

"Jim, you must tell me about the hike. So few of us did it. What did you see?" Rachel pulled Jim towards a huge armchair. He looked at her prominent breasts and quickly launched into a summary of the trek.

"Wasn't it strenuous?"

"It was a bit of a slog. You could feel for Shackleton and his companions."

"Didn't they do it in winter?"

Jim said that was so.

Rachel anticipating his leaving her said:

"I know you're interested in that gold robbery. Did you know that some of us were at a gold symposium the day before we left port?"

That group again. Their knees were touching. Jim couldn't seem to move his.

"Is there a connection between that symposium and the robbery?" asked Jim.

"I don't know. I thought you might know," said Rachel, giving him a slight press of her hand.

So much for his subtle inquiries. He stammered:

"Peter said he was at the symposium. The robbery seemed to be important to him so I've been asking a few people about it." Actually a lot of people on board, thought Jim. "Are you interested in gold?"

Rachel smiled and said:

"No, not that method of acquiring it. I thought of Peter and his terrible accident, and then I remembered he was at the symposium." She squeezed the inside of the knee opposite her.

*

A small white wine or something more sanguine. Didn't sanguine mean optimistic not bloody? Carol thanked Sandy for the Bloody Mary.

Boyd broke in with: "So you saw the two love birds?" brought a "FU!" to Carol's lip. She stifled it as she headed outside. He was going to get it. Maybe Jim as well. They always wanted their cake and eat it. It didn't make sense but the expression fitted the occasion. She watched the white-chinned petrels. Their relationships seemed OK. She wondered about hers.

After nursing school Carol had married a handsome doctor who needed care from other nurses as well as her. She divorced him after three years. There were one or two other relationships, but no one special.

Was this relationship with Jim a biological clock item, was he worth it, or was he another ruddy male playing the field? The second smoke got ground into the blackened ashtray. She would deal with Boyd first, and consider Jim later – if there was anything to think about. She liked him, but…After Ushuaia: a friendly farewell, a few desultory emails (more from her than him), and an end to the relationship due to distance and absence?

*

Jim wrenched himself away from his temptress with the excuse the captain had some Arctic slides for him to copy. Seated in the library he put his suspects in columns. The last name first plus the number of South American trips and any financial information the captain had gotten him. He would revisit the twenty-five or so possibles over the next day or so.

He could peep into suspicious cabins during lectures, once they left South Georgia. Maybe a bulletin on gold coins would be lying there or even a gold coin. Right. And then there was Carol to think about or use his imagination on. Before he retired Jim went and spoke to the captain.

"The injuries to Peter Tielmann's head were not what a straight fall would have made," said Jim.

"How do you know?" the captain asked.

"He had injuries to the front and back of his skull. I've seen injuries from falls before."

"The doctor wasn't sure. Stanley will give us a better idea of the cause of death."

"Maybe," said Jim, "Peter was getting close to the gold if it is on this ship. He was then finished off."

The captain's eyes flickered to a cupboard at the back of his cabin. "Why did Peter Tielmann talk so much about the bank hold up?" asked Captain Engstrom.

"Perhaps he was so interested in it so that it appeared he couldn't be in on it, or maybe he was genuinely interested in gold," Jim said.

Jim wondered again about the captain. Was he the brain behind the robbery, and Jim was there to root out any suspicious activities? "My crew is not involved," seemed simplistic.

"What about robbers falling out over the money, and Tielmann gets bumped off?"

Was that a deflection from the captain, thought Jim?

"It's possible," said Jim.

The captain continued: "Jim," he said warmly, "investigate the death as if it was suspicious. If the gold is on board it can wait.

"We'll keep Mr. Tielmann's death as an accident especially as the Governor of South Georgia would hold up this ship, the cruise and all the passengers if a non-accidental death leaked out. She could send us straight back to Port Stanley."

"The trip must carry on," said Jim.

"Precisely," replied the captain. "In Stanley with better medical facilities and a military doctor we will have a more exact cause of his death."

"That's true," said Jim.

"The body would then be shipped back to the States. Hopefully by then we," (you mean me, thought Jim), "will have got to the bottom of everything."

"And the gold?" asked Jim.

"If it is on board, it is not going anywhere," said the captain. He concluded: "I'm sure the death is not related to the robbery."

Jim was dismissed.

CHAPTER SEVENTEEN

The *Polar Adventurer's* anchor joined decades of whaling debris at the bottom of King Edward Cove. The clouds blew away from the surrounding dark mountains. Opposite the scientific station the remains of the Grytviken whaling station continued to rust away.

Greg started the day with: "'In the darkening twilight I saw a lone star hover, gem-like above the bay.' These were the last words written by Sir Ernest Shackleton before he died here in 1922. We'll have the traditional toast to this great Antarctic explorer at the graveyard. Then you are free to explore."

From fur and elephant seal harvesting soon after Captain Cook arrived to sixty years of whaling during the twentieth century to the start of the Falklands War and to the present eco-tourism South Georgia had had its share of history.

The visitors enjoyed themselves though some avoided Boyd's and the ex-BAS crowd's Zodiacs. The old bawdy songs broke any quiet contemplation of the wild.

By the old whalers' graveyard the staff prodded seals back and persuaded passengers not to stop for open mouth close-ups of eager toothed fur seals. Congregating in the whalers' graveyard the passengers were only concerned about one grave. By Shackleton's headstone paper cups of Irish whiskey were handed out, and "The Boss" was toasted.

*

Carol was not with Jim. She had headed off to Maiviken to photograph more wild life including a meat-eating pintail duck. He was left to photograph the old whaling factory on his own. The wooden plan where thousands of whales had been dragged up and cut up was long gone, but there were plenty of rusty orange-brown blubber cookers and other machinery lying around.

After getting little satisfaction from asking who was near the bluff at Salisbury Plain Jim headed back to the empty graveyard. He could now photograph the one granite slab of interest without having other bodies blocking the shot.

At a lunch of Scotch broth, fresh bread, and chicken curry there was room for layer cake. Jim sat with Arthur and Georgina. Rachel was further down the room with Mark. Jim asked about Shackleton and the Antarctic.

"After getting scurvy on Scott's first Antarctic expedition, Ernest Shackleton headed south again with his own expedition. He almost got to the South Pole. Later in a letter to his wife Shackleton said he turned back as he was sure she would prefer a live donkey to a dead lion.

"Shackleton's later *Endurance* expedition to try and cross the Antarctic was stopped by heavy ice. The ship sank, and after many months on ice the crew landed at Elephant Island. You have the facts on the voyage of the six to South Georgia and the winter trek across the island. For those of us who lived in the Antarctic we preferred Shackleton to Scott. "The Boss" got his men back alive.

"Of course, after we lived down south there was always a problem for us when we came out. You married right away, you traveled, or you returned to the Antarctic." Arthur smiled at Georgina, and then said to Jim:

"You're interested in that gold robbery like Peter, aren't you?"

Jim admitted that he was, and said: "What do you think about the idea that the gold is on board the *Polar Adventurer*?"

"Fanciful," said Arthur. "I can't see anyone, not even Boisterous Boyd doing that."

"Well, it's a prank that Boyd might have done when he was younger," said Georgina.

"Yes, but we're all too old now," Arthur said.

Was Arthur being devious as he talked about how old some of them were. Should Boyd be removed from the suspect ranking? Jim still wasn't sure. Perhaps Boyd's "accident" on the Salisbury Plain bluff was contrived. He should keep Rachel at bay, a bit more; otherwise she might cloud his inquiry. And Carol? He should back off a little so he could get some answers, or maybe not.

CHAPTER EIGHTEEN

By hanging back until the last Zodiac but one had left Jim avoided Rachel. He was a bit unsteady when he landed. Too much dessert, too much coffee or Jill's driving? At the landing site below the museum next to the beached *Dias*, an old boat, Jim attached himself to the young Australian couple, Shaun and Pam.

They entered the old whaling manager's house, which had been turned into a museum. Overhead hung a stuffed wandering albatross. It viewed dispassionately the humans below viewing exhibits. There was still a run on the souvenir and stamp items. Three young people spent their summer selling items to tourists. Post cards could be sent home from this out-of-the-way place. The outgoing postcards often left South Georgia on the same ship that the passengers were on.

Rachel held up a t-shirt in front of her slim body, and asked Jim what he thought of the yellow shirt on which three king penguins marched across her breasts.

"Seems, OK," he said, and as Pam and Shaun left, Jim quickly joined them. He would get mementoes later.

The two Australians were going to climb up the side of the mountain to take pictures of the cove below. They wandered through the rusty remains of the whaling station to the small white wooden church further back. The trio rang the church bell, and read plaques to Shackleton and others on the walls. Most church congregations were the summer visitors.

They passed an old soccer field and on the side of the mountain, the wooden remains of the Norwegian whalers' ski jump. Above them leaning slightly to the right, dark Mount Hodges showed its twisted layers of rock. The light opened as they climbed higher. A pale sun shone on the cove, King Edward Point with its glistening red roofs and the *Polar Adventurer* anchored in still water.

Below Jim could see passengers moving through the whaling station and along the beach. At least up here he was safe from Rachel. To his left he looked wistfully towards where Carol's group had headed over the hill to Maiviken cove. A slight wind blew around them. Sea birds below gave the odd cry.

The trio headed down to reach Shackleton's cross just past the King Edward base. Shaun mentioned that that man Moresby who seemed to have a lot of information about the south had said not to bother with Shackleton's cross. They had asked Boyd who said: "Do it!"

The couple were teachers. When Jim said: "Disculpe, ¿habla castellano?" their lack of response probably meant their Spanish was zero unless they were very good actors. His own Spanish was hard learned to make it easier on a Mexican holiday. Jim decided they were not the master minds behind the gold coin robbery, but noted them just in case.

And his own teaching job? He would have to say less about it. An American woman whose daughter was a teacher thought it highly unusual that he would have only twenty public school students in his class. It was a number that just came into his head when she asked about his class. He should do his homework. Weren't policemen even ex-ones always prepared?

At dinner Carol sat with the birders Bob, Ricardo and Alec, and a few others who had gone over to

Maiviken. Jim was not going to force himself on her. He avoided the usual Antarctic types and sat with a small British tour group. They had not traveled south before, so he eliminated them from his enquires.

On the *Polar Adventurer* Jim discovered different regional UK accents. This group was from near Newcastle in northeast England. They were Geordies. He had to strain to understand their language. It was in sharp contrast to the careful articulations of Arthur and Georgina. He was used to educated North Americans who tended to sound the same

Another thing Jim noticed was the dining room sound level at meal times. At breakfast the noise level was almost mute. An early rising was only for some. At lunch there was more conversation, and the decibels rose. By dinner everyone was breaking in with what they had seen and photographed that day. There was a cacophony of sound rolling around the room helped by Happy Hour drinks and the dinner wines.

*

As Jim left dinner for the bar a Dutch woman cornered him and asked him to go outside with her. He was certainly attracting the women. This woman like Carol smelled of smoke, but had a blunt no nonsense manner. She spoke very good English and introduced herself as Brigit from La Hague.

"My friend Margriet does not understand much English so she records the lectures. Her son back in the Netherlands will translate them for her." She paused and instinctively pulled out a cigarette. It was not lit.

"Yesterday after the evening recap my friend left her recorder turned on. Everyone had gone outside to see a whale blowing. Two people on the recorder were talking about gold. I know you and that man who had the accident were interested in the gold robbery."

So much for an unobtrusive investigation of the heist, thought Jim.

"Would you listen to it and return the recorder to Margriet when you are finished?"

Jim thanked her and retreated to his library lair. He listened. One man was Spanish sounding, a Filipino, a crew member? The other man was more educated, English or American though the recording quality was not too good. Did that mean no women were part of the robbery though a woman could be the brains behind the scheme? Surely the Dutch women weren't behind the robbery and used the recording to head him off in a wild pursuit? Jim headed to the bar.

*

The bar group, well established as to personnel, place and time, kept Sandy busy. Doug held on to his glass of Chilean Sauvignon Blanc. He noticed that Boyd had more than his usual number of drinks. Doug had counted at least three glasses of malt whisky going into Boyd since he had arrived. Boyd had been busy at Happy Hour. Was there no limit to his capacity?

Doug suddenly asked Boyd about the fund that he had lost so much money on.

"Who made money on that Antarctic Trust Fund? Have you got any information on it?"

Boyd snapped: "No!" and swallowed some McCallan. When would this damn ship lay on the decent stuff?

The Australian circled in again. "I wonder how one could find out?"

Before Boyd could snap another reply, Frank stepped in with:

"Probably one of the financial institutions could tell you."

Doug wondered why Frank was answering Boyd's question.

Boyd said: "It's all ice long under the bridge."

Ron diverted the conversation and asked if any of them had been here when there was whaling going on.

Arthur said he had one brief visit when Leif Harbour up from Stromness had flensed the last few whales before all the land based stations stopped whaling. And the reason for that? As normal, costs and diminishing whales.

"This island," said Georgina "had been used for killing animals. Today it's for us friendly tourists who don't kill."

Jim had an image of a blooded Peter being carried back to the ship. He noticed Rachel waylaying one of the younger staff members. Her green shimmering dress moved well as she did. Ed came out with:

"She's a cougar, isn't she?"

Boyd added: "More like a saber-tooth tiger."

Georgina: "Are you men intimidated by her?"

Ed said that they were only having a bit of fun.

"At a woman's expense?" was Georgina's rejoinder. The males examined their drinks.

To make a bit of a recovery Ed asked: "What happened to the body of that guy who died on the Sheldon Expedition? Was he buried there or was he taken back to the UK?"

"I expect he was buried near where they found him," said Frank.

Ed nodded as if that was all he needed in Antarctic knowledge.

Jim left for the smokers' deck to see if he could make up with Carol. He stepped from the lighted corridor into pitch blackness. He could see the Southern Cross hanging above. The Milky Way swarmed with unfamiliar stars and constellations. He found Carol by the yellow tip of her cigarette. Jim assumed her hiking trip had been a success.

By the way of building bridges he asked her if she had seen the Southern Cross. Carol said she hadn't. Jim pointed it out and the less than easy way of orientating to the south. It took a few tries on his part, and following his arm with hers he had some success in more than finding a constellation. His Southern Hemisphere research had paid off..

"It's not as easy as the Plough for directions," she said.

"Oh, you mean the Big Dipper. I suppose finding good water was important to early North American pioneers, and plows were more important to the English."

The lights were turned off to stop birds crashing into the ship at night. The rest of the cove was dark. There was a bit of light to the northwest. The wind rattled a few stays. Jim and Carol were content to lean side by side on the railing and peer up at thousands of stars sparkling above them in the clear black sky.

CHAPTER NINETEEN

After the "Bing-bong" broke through the torpor of the early morning another of Greg's quotes was thrown around the ship: "'King Weather is the tyrant of these latitudes, and he rules South Georgia with ruthless despotism.'

"That quote by the Australian Frank Hurley, a photographer on Shackleton's *Endurance* expedition, is a heads up to be aware that this is still South Georgia, and the weather can change in a moment. The sky is clear, but the pressure is falling.

"As you are all aware we are heading into St. Andrews Bay. If you haven't seen enough king penguins you will today. Shall we say 100,000 pairs give or take a few thousand either way, depending on this year's food supply? We're here all morning and then head south to Gold Harbour in the afternoon, our last South Georgia stop."

Jim decided to sit with the Californian couple he had first asked about the original robbery. He might ask about their South American contacts. Before he could get there Mark joined the pair. They exchanged pleasantries.

Jim McKinnon put down his French toast and one coffee. He avoided having too much liquid before meals, as there was nowhere to relieve yourself once you were on shore. He nodded at everyone. There was a bit of silence. Jim plunged in and asked Mark:

"Have you met Jacqueline and Richard down south before this?"

Jacqueline broke in with a firm lawyer denial: "No, we've only met on this trip. And before you ask we have no information on that gold coin robbery."

Jim caught off-guard, reddened: "Oh, OK."

"I just heard about it. That's all I know," said Mark cutting up his French toast.

Jim rallied with: "In Canada we have it with maple syrup."

"Yes, it is rather nice that way."

Rachel made her entrance, sat next to Mark, and beamed at everyone. Jacqueline and Richard looked at each other and continued to eat their rolls and jam. Rachel brightly said:

"So, we're to see a quarter of a million penguins today. That should keep the picture snappers happy."

Jacqueline asked: "You don't take pictures yourself?" as she moved her Nikon camera with a body worth two thousand dollars to one side.

"Only a few snaps with my Olympus point and shoot."

Jacqueline coolly bored on with: "You must miss a lot of what's going on."

Rachel did not reply. Except for Jim and Rachel the rest of the table was loaded with expensive camera equipment. Jim, with his PHD camera (push here dummy) like Rachel's, refused to support her.

He understood her interest in him was not just his handsome body, but also something to do with the bank heist or was she was being used by someone else for that end?

Jim excused himself and said "Hi" to Carol as she came in late. He asked if he could join her on the St. Andrews Bay landing. She looked from the table he had vacated with Rachel to him. She gave a brief: "I guess so."

At the stairway down to the Zodiacs, waves lifted the boats up and down and slapped water over the base of the stairway. Jack from Northern Island carried a large photographic bag and a knapsack. He was determined to hang on to his bag rather than give it to a crew member. A staff member told him to get on with it:

" Use the sailor's grip, there's others waiting."

Jack ignored this and stepped into the dropping Zodiac. He fell onto a vocal Pamela: "Christ!" She pushed him off. Jack stumbled across to the other pontoon and clumsily slid himself and his luggage along the wet surface. Pamela gave him a withering look. She changed it to pity as Doreen carefully followed her husband along the unsteady boat.

Jim and Carol wended their way through the throngs of birds along a long spit of sand. A rushing stream raced along their right hand side on its way to the sea. Hundreds of brown fluffy king penguin chicks crowded the edge of the stream that was lined with discarded brown feathers.

The pair found a piece of rough moraine that looked over the beach covered by a multitude of packed penguins. The way forward was blocked by thousands of penguins and another wide rushing glacial stream. Jim took a few snaps to get the feel of the sea of birds.

Carol's wide-angled lens could not get in the mass of birds. She said you needed a fish-eye lens. Carol took a sequence of pictures to be knitted together later on her computer.

Jack came slowly up their moraine, and dumped his bag on the penguin guano. He ignored Carol and Jim, and started pulling a tripod and a large camera and assorted lens out of his luggage. He had a fish-eye lens. Jack's next half-hour was spent moving around the top of the moraine. He moved around and in front of them. Jim looked at Carol and said loudly:

"Well, we'll be off and leave you to our spot."

There was no response from Jack. At the bottom Doreen wandered along with another couple, seemly glad to be out of the way of her husband's passion.

Like balky school kids the passengers trailed back along the beach, finding yet another excuse for a photograph that could not be missed. The wind picked up and the Zodiacs had to be held close by staff and crew to get everyone aboard.

The lunch had a German theme. Jim took red wine soup, warm potato salad, a bratwurst, and joined Carol at Arthur, Georgina, Frank, Ron and Ed's table. With Peter's death he felt compelled to take more responsibility for the investigations, and that meant more questions. Georgina gave Jim and Carol a perky smile, and said:

"Come and sit down. We all know each other. Those bar sessions certainly help."

Her husband looked amused. He was less amused when Jim asked him about his connections in South America.

"Why?"

"I would have thought with the number of times you've been to the Antarctic you must have made a lot of contacts in Argentina and Chile"

"No, I haven't." Arthur cut up his bratwurst, added bright yellow mustard and didn't stop eating.

Frank started talking about scenic Gold Harbour. Jim left off his inquiries. Carol looked at him quizzically. Jim told her later that he was doing a little research on tourism in South America and the Antarctic. She gave an: "Oh, yes."

CHAPTER TWENTY

The wind increased as the boats headed to what little shelter there was at the Gold Harbour beach. As Greg gave each load of Zodiac passengers instructions about departure times and what could be seen at Gold Harbour, he added: "Don't stroll too far, in case we have to leave quickly."

The visitors headed to see their favorite species and settled down for an hour or so of observing. The wind whipped the fine sand around them adding to the swirling spray from the waves. As the passengers spread along the beach Greg looked at the slate grey clouds which rose steeply from the horizon and were moving in quickly. Jim wondered whether Peter would have liked this place. It had gold in its name even if it was only from iron pyrites.

Carol walked past most of the king penguins and headed up a slope that overlooked the Betrab Glacier whose snout clung to a polished rock cliff. A small lake lay below. Jim trailed along, but did not impose. She looked at him a few times. There was no smile on the wide lips, but no frown either.

Behind them came a slower Boyd, and behind him, Kim, the awkward woman from North London, whom Jim had studiously avoided since the first meal. But maybe he should talk to her in case she was the one behind the bank hold up

Jim was enjoying the rising wind, the squawking penguins, bleating young seals, the odd grunt from wallowing adult seals, and even the whiffs from their obese bodies. The only hardship was that he needed to pee. He had forgotten to go before leaving the ship.

Periodically there would be roar as a piece of the glacier fell off the black shiny wet cliff into the lake. Carol set up her camera equipment on a flat rock to catch the next thundering mass of ice. Jim sat on a nearby rocky lump by the cold water and looked up at the clouds moving rapidly over the mountains. Kim moved over rocks along the lake shoreline. Boyd had stayed up on the top of the moraine rather than hike down to the lake.

Along the main beach the wind increased in velocity and waves raced in. Greg snapped at his staff to round up passengers. Despite the wind and blowing sand the visitors were tardy as ever in returning. It was not wet enough to make them want to head back so soon. Staff kept explaining about the worsening weather. The price of their cameras and the trip made the passengers balky.

The drivers kept their outboard motors running. The Zodiac bows were pointed into the beach. Two crewmen and staff in hip waders held each boat and swung passengers' legs on to the pontoons. Short-legged people were lifted straight in. The waves crashed on the port sides and drenched those struggling to get in.

Once loaded the driver would back out into the waves, point the bow into the wind and roar slowly back to the ship. Most people were soaked. As the numbers on the beach dwindled, Greg waved frantically to the last stragglers and radioed his staff. Elsa, the deputy, counting heads as they left, had got down to the last dozen.

"I'll do one last scan at the south end," said Elsa. John the geologist had radioed that there was no one left. The numbers did not gibe. John brought his last few to the landing site. The wind blew along the beach with more ferocity. The wild life including one large brown male elephant seal lolling in the waves carried on with their lives.

Elsa nodded at John as she passed, and pushed into the wind. She headed up the moraine along a small stream. At the top where the wind increased in fury she found Boyd sheltering behind a rock. She told him: "Hurry back to the Zodiacs!" Elsa waved at Carol and Jim to come up. She noticed Kim on the far side of the lake near the icefall. She signaled. There was no response from Kim.

Elsa scrambled over the rocks to where Kim was looking at a house-size piece of ice that was about to plunge into the lake. Smaller pieces of ice bobbed around the fall site. Elsa yelled to Kim: "The ship's leaving!" She did not think warning about the overhanging ice would make any difference. Kim reluctantly moved back along the side of the lake.

When the two women got to where Carol and Jim had sat a large chunk of the glacier slipped off the wet cliff and crashed into the lake. Kim said: "Oh," as the wave of water whipped across the lake towards her. Where she had been standing before was a mess of broken shards of rock and ice. Elsa said nothing.

Horizontal rain was added to the wind. The waves smashed into Greg's Zodiac. He left the survival equipment, John, Elsa and the four passengers for the final boat. Greg's Zodiac pointed into the waves as water slipped over the bow. Progress despite the 45 HP Yamaha motor was sluggish as the boat crawled towards the ship. Despite keeping the Zodiac to the lee of the *Polar Adventurer* it took two attempts to get everyone off and up the stairway. Greg radioed to Elsa to wait.

On the beach the six, backs to the pounding weather, pondered the thousands of impassive penguins standing around. Elsa and John discussed whether to move or not. Their boat despite the survival equipment would ride high. Boyd overhearing this remarked:

"These boats never flip, do they?"

John said: "No, they're unsinkable. Well, hardly ever!"

Elsa looked at him.

Kim said: "I'm soaked! Couldn't we give it a try?"

"In a bit," replied Elsa. The bit lasted thirty minutes. Elsa radioed Greg that they were going to leave. Elsa pushed the Zodiac into deeper water and loaded the passengers.

She scrambled on board. John revved the motor and turned the boat into the wind. They chugged into the blow. The prow repeatedly rose with oncoming waves. A large wave raised the front of the lightly loaded boat out of the water. A gust of wind caught the underneath and pushed the boat vertically into the air. Helped by the racing motor the Zodiac flipped over backwards. One moment Jim was clutching a wet pontoon rope, the next, equipment and oars rained down on him as he plunged into the sea. He closed his mouth as water clasped him in a cold embrace.

Jim coughed, gasped and shuddered as waves beat over his head. The life jacket bobbed him up and down as he searched through the freezing water for the Zodiac. The boat, its shiny keel, now on top, drifted with the wind. Jim was soaked, frozen, and his waterlogged boots were dragging him down.

He counted heads and was relieved to see Elsa clinging to the nose, and Boyd, John and Kim clinging to the side ropes that were under water. Jim yelled: "Where's Carol?" She suddenly popped up by the side of the Zodiac swearing and spitting as the waves rolled over her. A sodden Jim and Carol looked at each other with a mutual: are you OK?

The prop was stuck up in the air and silent. The kill cord attached to John had stopped the engine. Elsa yelled: "Hang onto the Zodiac and kick your legs!"

Jim had an odd thought: was this what he had paid all that money for? And it didn't matter if he peed now. Chilled by the frigid water they kicked towards the beach. Elsa was the first one to stand up. She leaned into the beach and slowly the rest found their feet and pulled the upside down Zodiac onto wet land. John pulled the anchor from underneath the boat and buried it.

Driving several penguins out of the way John pulled emergency supplies out of the safety barrel. Elsa and he handed out two silvery emergency blankets to each shivering passenger and told them to strip. John then squelched down the beach through the wind, rain and birds to see if the two kits with tents, food and stoves had drifted in.

The radios were waterproof. Elsa contacted the ship. The wind reached gale force. The *Polar Adventurer* faced into the storm and ran its engines. The six would be staying ashore tonight. With an emergency blanket around her Elsa got the others to walk slowly around in one spot, but close together like musk ox, or as she said: "Like male emperor penguins who do this for two months in far colder temperatures."

Though as Boyd pointed out: "Some of those penguins don't make it." But he continued walking in a small circle.

John found one kit lying on the beach, and dragged it back through the massed penguins. Elsa and he pulled out the two tents, and gave a waterproof hat to everyone. There were only enough dry socks for the four passengers.

"I'm going bare footed," said Elsa, "It'll be warmer." And promptly pulled off her water-sodden waders and soaked socks.

Cold and wet Kim moved tightly up and down in one spot, with a pained look on her face. John handed her a packet of toilet paper. She disappeared behind the nearest rock.

The other three stripped down to their wet underwear. Covered with blankets and looking like large silvery penguins they helped take out more emergency supplies. A tent was raised, a tarp put on the wet sand, and a stove lit. More blankets were piled in. The wet five shuddered into the cramped tent. There was enough food for thirty people.

Boyd: "So that means we've got food for five days." No one replied.

A pale soaked Kim stumbled into the tent shivering. She collapsed on to some emergency blankets, and muttered. Elsa pulled off Kim's blanket, ripped off her underclothes, and opened the large zippers of a red hypothermia bag. She stuffed Kim into the bag and zipped her up. Kim's breathing had slowed down.

"Boyd, lay along side her, and keep an eye on her."
"Why me," Boyd asked.
"Do it," was the terse reply.

John heated green pea soup. He lit two candles for more warmth as the wind banged on the tent's fabric. There was some light outside, but John turned on a flashlight for comfort.

Soaked, they slowly warmed up and crouching close to the roaring stove ate freeze-dried beef stew. They listened as Elsa gave Greg an update. He told her that the pressure was still dropping. The ship would not abandon them. Boyd blurted out:

"I guess I don't have to sue anyone then."

"How's Kim?" asked Elsa.

"She's shivering, drinking soup, and requesting that I don't get too close," said her caregiver.

"We'll have to hire you as the ship's nurse."

"Not bloody likely," Boyd retorted.

Elsa and John took four-hour shifts to listen to the radio. With John's length and Boyd's girth, and the six of them the walls were touched. Water seeped in. Jim was damp enough already. He thought about the smaller tent.

"Do you want to share the other tent?" Jim asked Carol

She looked at him as if wondering what his motives were. But Boyd had gone outside twice in an hour as he put it "to see a couple of penguins". Each time he was roped up by John in case he couldn't get back – Carol thought that would be nice – everyone got disturbed. She looked at the large wet Boyd with distaste. Carol broached the idea with Elsa who still remained cheerful despite the sopping conditions.

Elsa said as John and she had to take turns being awake, and she needed to check on Kim's temperature it made sense to have more room and not get wet. John got the two-person tent, out and the three of them hurriedly erected it, as the wind and rain pelted them. As the two dragged blankets, rope and some food and water into the small tent, Boyd had the last word:

"Can those two be trusted?"

No one bothered to reply.

Under several blankets Jim and Carol lay there not quite sure what to say. Jim had had romantic notions of strolls along beaches loaded with penguins, not lying damp in a rain soddened tent. He mentioned Boyd's face when he had to lie next to Kim to keep her warm. Carol's dark damp hair plastered her head. She said nothing.

"I thought it was funny."

Carol was silent for a while and then said:

"You know his real name is William?"

"I saw that on a passenger list somewhere. Maybe he doesn't like William, Willy, Bill, Billy or any of the other variations."

"No, that's not it."

Jim lay there and waited. Finally Carol said:

"He was called Bill many years ago on an expedition, the Sheldon Expedition. Since then he has always gone as Boyd."

Again she stopped and lay there breathing gently.

"He was a young, rich, and only on the expedition because his father gave money to Eric Sheldon. From all accounts he was useless. But he used the year down south to get on bases like McMurdo and others to build up his Antarctic résumé. Boyd or Bill as he should be called has drifted on his limited Antarctic expertise for years."

Carol paused and then blurted out: "When we get to the Antarctic I'm going to humiliate the bastard in front of the whole ship!"

"Why? He's a bit of an idiot, but why so…" Jim couldn't find the exact word. He waited. There was more to come out. The reserve – reservoir? – was breaking.

"Another young man was on the Sheldon Expedition," said Carol. "Boyd and he got caught out in a storm. Boyd panicked and fled back to base with most of the huskies. The other man struggled through the storm to a refuge hut with one dog. The weather remained stormy for several months. There was no way he could get back to base, or the base could get to him.

"When the Sheldon Expedition left to pick him up, they learned that the Argentineans had not stocked the hut with food the previous autumn. Eric Sheldon landed. He went to the hut, and…." Here Carol started sobbing.

Jim suddenly realized who Carol was. He put his arm across her and held her as Carol wept. After a while she stopped and burst out with:

"There was no bloody food, and he couldn't reach any wildlife! He starved to death!" She cried into her blankets, tears and mucus flowing down the side of her face.

Jim handed some tissues to Carol and held her. He ventured two words:

"Your father?"

"Yes, damn it! All he left my mother were some letters saying what happened and how that bastard got him into the situation. He knew he was not going to survive." Bitterly she said: "The letters were all I have of him. And they weren't even for me. I was only a baby." And then: "Christ, I must look a mess." Carol turned away from Jim, blew her nose loudly, and wiped her face with a small towel.

"You don't," said Jim.

"Don't what?" Carol retorted.

"You don't look a mess."

"I'll be the judge of that, McKinnon."

He asked where would be a good place to expose Boyd.

"The first stop on the Antarctic mainland, not on some poky little island. And why are you taking your arm away?"

Jim faced Carol and stroked her face. "Because of this."

She attempted a smile.

Their lips met and held for some time. After while Carol said:

"Thank you."

But before he could continue Carol told him that she was going outside, he should rope her up, and then she was going to get some sleep. A bit deflated Jim did as he was told.

Later Carol kissed Jim briefly, and told him that as Mozart said: "My rests are as important as my notes."

Jim's reply was: "I could do with some notes."

Carol patted his face and pulled the blankets over her head.

CHAPTER TWENTY-ONE

Jim slept fitfully as the wind knocked against the tent walls. Who was on the bluff at Salisbury Plain, a passenger or a crewmember, and had they killed Peter? The Spanish sounding man on the recording, crew or passenger? Did one of them finish Peter of with a rock after Maisie went for help? And had Peter found the gold, or had he been too nosy about where the gold might be?

Outside the light came early. Carol slumbered on, with an occasional snoring snort. Jim broke open an almond emergency bar, and chewed and sucked on it. He thought about the capsizing, Carol's revelation, Boyd and the investigation. Nothing was straight forward except the ship's itinerary.

Carol yawned, stretched, and looked at Jim as if not sure who he was. Then she smiled. "To quote Captain Oates: I'm just going outside. Unlike that fourth man on Scott's ill-fated trip back from the South Pole, I shall return."

"Do you need roping up?"

"No, the wind is only steady. I'll hang on to some penguins if it picks up."

After gnawing on high-energy bars and drinking the emergency water with its slight plastic taste, the pair joined Elsa and the others for breakfast.

"Did you two sleep or what?" asked Boyd.

Carol ignored him, and asked the others how their night had been.

"Apart from a lack of sleep," said Elsa, "not bad."

Kim praised Boyd for his presence and his help.

"I feel so much better. Boyd has been wonderful."

There was no comment from her caregiver. John said he was glad Carol and Jim had their own tent. Boyd tended to thrash about a bit.

"He kept me warm," said Kim, and grinned at Boyd as he sipped his cup of black tea with acute interest.

A Zodiac arrived with Greg and George, the staff photographer. Elsa explained how they had spent the night.

"I want a full report," Greg said. After George took the required group-survival photograph next to the upside down Zodiac, the group packed up. Greg's boat towed the righted Zodiac back to the *Polar Adventurer*. It was a relief to enter the mudroom to dump their wet clothes.

The survivors headed for the showers, dry clothes and a second breakfast Leon the hotel manager made sure they were well taken care of. There were a lot of questions from other passengers of how their night had been, and had they been warm enough? The doctor gave them a quick once over.

The *Polar Adventurer* headed southeast, turned southwest around the end of South Georgia, and out into the Scotia Sea, and pointed to the Antarctic Peninsula, two days away. The island's black mountains, and white glaciers pouring into the sea, receded into the distance. A few sea birds followed. Jim looked at the gym and the gym looked back. There was so little time, and he was a bit weary for some reason.

After breakfast Jim and Carol fended off more questions on their overnight experience, and went to the bridge to look at birds swooping past the windows. Alec had his usual port side position with Bob, the staff birder. Henryk the third as Carol called him was the only officer on deck.

Doreen, Jack's wife, slid open the side door and stepped on to the bridge. She looked lost. Doreen asked where the steersman was. The third officer asked

"Would you like to steer the ship?"

She nodded. Henryk unscrewed the steering wheel and passed it to her. She held it tentatively and gave a faint smile.

When the passengers had gathered Greg asked for a round of applause for the six heroic survivors. Boyd raised his arms like a successful boxer winning his match. The others grinned sheepishly.

"Our emergency supplies worked well?"

Jim mentioned that the biscuits were questionable.

"But you had enough food?"

"Definitely."

Greg talked about the next two days at sea:

"Keep an eye out for the really large tabular bergs. Some are several miles long. They have broken off of the Antarctic shelf ice. And at 60 degrees south we will truly have made our Antarctic arrival, with, of course, a celebration. Probably sometime tomorrow.

"I'm going to repeat the titles of the lectures for the next two days, as some of you for some reason missed the recap session last night.

Doug wondered why Boyd despite his forced overnight camp looked remarkably healthy.

*

Colin the elder staff historian presented his slide show on early Antarctic expeditions. One German man asked him if there would be more on Robert Falcon Scott. Colin said no, Shackleton was the main explorer in this part of the Antarctic.

The usual black and white posed pictures of Scott, Amundsen and Shackleton were shown. The best one showed several men struggling to pull and push an overburdened sledge through soft snow. As Colin said it was a pity neither of the Brits used huskies as much as Amundsen did. They might have got to the South Pole before the Norwegians and saved themselves from exhaustion, and for Scott's men, death.

The historian discussed early Antarctic sealing, the lack of interest in the Antarctic at the end of the nineteenth century, and the twentith century rise of whaling and scientific exploration. Now Antarctic science had been joined by a much larger activity, tourism.

There was always the question for Colin of the effect of humans on the Antarctic.

"Hasn't the temperature in this part of the Antarctic gone up two or three degrees Celsius during the last few decades?"

Colin said: "In other parts of the world when the economy goes down the concern for the environment drops. It's less so for the Antarctic where the trips keep on coming. Most Antarctic visitors have money."

Another typical ecological concern was:

"What is our carbon foot print for this trip?" asked Shaun, partner of Pam, the Aussie couple.

Colin stated a ball-park figure of four months of driving at home equaled one trip to the Antarctic, and suggested that if people wanted to discuss the topic they should move down to the end of the lounge. Some passengers didn't want to feet uncomfortable with so much emphasis on the environment. .

Colin was the ringmaster. With the Aussie couple, Carol and Jim were ranged against Boyd and several ex-Antarctic types. The three Australian amigos, Doug, Ron and Ed, watched on the sidelines.

The ecological arguments had a religious feel to them. The staff tried to get passengers to avoid getting too deep in to either religion or politics, though the environment covered both.

Some passengers needed to flagellate themselves about what had been done to the earth: "We have polluted, punish us!" There was no obvious villain. We were the villains. Or was it those over there who don't care about what happens to the earth were the villains? And could tourists be environmentalists if they still wanted to travel the world?

Carol opened global warming by mentioning that white egrets for the first time nested in England. Jim added that robins, the North American variety, were seen in Canadian Arctic for the first time, and the locals had no name for them.

"So by being down here you're helping the egrets and the robins," said Boyd.

"Well, I paid carbon footprint credits to offset my polluting travel," answered Carol.

Frank lifted a foot and said: "My footprints are pretty big, I should pay lots!

"And the good old days saw us dumping our Antarctic garbage into the nearest sea ice tide crack."

Pam asked what happened to the ship's waste. Colin said that the foodstuff was ground up and pumped out. The non-perishables went back to Ushuaia.

"And then?" asked Pam.

"They're dumped in a landfill. They don't have recycling yet."

"So we're affecting South America as well as the Antarctic," said Carol.

"The rich make the most mess. That's us," put in Boyd. "You could always stay at home," looking at Carol.

"And what will you tell your children, when they ask you what did you do to save the planet?" asked Pam.

Boyd turned slightly and said: "I don't keep track of all of my offspring so I can't say. Maybe their mothers could talk to them about that."

Colin mentioned that the numbers of tourists going to the Antarctic had jumped from the 1960s of several hundred to nearly forty thousand a season at present. There were controls on how many people could land at certain Antarctic sites.

Pam said: "I suppose we're all guilty of damaging the environment here. At home a baby in Australia can fill a land fill with half a ton of throw-away diapers."

Ron piped up: "Thanks for that poopy home truth. And if the world's temperature is going up how come we're all putting on weight as if there's an ice age coming?" He glanced at Boyd's bulk.

Boyd said: "I think we need more people down south not just the greeny-weenies. It's the fifth biggest continent. There's lots of room, for God's sake!"

"Most people only go to the smallest part, the Antarctic Peninsula," put in Colin. "It's the nearest part of the Antarctic to most of the world. There's a lot of wonderful scenery and it has the most wildlife. But it does get crowded with ships."

"Couldn't we limit the numbers each season?" asked Carol. "Say have a lottery for who gets to go south.

"I say bring 'em all," butted in Boyd. "Even millions of Chinese." Despite his xenophobia, Boyd liked to be in on the winning side of an argument. "Think of the money the cruise ships could make. So more the merrier.

"We should build condominiums and hotels all over scenic parts of the Antarctic," carried on Boyd, "Course they would only be used during summer. In winter it would be too perishing cold for most tourists."

"So more pollution in Antarctica," said Carol grimly, "as we trample on the last piece of a pristine world."

"Oh, I'm sure they'll recycle," added Boyd, off-handedly. "If a train's thundering down the track, like all those people wanting to go to the Antarctic, you don't stand in its way."

"And if it's going off the track?" asked Pam, beating Carol to a retort.

Before Boyd could counter there was a yell from the aft deck:

"Whales on the port side!"

There was a rush to the outside. Like most whales seen, they were distant, and only showed a bit of black on the surface for a short time. The shape of their blows at least allowed Mike, the Scottish animal expert, to say they were fin whales, a mother and calf. At the bow those with long camera lens watched patiently for further resurfacing. Jim felt a conflict between the desire to see a whale and the tedium of waiting for it to appear.

For some the open sky, sea and wildlife dulled the mind. Maisie the eager American woman who had hung around Peter had been suggesting games for several days.

"Isn't time we did something else than just watch birdies? I mean there is more to life."

One lounge group huddled like a football team stood around a box of games. Having been at sea for a week and a half it was time to play bridge. There were only so many hours in the day that people wanted to look at wildlife and scenery. Four women, one of whom was Pamela, immediately sat round a small table, paired up and got down to bidding.

The keen woman was shut out; Maisie annoyed people. Her past friendship with Peter was no longer considered significant. Concentration not chatter was needed. Lectures and meals could come and go, but a trump call and winning tricks supplanted the rest. Pamela's well brought up tones rang through the lounge: "You did a simply, *marvelous* job!" "Well done!" "I am so sorry!" The other three tolerated the outbursts. She was successful in most of her contracts.

Other activities followed. One slim, fit American sixty year-old woman started a yoga group before breakfast. A large jigsaw puzzle was laid out on a long lounge table. The pieces were only held back when staff members pulled down the blinds and commenced a lecture.

For Jim despite knowing who was at the gold symposium his ranking of the suspects had not changed. The list proved nothing either way. Guilt seemed to be the only certainty, but who carried the most?

*

You know who this is by now. My cabin was disturbed. Some one was trying to "read my books". Vibrations were picked up on my mobile phone (cell phone, if you like). Some one was investigating my gold. I thundered down the corridor making a lot of noise. I saw the back of Leon leaving my cabin just before I got there. Some rather large steps will be taken.

CHAPTER TWENTY-TWO

The whales disappeared. The sun and clouds and a few birds remained. Jim needed lunch and some answers. Carol and Jim took beet soup, pizza, and, for him, quite a few raw vegetables. Mark asked why Jim was so interested in the Ushuaia bank robbery. Jim said that Peter had been keen on getting some answers so he thought he should carry on the questioning. It sounded a little lame.

"You seem to be asking a lot of the questions."

"Peter was the one who was the most interested," insisted Jim.

"The only person who could have been in on it would have been Boyd. It would be the sort of caper he would get up to." Mark then said he needed to talk to Frank and Arthur, and got up and left.

"So why are you so interested in this robbery? asked Carol.

"Can I tell you later," said Jim. "I would like to share but I am beholden (what a great word thought Jim) to someone else."

"Rachel?"

"Good God, no! She's got Jack over there."

Jim had already interrupted one clutching embrace between Jack and Rachel with an "As you were!" in the library. Rachel had countered with: "Can I help you?" There was no help intended.

Carol turned to the pair huddled over their soup. The odd loud guff came from Jack, from Rachel a beaming smile. Doreen sat off to one side, glumly eating her lunch, and occasionally making a short comment to another couple. Jim wondered if Jack was behind the heist and was using Rachel as a prop, or were they both in on it. But the recording was of two males. Unless Rachel was the mind behind the masters.

"Men can be so lousy. I hope that doesn't include the present company."

Jim smiled at her. He tried to think about the hold up and Peter's death at the same time.

"I was hoping I was wrong about you," said Carol, interrupting his musings.

Jim apologized and said he was thinking about the afternoon's presentation on Antarctic geology. Would she be there? Carol said she would give it a miss, birds were more interesting. She would see him later. Carol gracefully navigated through the tables. Arthur brought his dessert over and asked if he could join Jim.

"I really don't think anyone on board was in on that robbery, especially us Antarctic types."

"Not even Boyd for a prank?" asked Jim.

"Certainly, but thirty years ago not now," said Arthur as he headed away with his crème brûlée still not finished.

Jim meditated on Boyd not having any curiosity about the hold up, Arthur insisting that Boyd was not capable of it, and Mark saying Boyd could have been in on it. The investigation was no closer to being resolved.

After an afternoon tea, coffee and cake break, (come for a coffee and cake cruise to put on weight Jim thought), the staff photographer arranged for people to show their best South Georgia slides.

Some twenty laptops were laid out on auto display. There were a lot of penguin shots. Some close-ups showed penguin eyeballs reflecting tourists. Jim admitted that his snaps were not in this class though his satisfied him. Carol said the two Californians had very professional layouts.

Malcolm Moresby, the old Antarctican who droned on an on about his time down south to Jim in Stanley, showed some fantastic red and gold sunsets.

"Are they from this voyage or did you slip 'em in from previous trips?" Frank asked. Malcolm spluttered a denial.

Doug wandered listlessly around with a club soda, (or was it pure vodka?), despite Leon the hotel manager saying: "Drinks should not be near the laptops!"

Near the bar the young Australian couple, Shaun and Pam, looked through their slides. They weren't showing any pictures. They had taken so many photographs they had not had time to cull them. Jim was curious about any long distance shots of the bluff at Salisbury Plain. Shaun brought up the best one. Jim said:

"See that person on top of the bluff heading to the glacier. That's probably Peter, but who's the other figure behind him? Most people went only as far as the bluff and stopped."

Carol said:

"The jacket color is not a passenger issue. Is it a crewmember?"

Some crew had landed for a break that afternoon. What had the captain said, mused Jim: "My crew are not involved". He asked if he could copy the slide to his thumb drive. Carol and Jim headed out for an afternoon smoke session for one. Jim wondered about the second person on top of the bluff. What had happened to Peter?

Jim put his hand on hers and felt no resistance. She looked out at the waves and the few giant petrels, and hummed. Her hair smelled of smoke and salt. Jim stood as close as he could. He wondered if there was a connection between his investigation and Carol. She must have quite a lot of money if she had her large cabin. There had been no financial information on her from the captain. Was the captain being selective in what he gave Jim? Was she behind the gold coin hold up? He dismissed the idea and then it returned.

Later Jim blew up Shaun's photo. The person behind Peter on the bluff was a female crew member, Rita, who cleaned his cabin and others along the waterline. She had not been on the Dutch woman's recording.

Jim knocked on the captain's cabin door. No answer. He moved to the bridge, and asked if he could see the captain's Arctic slides.

"What, *now*?" was the querulous question.

"Now," said Jim firmly.

In Captain Engstrom's cabin Jim mentioned Peter's suspicious death, showed a copy of the Salisbury Plain bluff slide with Rita directly behind Peter, and a copy of the Dutch woman's recording of the two men talking about gold. One of the two had a Spanish accent. Jim tentatively broached the idea that one of the Filipino crew men could have been in on the gold robbery.

"I do not think so," said the captain to Jim's last point. "Very few Filipino's speak Spanish nowadays."

"Someone else on the crew?" ventured Jim.

"Certainly not. However, on another matter a military doctor in Port Stanly examined Peter Tielmann, and the x-rays confirmed our suspicions ("it's ours now not mine" thought Jim). There were two separate traumas to the skull. The second one was made by someone with a sharp rock."

A second official admission came:

"Mr. Tielmann's death was probably due to the gold robbery."

"The gold's on board?" asked Jim.

"Well." The captain had a small cough in his throat: "A day or so ago a couple not related had a romantic trust in a lifeboat."

""Tryst?" said Jim.

"Yes. They disturbed some packages of gold coins. Fortunately the couple came straight to me rather than hiding the fact and the gold. I told them their secret was safe with me, as was the gold.. Any word of this incident to anyone would mean an Argentinean prison experience as well as some difficult explanations to their spouses."

"They agreed?"

"They saw the wisdom of my suggestion."

"You have the gold?" asked Jim.

"I have the gold in a safe place." His eyes flicked over towards a locked cabinet.

Oh, thought Jim. Is he really behind the robbery or is he just being officious?

"I will question Rita on what she was doing on that bluff. Maybe it will lead to the real culprit."

"Were the gold coins in plastic tubes? Jim asked.

"Why," asked the captain.

Jim said that Peter had mentioned that that's how they were usually carried.

The captain admitted there were a few tubes. He then waved a dismissive hand at the passenger. Jim felt half thwarted and half satisfied.

Peter had been right about the gold being on board. Had he got too close to the lifeboat, and had to be removed? Where did Rita come into things? Jim listened again to the two muffled voices on Margriet's recorder. One was an educated man, British or American. The other deferred to the first, and spoke English with a slight accent. Gold was mentioned. Something about keeping an eye on the situation, whatever that was. The voice came to Jim:

"Welcome aboard, Mr. Stringer!" Leon the hotel manager. He was with the crew and the passengers, and took charge of the running of the hotel side of things on the ship. Jim knocked again on Captain Engstrom's door and said:

"That recording? Leon the hotel manager."

"Faen!" the captain replied.

That was a pretty crude response from a normally controlled captain thought Jim. The English equivalent was also a four-letter word beginning with "f".

CHAPTER TWENTY-THREE

Daniel the head waiter brought Rita to the captain and left. She sat down on a small chair.

"You pushed Mr. Tielmann off the bluff at Salisbury Plain."

"What is bluff?"

"The hill behind the beach."

"No, I stayed on the beach with the other crew people."

"Here is a photo of you and Mr. Tielmann on the hill."

"No!"

"Why did you push him?"

"I didn't!"

"He jumped on his own?"

"Yes, I mean no. I don't know."

"You were there. What happened?"

"Nothing. I saw him then I came down."

"In this photo you are right behind him. Look!"

Rita turned away as the photo was thrust in her face.

"You pushed a man to his death, and hit him on the head with a rock. You will be handed over to the Argentinean police. When convicted you will spend several years in a rather unpleasant prison. And what will happen to your two children back in the Philippines? Ages seven and ten, are they not?"

"Nothing will happen to them!"

"Will your parents look after them, or will they turn them out on to the streets?"

"No, they wouldn't!"

"You will not see them for a long time."

Rita burst into tears. Captain Engstrom let her cry for a while. He was not going to spoil things by telling her that the British not the Argentineans dealt with South Georgia.

"While you are thinking about your children's future listen to this recording. Who are these two men?"

Rita through the tears streaming down her face said she knew one was Leon.

"Was he the man who told you to push Mr.Tielmann?"

She hesitated. The captain talked a bit more about the "amenities" in Argentinean prisons.

"Tell me everything."

Slowly Rita told of having some drugs on the last trip, only a little you understand? And how Leon had caught her. He then told her to give that man at Salisbury a little push. That's all she did. She didn't think anything would happen. More tears flowed.

"And when he died?" asked the captain.

"Leon said it was my fault, and I had to do what ever he told me.

"I can help you with the Argentinean police. It will be an accident," said Captain Engstrom quietly, "but you have to help me. Was that a "yes?"

A murmured "yes" came out.

"Who is the other man on the recorder?"

"I don't know. Only Leon told me what to do."

"Right. One, you will sign this paper. Two, you will tell no one what happened here, and three you will go back to work as if nothing has happened. Is that understood?"

Rubbing her tears with her sleeve Rita left the room. She sniffed steadily down to her cabin. She got into her bunk without undressing, and wondered if her children would be safe. Josie her cabin mate did not question her.

*

The waves outside were still benign. Most passengers were at dinner. A few coughs picked up in Port Stanley croaked the air. Most eaters tucked into Argentinean steaks with a hot pepper sauce and fried potatoes. A few had the tofu vegetable skewer. Jim wondered about Carol's healthy eating habits and her smoking. They sat with a tour group from Australia. Jim felt he needed a break from the Antarctic regulars.

A shortage of places had Frank, Jacqueline and Richard join them. Carol congratulated Jacqueline and Richard on their photographic display. The Californian couple relaxed as Jacqueline and Carol talked about the pros and cons of their respective cameras and lens. Jim turned to Richard and said that he was not really into photography. Richard admitted that Jacqueline was the cameraperson, and asked:

"Are you still checking on that robbery?"

Jim said that he was. Frank put in:

"Boyd would probably be your man. That's the sort of prank he would get up to. He's got too much time on his hands."

On the way out Shaun asked Jim and Carol if they had seen his silver laptop. It had disappeared from their cabin. Shaun had reported the loss to Leon who said he would spread the word around about the loss.

Jim and Carol passed Jack and Rachel having a lounge tête-à-tête. Jack had told Doreen to join the jigsaw puzzle group. He had business to discuss with Mrs. Weinberger. Doreen moved slowly down the lounge. As Carol and Jim moved past their table Jack sang out: "Lucky Jim! How I envy him!" As Rachel nudged him, Jack said: "You haven't heard that, eh?"

"It wasn't that funny," said Jim as he marched a smiling Carol away.

On the outer limits of the bar area Georgina and Pamela shared a jug of sangria. Pamela nodded towards Jack and Rachel:

"A marriage breaker, that woman."

"And high maintenance too," put in Georgina. "To paraphrase what they use to say about living in Alaska: The odds were good for a relationship, but the goods were odd."

The inner bar circle had the usuals, with the occasional truant from a group tour. Frank pulled up with his rum and coke. Ron asked him about the Sheldon Expedition that Boyd has supposedly been on and the man who had died there. Boyd was not around.

Frank said: "I've heard a bit about it, but Malcolm knows more." He spied Malcolm Moresby heading to his usual middle of the lounge spot where he could disperse Antarctic wisdom without hassles from the other so-called Antarctic experts.

"Mouldy!"shouted Frank. "We need your Antarctic prowess over here."

Malcolm altered direction like a large liner forced to veer off course.

Frank asked him: "Boyd was on the Sheldon Expedition. But he wasn't there when that chap died?"

"I don't think so," Malcolm's replied.

"How did that bloke die," asked Ron.

"Well, his companion returned to base with most of the team, the lone husky turned up at the base a few days later, and the weather stayed warm and stormy. The fellow at the refuge hut couldn't get back and no one could get to him."

"And did he have enough food?" asked Ron.

"There was no food. The Argentineans hadn't stocked the hut the previous autumn and the seals stayed on ice floes too far off shore to get at," Malcolm said.

"What about penguins?" asked Frank. "They're pretty rank tasting but if you're starving…"

"No, they were all nesting on rock outcrops further south. There were just glaciers around that area," said Malcolm. "He had no food.

"Anyway, here's the man of the hour who was there."

As Boyd hove to with Kim like a small tug at his side, Carol tightened her grip on Jim's arm, and spoke into his ear:

"As you said, Jim, this ship is too bloody small."

He touched her hand. He hadn't used the term bloody. You could take the pedant to the Antarctic but you couldn't take the pedant… He told himself to quit it.

Frank said to Boyd: "You had left the Sheldon Expedition before they found that dead man, hadn't you?"

"I've no idea what happened," Boyd said sharply." Boyd turned towards Kim. He wondered if he would have to drink elsewhere. There was always his suite.

Carol's fingers had left marks on Jim's arm. He moved the pair of them outside. As they left they heard Malcolm say:

"He starved to death."

Tucked in the dark of the stern and after a comforting cigarette, Carol looked at Jim and kissed him. Her body fitted nicely into his. He held her. She gently pushed him away and said she would have an early night. There was still another day at sea. When Carol had left for her suite Jim thoughts moved from Carol to the investigation and back. He could see neither clearly, though he knew which he preferred.

Back in the cabin Martin mentioned that some people had been a little tense at the old alcoholic ranch. It must be the long voyage. Can you image he said being with that lot on a voyage that went on for months?

"That Sheldon Expedition keeps the bar entertained," said Martin.

Jim nodded and thought unlike the gold heist it was interesting. He was engrossed in thoughts about Carol, Rita on the bluff, the missing laptop and the taped conversation.

On turning out his light Alec blurted out:

"Your Carol did well this morning."

"What was that?" asked Jim.

"The argument about stopping humans going to the Antarctic."

"Oh, yes." She had said limit people going to the Antarctic, thought Jim, not stopping humans going down there.

CHAPTER TWENTY-FOUR

Jim woke to ominous tapping along the hull. Then it came to him: growlers, chunks of ice from broken up icebergs. Greg's morning quote was: "The ice was here, the ice was there, the ice was all around. It cracked and growled and roared and howled, like noises in a swound."

He added: "One, before anyone comes to reception and asks swound means faint, and two, please come up on the decks. We have icebergs as far as the eye can see."

Martin turned over and said if you've seen one berg you've seen them all. Jim hurriedly got up to see if the Antarctic icebergs were any better than the Arctic bergs of years ago.

In a cold grey morning passengers hung over the railings and the bow. A sharp wind cut into those still in pajamas. Stretched out lighting up the sea and reflecting up in the distant sky were hundreds of icebergs. One looked like a white aircraft carrier and ran for what seemed like miles. The shapes ranged from tables to castles to sloping roofs to spires to unshapely lumps of ice.

Waves ran up the sides of the bergs and shot white water high over the tops. The older icebergs already sported ice caves as the sea worked away on the rock-solid frozen water.

On the bridge the captain, the duty officer and a lookout man studied the icy obstacles. Using fine controls to the engine room the captain weaved the vessel slowly through the ice.

Ron said the gazing passengers were like Cortez's men: "Silent, upon a peak in Darien on first seeing the Pacific Ocean."

"Oh, yeah."

"Keats," Ron said.

"Sure," was the response.

Later passengers gathered like hungry giant petrels around the breakfast buffet. Some still carried their cameras. Some were still wearing pajamas. Boyd leaned past Jim as if annoyed. Perhaps he had heard the arguments of whether Boyd was behind the robbery. On seeing the warming eggs Boyd exclaimed:

"I love the smell of raw eggs first thing in the morning. I know, I know, originality is always suspect."

Outside the dining room Jim met up with Carol, and gently asked:

"Want to join me for a gym session?"

"Gym, Jim? While the birds are scarce I want to keep birding."

"How about a lecture date on some early Antarctic explorers?"

"You can certainly know how to get to a girl's heart."

*

Leon received a colder reception than what was outside, the second morning on the Scotia Sea. The captain had phoned. Leon arrived promptly and was surprised to see Bernard. Normally the first officer would be sleeping after his early morning watch. He looked tired as he wrote. There was still a noon watch to be carried out on the bridge.

Captain Engstrom spoke immediately: "This is about the death of Mr. Tielmann."

"That was shocking,' Leon said.

"Quite. I'm having all officers' quarters searched to ease my mind about the accident. For the company's liability we must cover all bases. Was that acceptable?"

Leon nodded. Why his cabin. Anything suspect was elsewhere.

"Petr will search your cabin." The captain phoned the second officer. "There is more. You did not land at Salisbury Plain, but how did Rita Agati get permission? Hotel staff rarely get to leave the ship."

"I don't know," said Leon.

Captain Engstrom's lips almost made a smile. "The signing officer was you. Can you explain that?"

Leon shifted in his seat. "No."

"Listen to this recording. Who are these two men?"

Leon listened and said nothing.

"One of them is you."

The hotel manager clasped his hands together and nodded.

"Would you say yes or no? Do not nod."

Leon said yes. The first officer wrote it down.

"Who is the second man?"

There was no reply.

"You are both talking about gold. Why?"

Leon muttered he could not say.

"Why not?"

There was a shrug. After a pause the captain repeated his question.

"I cannot say," was the answer.

"Cannot or will not? asked Captain Engstrom.

Another shrug. Leon looked everywhere but at his interrogator. The cabin felt warm. The captain waited. For inspiration, for Leon or for the second officer. It was the second officer. He handed an item to the captain and said that was all he found.

"Leon Rosa. I have a slide from a laptop. This is yours?" He showed the slide to Leon.

"Yes. Someone gave it to me."

"Who was that?"

There was no reply.

"Mr. Shaun Richards' laptop went missing. When it turned up this slide was gone. He had not given the slide to you."

Leon sat silent.

"The slide shows Rita Agati on top of the bluff standing behind Mr. Tielmann. Why do you have this slide?"

The silence stretched around the cabin.

"Miss Agati said that because you found her with some drugs you forced her to push Mr. Tielmann. She signed a statement here."

"She's lying! Just because I caught her with a whole lot of marijuana."

"Miss Agati admitted she pushed Mr. Tielmann on you orders. You have admitted nothing. And will not say who is on the recording that points to that Ushuaia gold robbery, and you have no answer as to where you got this slide." Captain Engstrom looked at the first officer and nodded.

He continued: "Leon Rosa, you know a lot more that you are saying. The Argentineans at Ushuaia will get more out of you especially where the gold is hidden. The first officer will escort you to a special cabin. A guard will be set outside your door. If you try to leave, you will be locked in a storage cabinet down in the engine room."

The captain waved a hand. His chief officer marched a pale Leon out of the cabin. Captain Engstrom pushed his hands through his thinning hair, and thought maybe he should retire. Antarctic peace, indeed.

*

Colin the historian described the serenading of an emperor penguin with bagpipes by Bruce's Scottish expedition. Also at the beginning of the twentieth century a Swedish expedition under Nordenskjöld had to stay for a second winter, when the ship was crushed by sea ice.

Later Carol took up her post on the rear deck to watch for the odd seabird flitting between the icy shapes. Jim entered the tiny gym, selected a stationary bike and pedaled away as the *Polar Adventurer* plunged up and down. The down pedal was easy, the up, hard. A sideways way motion made the exercise interesting. There was a Frenchman, pounding in different directions on a treadmill. They nodded with a mutual feeling of superiority.

After a long fifteen minutes Jim cut the erratic exercise short and headed to the library. In some ways it was nice to have only a couple of ideas to worry about. Since they were in an isolated part of the world he ignored the woes of the rest of the world. He was on holiday, despite his assigned task.

Jim needed to bounce ideas off of someone. He should trust Carol? They liked each other. Was Carol too closely tied in her dislike of Boyd to have a clean bouncing surface? She might even be the brains behind the gold robbery. He dismissed the idea.

He might be able to talk to Shaun and Pam. Jim found it interesting that they had found their laptop, after it was reported missing. The slide of Rita standing behind Peter on the bluff was gone. Jim gave a copy to Shaun. He wondered what would happen to Leon after the captain finished with him.

Who was the second man on the recording and were those two the only gold robbers? Boyd's snobbish manner with many of the hotel staff would have clued Rita if it was him on the recording. The low voice sounded educated North American or British. The recorder was rather a cheap affair.

The library had a few nodding off, heads tipped over their journals, the written proofs that they had been to the Antarctic. Others read the selection of books: Antarctic, Arctic, South America, birds, sea mammals, and heavy art tomes. A few travelers still had their nametags on.

Jim sat in a comfy leather armchair. Most passengers denied having anything to do with gold, the robbery, Spanish connections, or had no knowledge of what had happened. There was a feeling that Boyd was behind everything. However, as Jim's father use to say just because it's a black dog doesn't make it a black Labrador.

No one showed any interest in confessing. Just like when he had been with the police his investigation was impeded by disinterested citizens. His felt his task was more like tackling an iceberg than an icicle

Greg announced on the PA: "Those who want to tour the engine room before lunch should sign up at the reception center. First come, first served."

Jim broke away from his stalled thoughts and headed to see if Carol was interested in tour below decks. She wasn't. She would see him at lunch. He joined the group giving their names to Elsa.

They congregated one level below Jim's waterline cabin by the crew's quarters. As the group descended another level on open metal stairs the heat and noise rose. Engineering crew and officers stood around as the passengers trooped by.

Periodically a staff member would point out the engine controls linked to the bridge, the two massive diesel-electric engines, and auxiliary plants that produced heat, light, and water from a reverse osmosis system. Unless someone was right next to the staff member little could be heard above the steady roar of machinery.

While admiring a machine shop loaded with tools and equipment he could only wish for, Jim found Frank behind him. He tapped Jim on the shoulder and pointed up a level and to his ears. Oh, too noisy here.

Jim followed the Brit up an expanded metal stairway that he not seen before. They entered a darkened empty mess room. There Frank turned on Jim forcing him to step backwards:

"Stop asking bloody questions about that stupid robbery. You're a bloody nuisance. People are here to have a holiday. Leave it, damn it!"

Jim tightened his fists. He felt like hitting the older man and he felt very hot despite the lack of a physical threat. Jim turned and thumped heavily down the stairs to rejoin the tour.

This was a definitely a change in Frank from yesterday. Then he had talked about Boyd possibly running the heist, and he seemed friendly. Had someone talked to him, or was it a case of what Martin called testiness on a long voyage? Was Frank a flip-flop sort of guy? Nice one moment, bitter the next? Or was the outburst a ruse to put him off questioning the man himself. Was Frank behind the robbery?

Jim must be getting somewhere even if he wasn't sure where. He wasn't going to quit. Maybe listen more, ask less, and something would turn up.

The ship ran steadily into the east moving waves. Carol had seen the odd Antarctic petrel, an indication that they were nearing the Antarctic Peninsula. There was an afternoon Antarctic barbeque as they crossed the sixtieth parallel, proof that they were in polar waters. Jim made some effort to cut down on lunch though he still had to have fruit and a cake dessert on top of the soup, two meats and some risotto.

Jim and Carol sat down with Pamela and Georgina. Pamela said she had been talking about her trips to the Antarctic.

"How do you as a teacher find the trip? And please do not say educational."

Jim remembered his fake role and said: "As the only one on board without an accent I've found the trip mind expanding and fantastic. I find myself examining the scenery, the wildlife, the people and myself. It has been an eye opener. It will be an experience I will relish telling my students when I return to my school."

The studied silence told him that the original question was not an opening for sarcasm, gentle or otherwise.

Jim carried on with his self-determined path: "Of course, this type of trip take's a lot of money. Us poor teachers only make enough money to go every ten years or so. Though if you have the money I could see that it would be nice to go, say once a year."

Carol looked at her piece of vegetarian quiche as another slice of silence descended.

"Not that I am against money. Some of my best friends are quite well off."

"Some teacher, I presume," said Pamela, "who made a *slight* killing on the stock market. One hopes those types will not be taking up space on an Antarctic cruise ship. There are quite enough people coming down here already." Her background of money and her moniker: Horne-French left little room to argue, as far as she was concerned.

Jim said that he was sure his wealthy friends had other places they would rather go.

"I'm glad," snapped Pamela.

Carol asked if Pamela's concern was environmental.

"Certainly not. We should be selective in who comes here."

"Why, is it based on money?"

"What else is there?"

Carol did not reply.

Jim looked around at those with wealth and age, and thought "I'll achieve one of those two for sure, probably not the former."

Jim's father had spoken about not letting the buggers grind you down even if they did own the grinder. Was Jim getting fed up with the investigation, some of the passengers, the trip, or what? How not to make friends and not influence people.

Before Jim could ask about another disruptive subject: the gold robbery, the two women made an abrupt departure. Georgina mentioned having tea. Pamela hoped the quality was better today.

Carol looked at Jim and softly commented: "A little touchy, are we?"

Jim stared at her a moment and said: "I guess I'm feeling fed up. I'm not usually this way.

"No?"

"It's OK when I deal with people at work. I suppose I'm relaxing on this trip and don't give a damn."

"You don't have to beat yourself up. The change will make you a better person. I like that."

"Thanks."

They retired to the bridge to check on birds, whales and icebergs. A few others had joined them in checking the horizons. On the green radar screen the six-mile sweep moved around showing blotches of yellow, icebergs several square miles in area.

Jack and Rachel entered the bridge with a loud clatter. Jack squeezed his way through several passengers around the radar screen, his camera held out like a battering ram as he focused on the defined icebergs. He swung his camera blocking several passengers' view of the GPS screen with its yellow line showing the ship's course.

"That should show those blighters at home what a real voyage is like, not like those softies on their trips to the West Indies."

Rachel's eyes shone: "Spoken like a real man."

Ed standing next to Doug and Ron slipped in with: "You've had lots of experience of 'em?"

Before Rachel could reply, the first officer, Bernard, reprimanded them for making too much noise on the bridge. Jack pulled Rachel away and laughed: "Heel, tabby, heel!" They departed for less quiet climes. Could those two be behind the Ushuaia hold up, Jim wondered, their relationship being a cover of sorts. Or were they each playing the party passenger role. He moved them up a bit on his page of dubious suspects.

Bob, the birder, gave a talk on the gentoo, the chinstrap and the Adélie penguins. The origin of the first's name was unknown, the second had an obvious black chinstrap and the third was named after the wife of a nineteenth century French explorer.

Bob's slides depicted the different colors of guano, poop or shit. Pink was a meal of krill, white was fish, and green was no food at all. Some penguins preferred getting their stone nesting sites first and then a spouse. Others kept the spouse and then looked for a nest site. Both sexes looked the same.

Carol wanted to have a quick fag break, but was thwarted by the hotel staff and kitchen crew taking over the aft deck. Fat hot dogs spluttered on barbeques and the cans of Argentinean beer were suitably ice cold. A freezing wind picked up as passengers held warm sausages in long buns dribbling with mustard and relish. Most sheltered from the wind behind the lounge wall, where they could wipe their dripping noses.

Greg gave a few words on the success of the passengers having arrived in the Antarctic, and their endurance in having got this far. A few including Jim raised their ice-cold beer cans in a salute to the south. The expedition leader thanked the kitchen staff and the hotel staff for arranging the event. Some less hardy travelers made a rapid retreat to the lounge goodies and warm refreshments. The rest settled for another dog or more beer. Doug turned to speak to Ron and Ed, gasped, held himself round the middle and fell to the deck.

CHAPTER TWENTY-FIVE

Fortified with several south of sixty latitude beers and a few malt whiskies, Boyd talked of chopping up frozen seal with an axe.

"In those days I would get so hot chopping that even at minus twenty I would be bare-chested."

Mark babying his one martini smiled, contemptuous or friendly? Carol appeared and Jim gave her his best grin. He liked looking at her mouth especially the wide top lip and the bottom one which was soft and full, but smaller than the top.

"Yes?" she inquired.

Jim couldn't come up with a suitable answer. Arm in arm Rachel and Jack strolled past the bar group. In an aside Boyd said:

"I think she's well past her due date."

Carol looked at him. "Then *you* must be one of the living dead. No wonder you're single." She stalked off. Jim, smiling at the repartee, followed.

"Well," said Boyd, "that calls for another drink. Sandy, another live penguin here, this one's dead."

Sandy squeaked a cloth around a wine glass, replaced it slowly on the rack, and turned to serve a German couple. She listened carefully to their protracted drink requests. Boyd was left suspended between drinks.

"I could kill him. He can't relate to anyone but himself. I can't wait to destroy him."

Jim looked at Carol and took her hand.

"There's some good in him. Look when he stopped that fur seal from chomping on that Australian woman."

Carol turned on him. He quickly said:

"You're right. There's not much in him. He's a bull in a china shop. And, of course, being single he won't live as long as a married man."

She asked why *he* wasn't married. Jim mentioned his failed marriage, admitting his own faults not Janet's. Carol nodded and told Jim about her ex-doctor husband who needed the tender mercies of a steady diet of nurses.

"I would have thought you'd have had lots of better replacements."

"Thank you kind sir, but like you my hours have not been great for romance."

Then Carol said: "I told you about the few letters left to my mother. My father also left an old Leica camera and a few photos. It's not much of an inheritance."

"You've made your own inheritance with your job and this trip."

"I suppose so, and before you ask about my expensive single cabin the money came from an aunt's legacy. I needed a single. I don't share well."

Carol peered at Jim. He felt some urges that had been dampened the last few months. He postponed asking her how she learned about Boyd and the trip.

Jim and Carol put themselves at the end of an Australian tour group's dinner table. Rose was not feeling too well. It was her old complaint. The doc had suggested a few remedies, but she was being stubborn. "Typical," said one man. "Well, you should know, she's your wife," said another.

As they waited for the Argentinean trout and an unnamed vegetarian dish Jim and Carol talked about what they should talk about.

"We've done music. You'll have to come round to my point of view. So what's next," laughed Carol.

"There are always goals in life. What are yours?"

She hesitated. "After I have denounced Boyd, I'm not sure. And you?"

"I guess once I've had my break, I'll return to being a security consultant. I was a policeman before that. I'm not really a teacher. I've been telling people I am. I thought my police background would have put people off when I asked about the robbery."

"No, it wouldn't have put me off, but lying about it would have."

Jim looked at Carol and apologized for his deceit. She softened and asked:

"How about more travel, or a change of country to work in?"

"What are you suggesting?"

"Possibilities."

Jim looked at her.

"So, mate, is she your chick?" The husband of Rose looked at the two of them for an answer. Jim felt a tap on his ankle. Carol gave a half smile at the Aussie and concentrated on her vegetable lasagna.

*

Doug came to with a taste of vomit in his mouth. Had he cleared off all today's spam from his computer? His next thought was why does one bother with the stupid stuff in life when you're in real trouble? The doctor, Ron and Ed stood around his bed. The doctor he could do without.

"You had a bit of a fall there, fella. How do you feel?" The doctor had a friendly face and that intense searching look that doctors gave everyone, living or dead.

Doug head still spun. He managed a:

"Not too bad, I guess."

The doctor said: "I've seen better looking corpses than you, but you're making a comeback. You looked quite ill for a while. I would like to examine you if I may. Tell me where it hurts."

He took Doug's non-answer as an affirmative, looked at his mouth, and gently prodding around the chest and abdomen. Doug's yellowing eyeballs were peered at and Doug was asked if he had jaundice. There was a mutter about a touch of malaria when he lived in Queensland. The doctor extracted some blood.

"Will he live, doc?" asked Ed.

"Certainly. But I think he has a condition that he's not telling us about. How did you get a clean bill of health from your medic?"

Doug said nothing. He lay there breathing steadily, wishing everyone would go away. It always hurt more lying down.

"I'm going to leave you," said the doctor. "Don't stay too long with him," looking at Ron and Ed. And to the patient: "I shall return."

Ron said: "You gave us quite a turn there, mate. Do you want anything?"

"Some of those pills in my draw." Ed gave him a couple from the container.

"This stuff looks pretty lethal, Doug. Prescribed or proscribed?"

"It's only codeine for the odd pain."

"If you say so," said Ed. "You don't have too many left what ever they are."

Doug was going to have talk to the doctor when the other two were not around so he could get more painkillers. He would not give too much a way.

"So what brought this collapse on?" Ron asked.

"A bit of fatigue."

"Doug, you're good at most things, but lying isn't one of them. You look haggard."

"Wan," piped in Ed.

"Rough," followed Ron.

"And ugly," finished Ed.

"Hey, not that," managed the invalid. "OK, I'm not in top form as they say in England. I just need to finish this trip, and rest up."

"Why not rest up on the trip?" asked the rational Ron.

"I've got a few things to do," said Doug.

"Such as?"

"Don't pester me. OK?"

"Well, like the doc, we'll be back."

Doug closed his eyes. He needed to make up some convincing story to keep the doctor off his back.

Being mainly a roving seasick pill-pusher the doctor returned sooner than Doug wanted. The patient said he felt better. He had a stomach complaint, ulcers he thought, and he would see a specialist once he got home. Did the doc have any painkillers? Doug could have some Tylenol, but that was it. What had he been using before? Doug said Tylenol.

"What if the pain gets worse?"

"We'll come to that when it happens. Keep off the alcohol and fatty foods, and rest up. I'll drop off some antacids. I'll check what's in your blood sample but our facilities are a bit limited. You'll tell me your true condition in time. For the next day or so you should only land once a day. Zodiac cruises are OK if you keep warm."

Doug was left with a mild painkiller and the need to deal with Boyd. Rest was the only "activity" that would get him through. Maybe some hot and cold packs. Interesting how some of the symptoms of a stomach ulcer and "Pankie" were similar. He did not want to think about the pain getting worse.

*

Boyd propped up the bar at his usual spot. The blue carpet was faded where the heavy drinkers turned to order refills. Sandy topped up his glass. She depended on him despite his attitude. He turned to the circle of regulars and said:

"Stop me if you've heard this one."

"We have," said Frank.

Boyd carried on:

"A man falls in a crevasse. He's told not to climb out by the other men on the base."

"Why was that?" asked Ed.

"Well, everyone had to go and get their cameras. When enough photos were taken they pulled him out."

"Mind you, for emotional stress receiving a 'Dear John' letter was far worse," said Frank. "When the ship came in after eight months of isolation there was usually mail from ex-girl friends who were not prepared to wait any longer."

"One chap put the picture of his ex- on the dartboard and had some target practice," added Arthur.

Ed looked around: "What about, you know, sex in the old days?"

"There were girlie magazines if you needed them. But with no females there was less interest in sex. With me at any rate," muttered Frank.

"Oh."

Boyd turned to Doug: "Not drinking?"

"I'm drinking."

"Looks like ginger ale. When did you stop drinking booze?"

"This ginger ale is first for my thirst."

"Getting too old to hold your liquor? Mind you after your fall this afternoon, you should be more careful."

Doug's face reddened and said:

"I don't need to drink and look bloated like you."

"Well, someone's pissed in your drink."

Doug tightened up. Ron and Ed gently escorted him to a lounge chair. Ron quietly said:

"We hang together or we hang separately."

"What the hell's that supposed to mean?" Doug retorted. "I should have done the bastard in South Georgia."

Ron and Ed looked at each other.

"Are you sure the doc can't help you?" asked Ed.

"Leave it," snapped Doug. He slowly stood up and said he was going back to his cabin. It was confining, but it was less aggravating than being here.

*

The piano player played comfort music. Jim was not interested in it. He said:

"I'm enjoying this cruise despite certain people."

"I'm sorry if I've upset you"

They smiled at each other.

"You're doing it again."

"What's that?"

"That deep intent look."

"You're worth looking at."

Jim found her hand under the small drink table and for a moment their fingers conversed.

"Have we come to the end of our conversation?"

"How about food. Do you cook?" Carol asked as she slid her fingers away.

"I see a lot of fast food joints. I was planning on taking a cooking course when I got back."

"French or Italian?"

"Calories."

The conversations and drinking carried on around them as they waited out another pause.

"How about a change in career, say to nursing."

"I'm too old to change careers."

"So, Mr. Mckinnon, how old are you?"

"Forty."

"I knew a woman who got her university degree at eighty, so you've got some ways to go."

"And your change in career will be…?"

"I'll stick with nursing. I like artistic endeavors, but I need a stable job to come home to. Art rarely supports itself."

Jim moved the conversation away from the personal, his at any rate. "How did you know Boyd would be on this trip?"

"An old friend of my father's told me which cruise Boyd was on. I see you are a typical male wanting facts rather than giving empathy."

"I plead guilty of maleness, your honor."

"But you do listen."

"My penalty will be less harsh?"

"Perhaps. Anyway I want one more cancer stick before I retire to bed."

With me, thought Jim, the bed not the cancer stick.

Harry, the husband of Australian Rose of the "usual complaint" joined the bar batch. He grumbled to Ed that the tour rate was cheaper but it had its downside. They traveled as a group. Not that he was complaining about his wife, mind you, but a bloke likes to get away some time. Ed agreed. His wife was holding the fort back in Adelaide. He was enjoying himself.

"Mind you," said Harry, "where ever you are, there you are."

Ed feeling his drinks agreed. Ron wanted to look in on Doug again. They both left.

Jim could chat with Ed, verbally spar with Ron, but Doug was always on edge and probably too ill to be behind the hold up. Jim sat on the edge of the bar group and listened to old polar gossip. He wondered if his concerns would ever show any light rather than obscurity.

What does one do with Frank's "if in doubt there is no doubt"? Was that some Antarctic philosophy or too much booze? Then Arthur followed up with would they rather have an infirm body and a sharp mind or a feeble mind and a strong body.

"The amount Boyd's imbibed he would have neither," said Frank.

"Screw you!" came out of Boyd.

"Boyd!" said Kim.

"OK. Just a bit of Antarctic repartee."

A pause at the bar was broken by Ron's need for facts. He turned to Frank and quietly asked him about his limp. An Antarctic accident?

Frank said: "Yes, an icy slope."

"Any compensation?" asked Ron.

"No."

Passing by to replenish his glass Boyd butted in: "Come on Frank, shame your devil and tell the truth."

"What do you mean?"

"Sure there was an icy slope, but what condition were you in?"

"To repeat your comment: 'Screw you!'" said Frank. He grabbed his drink and moved down the lounge away from the bar.

"A few too many rum and cokes, I heard from those who were on base with him," said Boyd.

CHAPTER TWENTY-SIX

Jim surfaced in the morning. There was a lack of headway in his investigation of Peter's death and the robbery, but Carol and he were getting on fine. The captain would not be happy but he was. There was only a week to go before they reached Ushuaia. His priorities were shifting.

For the second time on the voyage he peddled a stationary bike above a sea that had a mind of it own and waves that changed course at will. Inflamed red and grey clouds twisted across the horizon. The sun was hidden behind a grey background. Greg's quote: "I go exploring because I like it and it's my job," broke into Jim's thoughts.

For their first Antarctic landing, Brown Bluff, Greg repeated the rules about distances from wild life, the disinfectant tray would be in place at each landing, and:

"You do not to take any thing in or out except memories and photographs." Greg looked round as if looking for a culprit. Jim wondered who would succumb to a dead penguin foot souvenir?

Jim joined Carol at the stern deck. They smiled at Shaun and Pam, nodded at Kim on the hunt for Boyd, and got a cool response from Pamela, and some of the ex-Antarctic people. He still needed to approach Pamela. She was on his list. Jim made sure he was a little closer to Carol than necessary. She didn't object. Jim asked her how she was feeling.

"I'm OK. But I may be a little difficult the next day or so. I've got to deal with Boyd. Can you bear with me?"

He said he could, but an image of Mandy's long legs striding over the rocks on the Fortuna Bay hike appeared. We always want more, he thought.

*

Leon had no thoughts of more or less. Outside his cabin Raul made eyes at Marissa as she brought Leon's breakfast. Raul was a little slow in opening the door. A nudge in his side produced a smile. The door opened and for some life changed. For Leon lying on his back on the floor it had gone. He looked peaceful. But there was no movement or breath.

Marissa put the tray down on the bed touched Leon and screamed. Raul looked around as if the answer was somewhere there. Marissa pulled the phone to her and pressed several buttons. One eventually reached the bridge. The captain arrived, looked at Leon and called for the doctor. Raul and Marissa were questioned and sent back to work. There was no point in telling them to keep quiet.

The doctor closed the door and examined the body. He smelled booze on Leon, looked at the empty bottle of sleeping pills and the dead whisky bottle, but said nothing about the cause of death.

Two crewmen took Leon to the sick bay. Captain Engstrom asked the doctor to give him the results as soon as possible, and then stomped off to his cabin to note down another death. The rumors of Leon's demise would fly around the ship whether he wanted them to or not.

Jim had a hurried breakfast. The only conversation was the speculation on why Leon died. After his meal Jim knocked on the captain's door and was invited in.

"There's something rotten about this ship!" Captain Engstrom's papers lay strewn around his desk. Like his thinning hair there was little order to them. "How can a tourist trip to damn Antarctica have two bloody deaths, if you will excuse the language?"

There was no answer to this rhetorical question.

"Leon?"

"Yes!"

"There must be a connection with that other man on the recording and with Peter Tielmann's death. I suppose there'll be an inordinate amount of paperwork at Ushuaia." Jim remembered back to his days on the force. More time was spent writing up reports than dealing with crime.

"And in London and several other places," snapped the captain. He pushed the offenders aside and phoned the doctor. "He's on his way."

"Too many sleeping pills and booze," said the doctor.

"Suicide. That was the cause of death?" asked the captain hopefully

"No," said the doctor. "The inside of his mouth was damaged as if someone had forced a bottle and a lot of pills down his throat.

"A tap to quieten him down before the medicine was administered. One of the passengers said his bottle of sleeping pills was missing, and there was a small knife wound in his back to make sure he stayed dead."

The captain swore then said: "This is also an accident. An overdose while depressed. We don't mention the knife wound. The knife would have been long gone. Has the food storage got room?"

"Yes." The doctor went back to his "patient". Before he left he asked about the other "accident". "That was not just a fall from a cliff?"

"No. We will keep Mr. Tielmann's death as accidental for the time being."

The doctor nodded and left.

"First, how did someone get the guard away from the door, and who was behind the killing? The first I can deal with. A bit of pressure on certain crewmembers will work wonders. You try and find the second. I shall certainly have more success than you."

Jim was dismissed. Jim had two deaths to investigate. Someone had stopped Leon from speaking about the robbery and presumably about Peter's death.

*

Once I got into his cabin I told Leon that he should have more of the gold. He had done all the groundwork in Ushuaia. He jumped at the idea. We had celebratory drinks. Large ones were poured. As Leon turned towards the Johnny Walker I smashed the back of his head with a rock brought along from Gold Harbour. The sock the rock was in would not see my feet again. Leon slumped to the floor.

I pushed the knife low and up into his back. A kidney strike. One must make sure. Hitting more times with the rock sock would have been messy. More whisky (his favorite drink) with sleeping pills was poured into him. A cursory glance would show overdrinking. The pills would later suggest a self-inflicted death. Only a close examination would disprove both the previous suppositions.

*

At the morning lecture Colin the staff historian spoke on the first scientific Antarctic expedition. The Belgian leader, Gerlache, named much of the landscape. His ship, the *Belgica*, got frozen into sea ice for over a year. Notables on the ship were the Norwegian, Amundsen, first man to the South Pole, and the American, Dr. Cook, who claimed to be first to summit Mt. Mckinley and the first to the North Pole. Both men helped the crew to survive their long sea ice imprisonment.

Bob the staff birder mentioned that at Brown Bluff if a skua stole a penguin egg or even a chick they were not to be whacked. Some other passengers had attempted this. The skuas had their own chicks to feed. If a penguin was a couple of feathers short of being an adult they would have to learn to be more protective the next season.

"Will we see any of the big emperor penguins that we've all seen on a DVD back home?" was a perennial question.

His response was: "You never can tell. Of course, for more money you could go down on a huge icebreaker at the end of October to visit an emperor colony." Bob added than a few million years ago some penguins were nearly six feet tall, so the emperor was not the largest penguin ever.

The last presentation was the expedition leader's on the requirements for landing in Antarctica. Attendance was mandatory if passengers wanted to land on Antarctica ice or land and not stay on board. Jack broke in with:

"So I've paid all this money to come down here and if I don't attend this spiel I can't land?"

Greg said: "That's correct."

Jack's reply was: "That sucks!"

*

Jim and Carol sat at a lunch table where there were mostly Americans. The food was a repeat of two weeks ago. The chef or the pantry was running dry.

The conversation around the table was on the dominance of American culture. Carol put in that more films were made in India than in Hollywood. The response was but who watched them? She gamely said:

"Maybe we should try."

Jim added that some Americans believed there was no other culture in the world but theirs. Joe across from him asked, didn't they call that "cultural envy?" Jim admitted as a Canadian that was easy to do.

There was a movement to the bridge as the ship neared Brown Bluff. Cameras photographed the milling mass of birds going to and from their nests. Black and white spotted pigeon-sized cape petrels, sailed over the grey waves. Slower white kelp gulls followed. Tiny hand-sized Wilson storm petrels flitted over the rolling water, their feet "walking" on the water.

A thick dark cloud covered the volcanic brown mesa-like cliffs ahead. Small icebergs rolled back and forth. Further out larger tabular bergs blocked the drifting sea ice. The ship had reached Antarctica.

"God, what an awful place!" Jim turned at Carol's voice, and smiled at her animated face. "Is this the holiday you promised me?" she asked.

*

The smell and the noise from the penguin rookery rode out to the ship. At the beach landing passengers strode quickly away to get some personal space for themselves. The voyage had brought out some irritations. Some people sat down and watched the scenery and wildlife. The passengers were fit though some of the husbands would have to take some definite steps if they didn't want their wives to collect on the life insurance.

The staff stood at both ends of the beach to limit wanderers. One grey spotted Weddell seal lay on its back close to the water snoozing. The penguins, gentoos and Adélies, continually collected pebbles for their rock nests. Some thieving took place. The more rocks a penguin got for their mate the better they were at bringing home the krill. The gentoo penguins with orange bills and pink feet were more colorful than the black Adélies. A few eggs peaked out under the nesting parents.

The Australian guy Doug stayed close to the moored boats. He still looked ill even though the doctor had seen him. Ron and Ed wandered off down the beach. Doug asked a staff member:

"Are we going to land at other mainland sites further south?"

He was told at least two more. Doug didn't give any reason why this was important.

A few young Australians were tossing snowballs at each other. The staff let them do a few and then suggested they head down the beach away from the nesting penguins.

Some people celebrated there seventh continental landing. One pair from Australia drank a miniature bottle of champagne using plastic glasses. For some passengers this continental landing was one more item to check off. Some had been everywhere and seen nothing.

One staff member mused on whether the Canadian guy and his English companion would remain a firm item He thought only the Antarctic gods could tell. Carol had also asked the staff member about continental landings rather than the more common island landings. He wondered why the interest.

A less firm item was Rachel and Jack. Jack was at play but would he go back to his mouse of a wife Doreen? Would she stay with the devil she knew or would she find the strength to make a break and sue for divorce? The staff rarely heard the end of these ongoing soap operas. The next trip down south produced more of the same.

On the beach a staff member had tried a little levity as Jack got out of the Zodiac. He didn't have a hat so the staffer said:

"No hat, no mitts, no service."

Jack glared and stalked off with Rachel. The staff members tried to keep the passengers happy, but…

Later Greg told staff members to start rounding up the reluctant residents. Not the feathered ones. One staff member found if he worked on Rachel it got the pig-headed Jack back quicker. As the staffer headed at an angle up to the base of the cliff he saw a pair of pure white snow petrels flitting around the rocks. Their eyes were jet black as were their beaks. Unlike quarrelsome doves in warmer climes the snow petrels were a sign that Antarctica was peaceful.

*

One question for Mike the sea mammal staffer was if the seal had spots how would you know if it was a leopard seal or a Weddell seal?

He said: "If it's got a huge head, a long neck and massive jaws with teeth, it's a leopard seal, Hydrurga leptonyx. It means water worker with small claws, but it has lots of sharp teeth. Keep away."

Carol decided to watch the sea birds for a while. Jim should join the Antarctic types. "Or should we call them the Antarctic tykes? I'll see you later." His hand flowed along her arm as she left. Jim joined Shaun and Pam the two young Australians for a drink.

Sandy at the bar showed them a 10,000-year-old piece of glacial ice a staff member had brought back from the sea near the landing. The lump hissed bubbles as it melted in its bowl on the counter. The ice would go well with their drinks.

Next table down the Californian couple, Jacqueline and Richard, sat keeping their own company. They were polite with others but were not overly social. Their eyes showed neither warmth nor coldness. There was no financial information on them. Jim thought the couple might be the ones behind the robbery.

Maisie the short woman who had been shunted out of the bridge games talked steadily to Kim, whose hair shone from much brushing as she waited for her lord and master.

"It must be pretty uncomfortable if you're a penguin sitting on piles of rocks for a nest. What do you think, Kim?"

She did not answer. Boyd had arrived. He called for his usual from Sandy and led Kim over to where the rest of the Antarctic bar keepers loitered.

To Jim it seemed Boyd never talked about gold or even made comments about the robbery. He only drank, propped up the bar, and projected his ample front, both the physical and the mental.

Mark moved into the lounge. He was a possibility for the heist, though he lacked wealth, a suite, and had said his Spanish connections were tenuous. He nodded at Jim but did not stop. He shed a little more warmth than Jacqueline and Richard, but little light. Jim had once asked him who knew the most about the Antarctic. Mark directed him to Arthur and Malcolm Moresby. Jim was about to pop the question of the Ushuaia hold up to anyone available when there was a:

"Penis! That's what I said," exclaimed Boyd. "You put a string through seal penises; leave them out side for the skuas to eat the flesh off, and then you turn them into cigarette holders. Some earlier tourists had paid dearly for them. 'Course, you can't do that nowadays."

"Have you actually tried it?" asked Frank.

"No, but I heard it was done."

CHAPTER TWENTY-SEVEN

The deed was done. Leon would have spilled the beans. (Why do the Americans have all the best phrases?). My gold is safe. I still have half of the hoard. The lifeboat part was unaccounted for: crew, passenger, captain, I do not know. The third quarter with some pressure in certain quarters will be mine.

Unlike, others my life has moved on. Mark, that's me, likes order; it holds back time. The hands of time can not be stopped, but they can be slowed down a little. Entropy resisted again.

Dinner was a very contemplative time. The day wound down. It was still broad daylight outside. Why *broad*? The sun glittered off the water and the icebergs, and around me the passengers discussed their first day in Antarctica. They did not realize the shifting that went on behind the scenes. The Antarctic was another landscape, an icy one, but one with layers to it, some opaque, some transparent.

*

Pamela said: "I still say it would be better if the Antarctic was limited to those with money and not the many. You have seen the ships queuing up to get through the beautiful Lemaire Channel. It might as well be Piccadilly Circus."

Arthur sitting with Georgina and Frank interjected that he preferred the more winding scenic Errera Channel to the dead straight Lemaire, but she had a point about the numbers of people putting pressure on the Antarctic Peninsula. Some restrictions whether financial, lotteries, quotas, or whatever should be put in place.

"But Arthur, you've had a chance to live here. What about those who have to save up for a small taste of the Deep South?" asked Georgina?

Pamela carried on with: "No, we cannot all have what we want. The uniqueness of the Antarctic is lessened as more travel here. It should be limited to the few." She waved vaguely at the unending Antarctic ice. "Don't you agree, Frank?"

Frank who had been working on a sponge cake laden with dulce de leche grunted: "I suppose so."

"Look at those teacher types over there spending money they don't have on a week or so of Antarctic travel."

"Actually, Pamela, the woman's a nurse," said Georgina.

"Same difference!"

Georgina gave a slight smile to Arthur, and sipped her milky coffee.

Jim and Carol sat with a French couple, and struggled with their high school French. Jim especially felt guilty as French was supposed to be one of the official languages of Canada. Jean and Marie's English was enough to get by on. Penguins formed a common bond.

Elsa announced that for this evening there would be a BBC DVD on Antarctic wildlife, to add to their impressions of this cold, hostile land.

'Will you be watching it?" Jim asked.

Carol said she would. She would see him afterwards.

Kim, accompanied Boyd whether he liked it or not, and in turn was followed by Maisie. As Frank said to Ed: "Boyd's harem."

Espying Carol, Boyd yelled out:

"Hi, babe!"

"I'm not your babe!"

"Well you could've been my daughter!"

"Not, in your wildest dream!"

Kim said: "Boyd, be nice."

"I'm so sorry," said Boyd eyeing Carol, and then turned back to Kim.

"Sorry! Next he's going to burst into tears. He could ruin things when I tear a strip off him in front of everyone," Carol said. "I can't stand this. I'm going to watch that film; I'll see you in the morning." She touched his non-drink hand and left Jim to his persistent question. Jim didn't think it was worth it.

*

Boyd thought it was a pity that Carol left. She looked good. He wouldn't have minded her as his daughter or mistress. He liked riling her. And her boyfriend too.

"What's that Kim kitten?" Kim had been yammering in his ear about seeing the Antarctic animal show downstairs. She headed off taking that Maisie woman with her.

He noticed there were only two Aussies from the trio. As usual the wannabe Antarctic heroes wanted to learn more.

Ed brought up a weird topic: "Have you ever wanted to murder someone on the ice?"

"Several, actually, but I never got round to it," said Boyd.

"Some men if they were fed up at the end of a long Antarctic winter would go and talk to the huskies," said Arthur. "The dogs always appreciated human company even if they weren't the greatest talkers."

Frank said: "I haven't murdered anyone in the Antarctic, but keeping a bottomless crevasse handy would have been useful. Or there's always the drifting ice floe."

The ice floe bit got Boyd thinking about an incident from a long time ago. Then the Canadian boyfriend broke up his thoughts by asking:

"Have you ever been threatened down south?"

Boyd bluntly snapped: "No, never!"

Georgina strolled by to get a refill from Sandy. Ed told her what they were discussing. "Why would you want to murder some one down here? Isn't the Antarctic supposed to be a peaceful place?"

Boyd wondered why that the group that Georgina had left, Mark, Pamela and that American couple, Jacqueline and Richard, were in a bit of a huddle. Were there dirty plots a foot? Or were they discussing the difficulties of keeping a good gardener back home. "I have a man. Comes in and does the rough. Found him on a local estate. I do the rest." A bit pathetic. Boyd thought he might sidle up and interrupt their coziness. A little mayhem was always worthwhile.

He wondered whether this would be his last major Antarctic trip. Boyd needed other outlets. Kim perhaps. She was a newbie. He could educate her to his way of thinking. Well, it had been a long way from

Murder in the Antarctic

Chiswick, Eton, his first Antarctic winter, a time with the Guards, and then those other Antarctic trips.

Boyd gave most people short shrift except for his Aunt Glynn Featherhyde. She had rather a lot of property, which eventually came to him. You had to push people to get them to do anything. Some would call it bullying. He was not sure why. A lot of them as Maggie Thatcher, our only decent Prime Minister, said were "wets".

Then there was that odd twerp like that Canadian who questioned him. He seemed interested in that Ushuaia robbery. Boyd had no idea why.

*

Jim looked around the lounge at the various groups. Outside, the sun was still above the horizon to the north. It was late. It did not feel like night. The Arctic was like that. You got a lot done during the long daylight hours. And little sleep.

Glaciers headed to the sea, dropping icebergs on their way. They at least moved although slowly. He felt that his investigative journey was at a standstill. The response to Jim about the heist was nil or unfriendly. When he was a policeman he occasionally used a firm adversarial tone. That was not possible here. The situation was unique, and he had no backup.

Jim was stymied. The dubious ones stonewalled, balked, blocked or ignored him. He leaned towards Boyd as being "it". It would solve the problem. There was weariness in asking the same questions and not getting anywhere, despite what had happened to Peter and Leon.

The ex-Antarctic guys Arthur, Mark, Boyd and Frank could have South American contacts to implement the holdup though Frank was not quite as well-off financially as the rest. Most passengers said they were in Ushuaia the day before the bank robbery and the ship's departure. There was time to organize the robbery.

Age? Were Arthur, Boyd and Frank too old? Though with Leon's help they were possibles. Peter had been a prime suspect for age and need, but was out of the running now. The three Australian men, (but Doug?) fitted the age category, but they lacked money and Spanish connections. The expedition staff had age and some South American contacts on their side, but they had neither time nor money to organize the heist.

Gender or as he preferred, sex? Pamela with help, Rachel with help from Jack, or even Carol? He had to keep an open-mind even if it was difficult.

Knowledge about gold? Most would want the gold, and could easily mug up on the forms it took, its value and its weight.

Jim thought about the Ushuaia end. Several of the possibles could have slipped away from the prison museum tour, done the robbery and then joined the national park visit. Some like Arthur, Boyd Frank and Mark had skipped the prison tour having done it several times before.

Jack and Rachel? Did they come together "naturally" or was the joining up contrived? He should ask if they were on the museum tour. They would say yes. Jim had no way of asking the tour guides in Ushuaia who was or wasn't on the tour. He had arrived too late to be on it.

And now Carol was holding him, (I wish she would), at arm's length. Perhaps the answer was another drink. The night was young, by looks if not time. Long-legged Mandy had strolled through earlier. He grinned at her as she passed. She smiled briefly.
He regretted his grin and thought about Carol.

CHAPTER TWENTY-EIGHT

The *Polar Adventurer* slid along the flat glassy Gerlache Strait. Sunlight poured down from a steel blue sky, reflected off white glaciered mountains, islands and capes, and bounced off many sunglasses. Further out a few minke whales, black finned, moved parallel to the ship.

Some passengers like Arthur were home again. Georgina asked "Why Brabant?" Arthur mentioned the first scientific expedition was from Belgium at the end of the nineteenth century so that white snow covered island became Brabant Island. And the strait they were sailing along was named after the leader, Gerlache.

Like Gerlache, the Frenchman Charcot a few years later needed sponsorship money, so he named places after benefactors who at least got some name recognition, even if there were no monetary rewards. Boyd, strolling along with Kim and a tagging Maisie, pointed out remembered features.

Jim and Carol sat with Pamela at breakfast. Carol commented on the brilliant white scenery bordered by black razor-edged ridges. Pamela agreed that it was rather naice. She carefully cut her triangled toast into sharp, small bite-size pieces. Jim asked if she was enjoying the cruise.

"Parts of it," was the reply.

"Which parts?" Jim persevered.

"The scenery."

Carol mentioned they had not seen any other ships yet.

"You will."

"Should there be more?" asked Jim.

"I would rather there were less," said Pamela.

"Seems a bit unfair." Jim was ready to roll. Pamela was not. She abruptly excused herself and left. Again his more provocative subject, robbery, was thwarted.

Carol shook her head. "Mr. McKinnon, Mr. McKinnon. What are we going to do with you?"

"I can think of several options."

"Keep those to yourself."

Greg said that the next landing site would be Danco Island:

"Be careful. There are ice cliffs as well as crevasses. A few years ago a retired millionaire took a stroll on a glacier along the Antarctic Peninsula. He became a millionaire no more. A crevasse death is no way to end your Antarctic trip."

The ship maneuvered around large icebergs straddled across the Errera Channel. Glacial ice plunged into the sea. Drifts of fresh snow threw themselves off hanging cliffs. The *Polar Adventurer* anchored in calm water near the mile long Danco Island. Jim thought of staying on board to look at a few cabins, but the bright shining blue sky and dazzling snow were a greater attraction.

*

Carol had landed with Jim in what for her was a late Zodiac. Jim had hovered. Carol liked him but he would have to wait. Gently Carol said she would rather walk the beach on her own for a while. He looked disappointed, but a touch of her hand got him clomping up through the snow with the rest. She was girding herself up for what she called her "Boyd bollocking." He needed to be ashamed in front of all the passengers at a key time like dinner. Carol was going to introduce herself, and then explain her real reason for the Antarctic trip. She wanted to lash into William Boyd Barrington's pompous hide, and expose him for the coward he had been all those years ago and still was.

She thought of a young man with little fuel for heat, no food, the hunger gradually taking over his thoughts and life. Had he chewed his leather belt? Carol had heard of people assuaging their hunger that way. But how long could you do that for? She replayed the scene of her father slowly dying in a small wooden hut, stranded on a barren icy coast.

Boyd loomed large in her father's dying. He had deserted Dave Bapton though in Boyd's account her father had left him and the husky team. She didn't believe it. Boyd had deliberately abandoned her father in an Antarctic storm. She thought of how she could kill Barrington down here. Was it in her? She was suppose to look after people not get rid of them.

Carol returned to her father's last few weeks of life. Her loss needed revenge. She had seen the pompous one trudging up the snow-covered hillside earlier. His females following close behind. Their loss. If you attach yourself to an arsehole you pay the price. A few warm tears came to her eyes.

Carol blinked at a large spotted seal. It opened its mouth. Large yellow incisors hung from its jaw. The seal raised itself up to face Carol. Bigger food than krill or shrimp could fit into that mouth. She stepped back as the seal lunged. The jaws grabbed her boot. Carol kicked. The seal hung on. Bob moved in and gave the seal a swift kick. As it turned to deal with the second intruder Carol dragged her foot away. Bob checked her boot for holes. Her foot wasn't punctured.

"There's only been one recorded human death, and we think that was a mistake on the leopard seal's part. But we don't want to push it. I'll stand guard and keep others at a safe distance."

Carol thanked Bob, and headed up the slope where some were still striving to reach the top. The younger set was already sliding down the hillside on their rear ends. She passed an ashen Doug who had got a little way up the trail and stopped. Carol asked him if he was OK. There was the usual male: "I'm fine."

At the top she found penguins nesting, and innumerable bird prints running down to the sea. Around the island the shining white Antarctic scenery glistened; it gave the illusion of warmth. Below the small bluish *Polar Adventurer* mirrored itself in the blue-grey water.

Some visitors followed a snow packed trail to the eastern side of the island overlooking the mainland. Drifting snow made a dry soughing sound. Staff members stood guard above ice cliffs and crevasses. There was an occasional roar off the sides of the mountains opposite as glacial debris broke off and joined the sea. Otherwise there was silence.

*

Jim had broken the quiet earlier by having a few words with the tall blond Mandy. She was from London. As she headed back downhill she had slipped. Jim grabbed her arm. She gently pushed him away, smiled a thanks and was gone. He remembered his decision of last night.

Arriving at the top of the hill Carol told Jim of her close escape from the leopard seal, and where was he when she needed him? He didn't say she had not wanted him around. After that Carol's camera preoccupied her. The correct lens always took time to fix. Jim was close but for him not close enough.

Back on board they stayed on the port side of the bridge as the captain guided the ship. He snapped quick commands to the third officer as they skirted icebergs through the winding channel. The ship moved slowly west back into the Gerlache Strait.

Bob the birder dispensed information on the next site, Port Lockroy. Though when Jack, with Rachel joined at his hip, asked about cruise ships sinking in Antarctic waters, Bob was a little reticent.

"I heard that one went down a few years ago. Everyone got off, but the ship went straight to the bottom in very deep water," said Jack.

Bob looked at him and said: "Oh, you mean the old *Explorer*. It hit some hard glacial ice north of here along the Bransfield Strait. Captain Engstrom is experienced in Antarctic waters so that won't happen."

"Shouldn't we have another boat drill or something," asked Rachel. She looked suitably concerned and clung to Jack's arm.

"No, no," said Bob. "One's all you need. We are perfectly safe. Our captain is very knowledgeable, and we have all the latest electronic gear. There's nothing to worry about." He smiled at Rachel and nodded at Jack. The passengers had to be kept happy. This was a trip of a lifetime. They had spent a lot of bucks.

Jim thought about Jack as a potential hold-up man. His lack of awareness of other people lessened his possibility as a suspect. He had not even twigged that Jim had been the guy he almost had a fight over when trying to sit with Carol. His South American connections were nil.

Ed remarked to Ron about how a sinking ship would make the trip really interesting.

"Especially freezing to death in a life boat," replied Ron.

Doug, wan-faced, didn't join the conversation. He was uncomfortable. He hadn't felt well that morning, and the afternoon would have too many people around to deal with Boyd even if he wanted to.

Standing next to Carol Jim looked at scenery and the odd sea bird, and wondered what he could do to get her more on side. Just time? Possibly. He felt somewhat slighted but he put this selfish thought aside. Then it returned.

Jim steered Carol to a lunch table with Malcolm Moresby and some other British passengers. Moresby gave details of expeditions that had been along the Antarctic Peninsula during the last century. He mentioned his own Antarctic experiences of living at two different bases. Jim thought there were some embellishments here, but he didn't correct Malcolm. The book on iceberg pictures was brought up. There was not much interest in it. When there was a break Jim asked about Mark and his Antarctic and South American interests, if any.

"He proceeds in his own fashion," said Moresby. "I don't know too much about what he does."

"And Arthur?"

Malcolm thought for a while and then said that Arthur had had a lot of southern experience.

"In financial areas?"

Again the reply was slow but it eventually came.

"He was involved in one or two Antarctic ventures and maybe in Argentina. He tended to have others as the front men."

"Was Boyd involved in that sort of enterprise?"

"Boyd! A buffoon if ever there was one. He inherited money but no finesse. His financial expertise is as limited as his awareness of the rest of the world. I've had to rescue him once or twice in the past though not with Antarctic deals, mind you."

Breaking Jim's train of thought, Moresby said he had visited Port Lockroy every year for the last five years. He always picked up at least one new souvenir. By this time the other passengers at their table had made their escape, and Carol had left for a smoke.

Jim wondered if Georgina could be a lead in to Frank, Mark, and anyone else who had been in the Antarctic. He would ask Carol if she would talk to Georgina about them. A PA announcement rang out:

"Killer whales at twelve o'clock!" Weaving between white floes were seven black triangular fins. One medium fin, led the rest including a tall male's triangular sail followed by smaller killer whales and one immature one. The yellowish white blotches on their backs contrasted with the black skin. Ahead on an ice floe a light colored crabeater seal was sunning itself.

Two of the adult whales paired up and surged forward. A wall of water rose in front of them. The wave hit the floe and the seal slid off. Fascinated the passengers watched as the whales grabbed the seal. Soon all that was left was red sea and bits of seal. The telephoto lenses showed a lot of blood and gore. And where there had been no sea birds multitudes flocked to the site like ants at a picnic.

The whales moved south in search of more prey and more education for the young. Mike mentioned the type of killer whales they were and what their next meal might be: penguins and seals including leopard seals. The incident had been a contrast to the benign Antarctic of sedentary seals and penguins.

Carol had stared at the scene and felt uncomfortable photographing the seal's death. Jim's excuse was that his camera couldn't have done the event justice. He decided to wait before broaching his request for getting Georgina to do some questioning.

On the eastern side mountains like black teeth rose up from the sea. The *Polar Adventurer* ran down the middle of a narrow channel and after an hour turned into a bay. On the right hand side was a small rocky island capped by a couple of huts. Glaciers and sharp peaks surrounded the site.

CHAPTER TWENTY-NINE

Greg quoted Apsley Cherry-Garrard: "'An Antarctic expedition is the worst way to have the best time of your life.'

"Port Lockroy will give you a taste of the primitive conditions in old Antarctica, but not quite as rugged as Cherry-Garrard's *The Worst Journey in the World* which I'm sure you've all read. There's a shop to buy Antarctic souvenirs."

At the old British scientific base fifty passengers landed. The rest waited on board. Jim had tried to go with Carol but his cabin number was not in her section.

Elsa firmly told him: "Sorry. Otherwise everyone will want to change."

He left Carol and moved down to his cabin to think. Martin was lying on his bunk listening to some music from some earphones.

"Would you be seeing the captain?" he asked.

"Should I?"

"I saw the captain looking at an email and he was fuming. He muttered about you and Arctic slides."

"I'll go and see him."

"Don't forget your laptop," said Martin.

Jim looked at him, grabbed the machine and headed out. The Arctic slide ploy was losing its edge. From what he had learned about Martin Jim didn't think he was a heist possibility. He knocked on the captain's door and heard a barked: "Enter!"

"Ah, you read my mind," said Captain Engstrom. "No gold has been recovered in Tierra del Fuego. Though the bank thieves of the Argentinean pesos have been caught. Most of the gold must still be around somewhere. Maybe only a bit was on this ship. I have done some searches but if the rest is on board the culprit or culprits can move it around to avoid being found. Have you any likely suspects?"

"My main one is Boyd. Not that he shows any sign of interest in gold or the robbery. Others might but I haven't seen and heard anything."

"Damn!"

Jim had no answer to that.

"The gold you found is still secure?"

Captain Engstrom snapped:

"Of course!" and dismissed his investigator.

. No Arctic slides were copied. There was no mention of the deaths of Peter and Leon.

*

On shore Frank, Arthur and Georgina wandered through the small wooden hut. Passing the mukluks, mitts and anorak hanging near the entrance, they reached a tiny kitchen.

"I learned to cook in a place like this," said Arthur, "complete with coal stove and tinned food."

"And does he cook now?" said Georgina. There was no reply.

Entering the radio room, Arthur said: "We could only send personal messages once a month, a limit of a hundred words."

"I think I've heard that before" Georgina said.

The group stopped in the ionospherics room.

"What is that?" asked Georgina, pointing to an old green machine loaded with dials and switches.

Arthur answered: "That's a radio ionosonde. It sent signals into the upper atmosphere and recorded what was up there. It was quite technical for the time."

"Oh," she said.

Arthur and Frank glommed onto the display of old sledging rations with enthusiasm

"Weren't those meat bars awful?" "The bars of chocolate were always a godsend!" "Ah, porridge with curry!" They fondled memories of their youth.

Georgina said: "The souvenir shop looks more interesting. I'll see you men later."

Boyd explained to Kim and Maisie that he had similar primitive conditions: coal fires, melting snow for water, and huskies, when he first came south. He had not been with this organization.

"Why not?" asked Kim

"I preferred the simpler private expedition."

"This outfit doesn't look too sophisticated," said Maisie. Boyd turned towards Kim.

Carol had done a quick tour of the base and decided against buying any souvenirs. Outside she snapped a young gentoo penguin that sat on her boots. Pure white sheathbills ran through the rookery picking up any debris that looked edible, including penguin poop.

A staff birder had told them that the penguin chicks nesting around the hut had a better survival rate than those further away. People visiting the hut kept the skuas away. So much for the negative effect of people on the Antarctic, Carol thought.

She avoided Boyd and his followers along the narrow corridors and rooms. Another reason to stay outside. She thought of Jim on board, and realized that more separation was needed for her to deal with bloody Boyd. Tomorrow or the next day. She could not leave it too late or she would look foolish. On board Carol told Jim:

"Port Lockroy will you give a feel for the old days." She escaped to her cabin.

At the landing site passengers clambered over large grey granite rocks, passed old whaling chains and a wooden Nansen sledge that used to be pulled by huskies. The Port Lockroy staff pointed out an old diesel generator in the middle of the souvenir shop, the bunk beds each carefully curtained off for limited privacy and the tiny bathroom. Baths were infrequent, as you had to melt your own snow for water.

Jim thought he could have learned to cook with all that canned food though whether his stimulus-deprived companions would have been satisfied he wasn't sure. Jim let Mandy squeeze past him in one of the narrow corridors. He was not trying to be attracted to her.

At her usual spot Carol puffed silently and savagely on a filtered Benson and Hedges. Jim waited until some of the puffing had slowed down. A question on how she found the base was: "OK". When the smoke was almost gone he popped the question.

"Would you ask Georgina about Mark and Frank's connection with South America?"

Carol looked at him: "Certainly not! Do you really think Georgina wouldn't tell them who was asking? I've got more important stuff on my mind." She turned away and almost dropped the butt overboard. Nothing overboard, south of sixty was the rule.

Jim apologized. He knew that she was under strain with Boyd. He shouldn't have asked. Carol nodded and looked at him. She was not smiling. Jim liked her even when there was tension between them.

They stared at the icy landscape that surrounded the small base. The ship was staying the night. Two other ships had visited that day, but the Port Lockroy staff did not expect any more until the next day. Port Lockroy was one of the top three tourist sites in Antarctica. If the odd small yacht dropped anchor it could wait until the next day to visit. That night the shore personnel would go on board for a free meal and drinks.

By Happy Hour the last of the Zodiacs had returned. The lounge was abuzz with the old Antarctic types retelling each other how much better life was in *those* days.

"I'm not sure I could have lived on tinned food for a year," whispered Kim to Maisie, as Boyd joined in the comments thrown back and forth.

Maisie said: "I sure we both would have put on pounds and pounds. I knew a woman who wintered in the Arctic, and do you know she started at a hundred and by the end of the winter she was up to a hundred and sixty pounds. And to this day she…"

Kim nodded and looked around the lounge. The three young women from Port Lockroy's summer staff were into the free wine, and were enjoying the same Antarctic stories they had heard from other ships. Georgina and Pamela sat away from the center of conversation. Arthur's wife kept a benevolent eye on him, and chatted about the mementoes bought that day. Mark sat near Jacqueline and Richard but as usual said little.

Jim was without Carol. She was going to have an early night. She apologized but was firm. He asked her to stay a little longer. Carol's lips tightened up:

"No. I'm not myself and won't be for a day or so. You listen to the old tales. Maybe you'll learn a thing or two."

Jim bearded Pamela, if he could use that phrase with a woman, and asked if she knew about the Ushuaia bank robbery.

"Of course," she snapped, "But why would I concern myself about it?" She carried on talking to Georgina. Jim went and sat near the two Australian doctors from Perth. They gave a polite hello. Jim decided on subtlety for a change and asked how this trip compared with their Antarctic trip to the Ross Sea. James said there was a lot more ice on the Ross Sea side of the Antarctic, but this side had greater variety of scenery and animals.

"They've both impressive."

Shirley asked Jim where he was from. He explained. Shirley thought it must be cold.

"Yes, though not as cold as most of the Antarctic in winter." He asked what they did when they weren't being doctors.

"Oh, we sail, scuba dive, and plan our next trip. The Amazon, wasn't that the next port of call?" Shirley asked.

"Either that or Belize."

Jim squashed any feeling of envy, and asked what the opportunities for teaching were like in Australia. Shirley thought not good.

"We produce too many of our own. I remember my mother telling about the large numbers of Australian teachers who went to Canada to teach in the nineteen sixties. Some never came back."

"Must have been the money," said Jim.

"That's normally the case," said James. "Are you still interested in that bank robbery at Ushuaia?" His switch in topics left Jim a bit off kilter.

Jim admitted he was interested. "I'm wondering if the gold was stashed on this ship."

James said: "That sounds unlikely." He did not have any nervous tics, or showed that he had anything to do with the gold, robberies or murder. Unless he was a good actor.

"You would be trapped on here if you had the gold," said Shirley. "Seems a funny thing to do on an Antarctic trip."

Jim agreed. He left them to go and listen to more ancient Antarctic lore from the bar.

Shirley said to her husband: "I don't think we have the whole story there. I wonder why he is so interested."

They sipped their wine and looked around the lounge. Ron and Ed joined them. They could always argue with these two about the best parts to live back home in Australia.

"No Doug?" asked Shirley.

"He's feeling a little crook. He'll be fine tomorrow," answered Ron, avoiding Ed's eyes.

*

After dinner I pleasantly requested Rita to drop by my cabin. When she was sitting comfortably I asked:

"Did Leon leave anything special in his cabin?"

She said no.

"How about something special in someone else's cabin?"

She blinked.

"Had he given you something to keep?"

More blinks.

"What was it?"

She said nothing.

"You're rather pretty."

Rita tried to back away from me.

"No, I'm not interested in you."

Nothing was said.

"Well? Did Leon leave anything in your cabin?

"He left some porno books in a bag"

"If I took them there would be more room for your things. Right?"

She rose quickly and led me to the cabin she shared with another girl. I bent my knees and lifted the bag. The books were certainly heavy in at least a couple of ways.

CHAPTER THIRTY

"Arthur, stop prating and come over here and help us with some of your Antarctic wisdom." Frank was supping drinks and supplying drinks to the three young Port Lockroy women. Their boss had told them that they could go and play on the *Polar Adventurer*. She would hold the fort back on the island. Unfortunately for Frank his fund of stories was running dry. The "girls" had heard them before and wanted more.

"So, Frank," oozed Jill, a tall slim blond from Birmingham, "what was it *really* like in those old days.

"Well, men were men…"

"And women knew it," chorused Jill, Babs and Rosemary. Jill looked at Frank and said she had thought she had heard that a few times.

"Arthur!" pleaded Frank. "Help!"

"Ok, I guess you need the real gen," Arthur, said strolling over to the trio.

"Yes, please," they trilled. Like the cruise staff their job was to keep the travelers happy.

"Once upon a time way back when, the old days were…"

"Those were the *good* ones," said Babs, a pleasant plumpish young woman from Edinburgh.

"Are there any other?" Arthur carried on: "Any way, once upon a time, a sledge team was heading up this long, cold, snowy glacier."

"Is this a scary story?" asked Rosemary, a short, fair-haired student in social work at Reading University. She was taking a year out to find herself.

"I don't do scary," said Arthur, sipping his beer, "I do truth. As I was saying, this team headed up the glacier and finally stopped at the top. Then the last of the three dog teams arrived. Where was the middle team?"

"In a crevasse" said Jill, beaming at Arthur, who tried to finish his drink and the story at the same time.

"You've heard this one?" he demanded.

"Oh, no!" said the three damsels.

Pamela leaned over to Georgina, and asked: "When do you send for the cavalry?"

"He's got lots of time to save himself," she said.

"So, the two teams went back down the glacier again, and half way down was a large hole. The second team had fallen into the crevasse and the last dog team had passed them in the mist and ..."

"You never mentioned a mist," was Rosemary's comment. A year out was much more fun than learning social hierarchies at uni.

"Eh, well I forgot that part," said Arthur. "At any rate they lowered the lightest sledger down the crevasse, a matter of some hundred and twenty feet."

"Not more?" asked Jill.

"Possibly it was a bit more," said Arthur sucking on his empty glass. "Any how, there at the bottom was a man with only a strained thumb and one dead husky. The whole team had fallen down this gigantic hole a hundred and twenty-feet, but they had hit several snow bridges on the way down. And everyone survived."

"Except for the one husky," said Babs.

"Correct."

"Of course, I don't want to spoil a good story by telling the truth, but I think it was the last sledge team that disappeared down the crevasse originally."

"Thanks for those unnecessary words of wisdom, Frank. I need another drink. I'm still thirsty." Arthur gave him a half smile and his glass. "I think for that comment, you should get the next round."

Frank counted heads and said he would get Arthur's and the trio's, but everyone else was on their own.

"You've been down here a few times," said Jill to Arthur.

"I've done eight winters down here."

"I guess you've seen lots of changes?" asked Babs. She still had her drink though Frank had handed her another.

"Arthur was there when there was husky travel. He then saw their demotion to a few pet dogs, and the takeover by snowmobiles," said Frank.

"You drove a dog team?" Rosemary waited expectantly.

"I was tied to the base at different stations, but I took a few trips. We would camp out on glaciers, radio back to base, sometimes without success, and do a lot of reading while waiting for the storms to pass."

"And the huskies," asked Jill.

"They curled up in the snow, and were fed compressed dog food once a day. They were happy. But sadly huskies were made redundant by more efficient planes and snowmobiles. Ah well, life changes."

"What's the biggest change you've seen since you first went down?" Rosemary was determined to get a firm picture of Antarctica. There might be a term paper in it when she got back.

"Tourists," said Arthur. "That's about it?" turning to Frank.

"I would agree with you. A few hundred fifty years ago to tens of thousands now."

"Is everyone happy to see the numbers increase?" persisted Rosemary.

Arthur did not answer, but Frank said that most people were satisfied. But there were always a few who were against the increase.

The conversation petered out. The three young women circulated amongst other strangers. Arthur went back to Georgina dramatically wiping his brow with his handkerchief. Jim tried to inveigle a few passengers to part with their knowledge of robberies and gold. He had no success.

*

Georgina asked if he had enjoyed himself. Arthur admitted he had. It's not every day that three young women hung on his every word. He got a free round out of it too. And Boyd was not there to hog the bar. Must be his old liver complaint again.

Sandy was certainly handing out the drinks. Life felt good. When Georgina said she was going to retire to bed, (nice word that, especially as he had been retired for several years), Arthur said he would hang around a bit more in case more expertise was needed. Georgina grinned and said "Of course".

Frank was nursing his rum and coke, a nasty habit he had acquired on his two trips down south. He was looking at the three youngsters chatting with passengers. One of the French men was hoping to get lucky. Arthur wondered how many offers they got with all those boats calling in: "Come up to my cabin and see my Antarctic mementoes." He imagined at least one offer per cruise ship. They were nice looking. And friendly. Arthur wondered who chose them.

He told Frank he would call it a night.

"That robbery at Ushuaia seems to have done its rounds," Arthur said as he angled past Jim who fell in step with him. "But it really doesn't have anything to do with our trip. So why not leave the whole business? We are all here for a holiday."

Jim agreed, and seemed to be giving the topic a rest. Yet there was a slight flicker in his eyes as Arthur looked up at him.

Outside they looked at the sunset redder than yesterday's, (or did everyone have selective memory for sunsets?), and watched grey fluffy clouds edged with pink and yellow float across the nine thousand foot white-domed Mt. Français. Arthur thought this would be the last nice day for a while.

He said:

"Being down here is not like going to a favorite place at home. Here you are experiencing the unusual. It cannot be replicated, and it never lets go of you."

"Even if you have been down here many times," Jim said.

"Yes, that's true."

They parted.

CHAPTER THIRTY-ONE

"Ice is nice!" boomed through the PA, earlier than normal. "Everyone should be up. We are going through the world famous Lemaire Channel. This is definitely what they used to call a Kodak moment. We sail this dramatic passage, and then we cruise "Iceberg Alley" near Pléneau Island to the south.

"There is a slight wind, the sky is overcast and the pressure is dropping. Otherwise it's another perfect day in Antarctica. Oh, and breakfast will be delayed until we are well into the channel." Greg's spiel finished.

Jim knocked on Carol's door, but she had already left. He went up to the bridge, and greeted her carefully. She had a pair of binoculars for distance and to be a little distant. The bridge was filling up as the *Polar Adventurer* passed Cape Renard on the port side. Two black rock towers rose from the sea, their tops capped with white snow.

"Ah, yes!" Colin the historian exclaimed. "Here are the famous Una's Tits. Many years ago a young explorer fell in love with a beautiful girl with a magnificent figure in Stanley. He raved about her as he headed off to the Antarctic. One wag fed up with the praise gave the cape its nick name." There were a few chuckles.

"You knew that already, didn't you," said Georgina to Arthur. He smiled with a nod.

Jim grinned at Carol. It was not reciprocated. He remembered Mandy's smile from yesterday and told himself to behave.

He wandered off to look at the charts. Some areas were not surveyed. Jim asked the second officer, Petr, about them. The officer explained that there were so many rocks underneath the surface that only a few well-traveled bays had been surveyed along the Antarctic Peninsula. The rest were left with warnings on the charts. When Jim asked him where home was he said Kaliningrad in Russia.

Outside the bridge Jim looked back and saw another cruise ship following them to the Lemaire Channel. He mentioned the ship to Mike, the sea mammal guy.

"We try to stagger our transit times so as to give at least an aura of being in lonely Antarctic though with this channel being only a mile wide and some seven long it is a little difficult. Every one wants to go through the Lemaire. I think you'll find that is the fifty-passenger *Professor Multanovsky*."

"How do you know?"

"We keep track of each other."

The Lemaire Channel took them past steep hanging glaciers, shear rock spires and cliffs rising from the grey sea on both sides. The passengers photographed the icebergs, glaciers, rocks, sea, and the odd seal watching the ship sail slowly by. The Antarctic lags gazed remembering the first time they had headed this way. They were still impressed.

Carol had little to say at breakfast. She looked gloomily at Jim tucking into everything that was offered. The Californian couple, Jacqueline and Richard, slid past their table Jim managed a small nod. They ignored him.

Mark placed a tray of toast and tea at their table. He said it had been a wonderful start to the day. Carol concentrated on her waffle. Jim assumed Boyd was on her mind. He maintained the conversation by asking if Mark had been through the channel many times. He said four times. It was always amazing.

Jim asked: "What did you do down here?"

"I had a couple of Antarctic winters as a meteorologist. Then it was law school, and international conferences that linked countries interested in Antarctic studies. There were twelve. Now the countries have more than doubled."

"Are you still involved in Antarctica? Jim asked.

Mark said: "No. I've moved on to other things." He nodded to them and left.

Jim was reminded of some one he knew at university who had been old and sure of himself even in his early twenties, and had never given much away.

Carol stood up. She was not relaxed.

Colin gave out a few items of interest. Why Pléneau Island? Jean-Baptiste Charcot had wanted his friend to go with him to Greenland. At the last moment in 1903 Charcot changed to the Antarctic. He received a telegram from Paul Pléneau: "Where you like. When you like. For as long as you like." Colin mentioned that after Charcot's first expedition his wife divorced him. Charcot made sure his second wife did not object to his next Antarctic expedition.

Ron asked the question that had been on his mind for some time: "How does one get one's name on an Antarctic map?"

The historian said: "You had to have worked down here a long time, been an explorer like Paul Pléneau, or you died here."

Carol thought of her father who had died here but on a small expedition with no government funding. Was that why his name was not on any Antarctic map?

Ed said to Ron he was relieved there were no lengthy lectures. It must because they were no longer on the open sea.

"I'm glad you worked that out," said Ron. "We can all relax, right Doug?"

Doug turned slowly and just looked at him. Ron wondered whether he should slip along to the doctor for some advice. Doug moved slowly and held his stomach when others weren't looking.

In his mind Doug could see finishing Boyd off. He had not been up to it at Danco Island. He couldn't even get to the top of that small hill. Port Lockroy was too busy. On a Zodiac cruise it would be impossible, and the afternoon at this Ukrainian base Vernadsky would be another crowded place. Maybe the next day at a quiet landing. After he would see the doc. But no confessions.

Carol felt better as the Zodiacs headed past Pléneau Island towards the mass of stranded icebergs. Most bergs shone with a brilliant whiteness even with an overcast sky. They reared up in pinnacles, spires and cliffs. The icebergs were jammed like a maze of streets in an old ice city. The Zodiac threaded itself between them like a skateboarder between trucks.

"As long as they're stranded on the sea bottom they won't tip over," said John, the geologist "As you know most of an ice berg's mass is under water. But with the change of tides and wind they could flip. We keep away from them, at about three times their height. If they tip we're toast."

Murder in the Antarctic

The Zodiac seemed to be closer than three times the bergs' heights to Jim. But the icebergs were beautiful. Dark and light blues, with some emerald green, intermingled with smooth overwhelming whiteness like squeaky plastic hacked out by gigantic knives. Some had completely tilted over, the carved underwater ripples lying on top. Caves had worked their way through some icebergs; the arches were photographed with Zodiacs on the other side.

Some bergs were crystal clear and lumpy: old ice that was near the end of its life. An odd piece of a small growler would frizzle and crack as the air inside popped. Carol used her camera on the icebergs and on the lines of blue-eyed black and white cormorants flying by.

"You can call them shags if you like." She twinkled a little at Jim, who grinned back.

They looked down through clear water where gentoo penguins zipped underneath their boat. "A streak of penguins," said Jim. Carol nodded. Occasionally the swimming birds broke the surface and porpoised along, dipping in and out of the sea.

Half an hour later Elsa radioed that a leopard seal was patrolling the outer parts of the "Iceberg Alley." John revved up the motor and headed closer to Booth Island. Three boats were already parked there. A large dark head made a vee shape as it moved through the sea. Dark eyes looked at the intruders. The leopard seal's sinuous body swished through the water but avoided the Zodiacs. Carol looked down at her boots, still tooth marked.

"The young ones will sometimes play with a boat. This one is older and larger. Probably a female," John commented as he sat on the engine housing staring at the seal's movements.

At the *Polar Adventurer's* stern dripping black Zodiacs were hoisted aboard. It was time to head south. Jim would give his, or was it the captain's investigation? one more try.

*

Three million dollars is far better than two million. I replaced Leon's pornographic tomes, rather pointless efforts, with some of my academic works relieved from my last place of employment. They covered the tubes of gold coins rather well. I didn't want anyone getting too excited over Leon's smut, and even more excited over finding all that gold.

Very early a.m. I placed the bag at the back of a hazardous material storage locker. The gold rested deep behind barrels of sand, buckets of detergent, neutralizers, respirators and protective clothing. The chances of anyone opening the locker other than for the odd pair of cleaning gloves, absorbent pads and pails was remote. Dangerous spills rarely happen. Others over-concern for safety benefited me.

CHAPTER THIRTY-TWO

"Why aren't we crossing the Antarctic Circle," Doug asked.

Greg, the expedition leader, had said that the Ukrainian base, Vernadsky at 65° 15' south, was their turnaround.

"To get to the Circle where the summer has twenty-four hours of light would take two more days of travel. And there's little scenery or wildlife to see."

"Couldn't we skip some landing sites on the way back and keep going south," said Carol. A denunciation of Boyd would have been fitting off the Loubet Coast where her father was buried. Greg said no. Jim wondered about the so-called flexibility of Antarctic travel where if conditions changed the timetable changed. Changeable if necessary but not necessarily changeable seemed to be the motto.

"Wasn't that southern area where the Sheldon Expedition explored?" Jim asked.

Greg said: "Yes, it was," and looked at the historian to give out more Antarctic information.

Carol noticed with satisfaction that Boyd for once had no comments. Jim gently held her hand. She slid it away. He hoped it was reluctantly.

For Jim the trip was rapidly coming to an end. There were only a few sites left and less than five days to Ushuaia. The gold robbery and the unfortunate deaths of Peter and Leon were unresolved. Captain Engstrom might have to take his lumps while Jim waltzed off into the sunset, hopefully with Carol. (No, not Mandy).

The historian, Colin, briefly described the Argentine Islands where the Ukrainian base was situated. The British had worked there for many years. The discovery of the hole in the ozone layer was first noted here. Then in 1996 the base was sold to the Ukrainian government for a token pound, as the British no longer had a use for it.

Ron asked about the Antarctic Chilean and Argentinean bases and their claims to the peninsula. Colin said that the three nations including Britain all claimed the Antarctic Peninsula, but since the Antarctic Treaty of 1961 there had just been scientific cooperation and peace in the Antarctic.

Jim decided on one more push. He bearded Arthur at lunch. No one else was at the table. As he moved the cheese and pasta concoction around on his plate Jim used an English cricket expression and opened with a strong bat:

"I know you said that we are all on holiday and the robbery should be left alone. But could the deaths of Peter and Leon be linked to the heist?"

"They were accidents. Why would they be linked to the robbery?" asked Arthur.

Jim said he was not sure, but it was curious that two people had died and there was the robbery.

"Why would those be connected to this ship?"

"I don't know," said Jim.

"So, leave it," snapped Arthur and picked up his plate and utensils and headed over to where Frank had come in. As his wife, Anthony and Pamela joined them; Arthur chuckled at something Georgina said. With this encounter with Arthur Jim revised his ranking of who could have done the gold heist.

Murder in the Antarctic

*

The first fifty passengers disembarked at Vernadsky. Jim's group went first. They had opened their own cabin number plates on the tag board by the exit. The number plates would be closed when they returned.

The Australian trio lined up in life jackets, cameras at the ready. On the gangway Doug turned to complain that Ed was pushing him. Ed said he had not touched him. Doug suddenly dropped face down on the sloping walkway, moaning.

Ed and Ron raised him up and brought him up on the deck. The doctor looked at a very pale and silent Doug. He told Ron and Ed to go ashore. The crew would take Doug to the sick bay.

"He didn't get a fair suck of the sav," said Ed to Ron as they headed away in their Zodiac He used less common Australian expressions when he was upset. "He hasn't complained much despite losing his wife and his money."

"He can snivel and whine with the best of them when he's a mind to it." Ron thought back to Doug's behavior. His lack of talking rather than his looks had bothered Ron the most.

Vernadsky was larger than Port Lockroy. Ukrainian staff took the passengers around in groups of twelve. The weight room with a large breasted blond pinup nailed to the wall was followed by a meteorological office, complete with old fashioned barometers with paper strips that got inked by a nib as the pressure went up and down. A base member explained that nowadays most Antarctic weather recordings were done with automatic machines. They didn't drink alcohol or miss observations.

The wooden bar built by the British kept Boyd and a couple of Ukrainian acquaintances happy. For the male visitors it was homemade vodka at a dollar a shot. For women, there was free vodka. The only stipulation was to contribute a piece of underclothing to the bar already festooned with bras and panties.

When Carol's group came in Boyd called out:

"Carol we need your undies. Can we put them next to these ones?" He pointed at a wide pair of pink panties draped tastefully across the top of the shining brown bar. Kim elbowed him.

Flushed, Carol pushed her way back through the crowd to the outside door. Her comment about going further south must have got to him. She stood outside on the rocks looking at the stationary icebergs in front of the base and the kelp gulls screeching overhead. Her fuming worsened as a voice behind her said:

"I'm sorry, Carol. That was uncalled for." Boyd looked apologetic. Carol blurted out a "Fuck you!" and stormed down to the Zodiacs waiting at the dock.

"Going back to the ship, already?" asked a staff Zodiac driver.

Jim found her looking hard at a rising pile of butts. He tentatively reached out to an elbow, which was angrily pulled away.

"That bastard! I'm going expose him. D-Day is today."

"D-Day?" asked Jim.

"Damn him Day!" Carol replied.

Jim looked a bit perturbed. "Is it time?"

"It bloody well is! I'm not going to wait any longer. I'm going to deal with him tonight."

Jim gently said that Greg had invited a few of the Ukrainians over for dinner and drinks. Maybe tomorrow when there were only passengers might be better?

"To hell with them! They might as well find out what an arsehole he is!"

Carol stubbed out the latest cigarette and said she was going to her cabin. She would see him at dinner.

*

The doctor probed Doug. Pressure around the stomach brought a gasp of pain from the patient.

"*Will* you tell me what is going on?" The doctor's narrow face looked keenly at the supine body that carried a slight fever. The examination was casual and friendly, but the doctor was going to find out.

"Well? I can guarantee you will not be going back to your cabin nor doing much else on this ship until I have an answer. You are a very sick man. Though you're probably know that."

Doug was reluctant to talk. But he was more likely to talk to the doctor than Ron and Ed. He wondered why one would rather tell a stranger one's problems than one's friends.

"I can give you morphine-based pain killers once you tell me what your problem is. How's that for good medical practice?"

The sick patient gazed at the ceiling. He talked about the pancreatic cancer and his determination to get to Antarctica. He didn't say why he was so keen.

"I won't ask how you got a clean bill of health. Anyway we can at least keep you semi-fit until you get back to your specialist. You will be having a lot of hospital time."

Not if I can help it thought Doug. As long as painkillers were available, legal or not. Hospitals were for dying.

"You've got a choice. The tablets are good for a couple of hours or injections that will knock you out for twelve. That's all we have on board."

"I'll take the tablets. No morphine pumps?"

"No. And with the tablets there's no sharing with any one else."

"I'm greedy and needy, doc."

"Some of the side effects will be similar to what you've got at present. Dizziness, drowsiness, and a feeling of being sick."

"Thanks."

"When I let you get up get up slowly. Oh, are you constipated or loose?"

"Constipated."

"I'll give you a mild laxative. You can stay here until after dinner. Daniel can send up a light dinner. I'll decide then whether your friends can see you and whether you can return to your cabin. You won't be doing any more landings."

As the doctor left Doug cursed himself for not dealing with Boyd sooner.

*

Jim looked for Carol. She didn't appear. He joined Shaun and Pam, the young Australian couple, who sat at a mixed table of Australian and British tour passengers. Everyone talked about the Ukrainian base and how it compared to Port Lockroy. Pam found the lack of recognizable words interesting.

Jim toyed with his fish pie, and thought about Carol and what might be called the double assignment: his and the captain's. A reluctance to keep on with questions about the robbery and especially the sensitive subject of two "accidental" deaths crept over him like a heavy blanket.

Carol arrived and ate her dinner quickly. As people started to leave she sprang up at the front. In a loud voice said: "Could I have your attention for a moment?" There were one or two supportive taps on wine glasses to calm the murmuring sea of voices.

She felt a lot of eyes turning towards her. "I'm sorry I have interrupted your meal. You'll want to get away, but I have an important announcement…"

The mob quietened further.

"As some of you are aware many years ago to the south of here," Carol said, "at the Antarctic Circle, a small private expedition, the Sheldon Expedition, spent one winter. But few of you know that one of the five men did not return home." Her eyes started watering. "That man was David Bapton, my father." Here she faltered, stopped then lurched on: "My father starved to death. He had been sledging across sea ice with another man. A storm broke…"

Here Carol looked at Boyd, pensively puffing out his cheeks. "At a lead of open water the dog driver turned the team around and left my father. The driver returned to base and later took an early ship home. In a small hut with no food my father died of hunger."

There was a hush. The punch line was coming.

"That driver, I won't call him a man, who left my father to die, was William Boyd Barrington!" Trembling Carol pointed at a speechless Boyd. Bursting into tears Carol ran from the room.

Shaken Jim got up and followed her. He did not see the passengers pulling away from Boyd as they left the dining room. Jim found Carol sobbing by the railing. He put an arm over her shaking shoulders, as she turned her head away.

*

The subdued lounge occupants talked about Carol's outburst, showed similar pictures of what they had seen that day, and wrote up their Antarctic journals. Carol's denunciation had lent an air of excitement.

After leaving Carol in her cabin Jim returned to the lounge. Boyd sat quietly tucked in a corner with a well-turned out American woman. Jim overheard the American woman say:

"It's golden and worth infinite money."

The Ushuaia gold? Jim brightened and edged closer to the pair.

"I've had enough of money schemes whatever the cause," said Boyd.

"But this one is essential," the woman said.

Boyd agreed and said he was sure it was important, but money needed for preserving Texas parkland was not for him. He supported enough parks back in England. The woman looked intently at him and said:

"Everyone should help."

"Certainly," replied Boyd, "but not me." He got up and moved majestically away.

Jim looked away as the woman turned towards him. He didn't want to get involved in other's concerns. He had enough on his plate as it was.

CHAPTER THIRTY-THREE

Vodka at Vernadsky, hung over at Happy Hour, and malbec at the meal, Boyd felt better at the finish of the day despite the embarrassment at dinner. His Ukrainian acquaintance Andrei had matched him earlier, but was slowing down as Boyd had another round of McCallan's. Was the thought of not going near the Loubet Coast, or was it Kim and the alcohol that was making him feel better? He kept up a joking front with Frank. Other member of the Antarctic group Arthur and Georgina plus Mark and Pamela seemed less keen to join him.

Pamela had made some remark about limiting people going to the Antarctic. Boyd, of course had to comment: "I'm no bleeding hearted environmentalist. If there's money to be made bring 'em all." She left in a huff. "Sod 'em!" thought Boyd. He was glad Carol was not around though the boyfriend was sitting with those two awkward Australian types.

"Did you hear the one about the army mechanic out on a field trip?" Boyd pushed the question out, as Sandy placed more drinks on the counter.

"No," said Frank, who thought he had heard all of Boyd's stories.

"This chap was on a jolly out on the ice. Jolly? It's a short holiday away from the base." He answered Kim, and said: "He's out with another chap some where up on a godforsaken snow-bound plateau. They're stuck in a blizzard."

"Another one?" Andrei was trying to keep up with all the old stories.

"Of course. Any hoo, this mechanic comes on the blower and says 'It's fucking windy up here. How's it with you?' The base leader comes back on the radio and says there's to be no expletives when on the air."

There was a slight pause while Frank explained expletive to Andrei.

"The army guy comes back with: 'What's a fucking expletive?'"

Roars from Frank. Smiles from Kim, Andrei, (who half understood) and others standing around. Sandy wiped the counter and shook her head.

*

Ron and Ed stood on the outer circle of booze. They had had a short visit to the sick bay. Doug was to stay there until the following day. Ed told him about the feeding frenzy at dinnertime over the five different flavors of ice cream, the chopped nuts and sprinkles, and the raspberry, chocolate and apricot toppings. Ed had said they must have gone through a lot of ice cream. But not enough said Doug. When Ed asked him what he meant Doug said sharply:

"If a certain someone dies you'll have to eat lots of ice cream."

"You're not going to die."

"I was talking about that bastard, Boyd."

"He's a pompous ass," said Ron. "We knew he had a hand in the Antarctic Trust Fund. But why the anger?"

"I wanted to finish him off. He's caused me too much pain."

"You want to kill him?"

"Yes," said Doug half rising from his bed. "Kill Boyd! I want him dead! Then you'll have to eat lots of ice-cream." He sank back with a grimace.

Ron and Ed looked at each other.

"That's why you wanted background information on Boyd, and why you wanted to come on this trip?" Ron pieced together Doug's behavior over the past month or so.

"What do you think!?"

"You're being a bit drastic. We're not even sure if he was behind that fund that we all lost money on."

"Of course it was bloody well him! How do you think he got all the money to go on all those Antarctic trips? I've left it too late!"

"What were you going to do?" asked Ed.

"Kill the blighter. Knock him off a cliff, push him in to a crevasse, what does it matter?"

"Shouldn't you discuss this with the doc tomorrow morning? Your illness, might be affecting you." Ron tried for the sensible approach.

"By the way," said Ed out of curiosity, "What is your ailment?"

Doug having vented his spleen managed: "It's none of your business. It's between the doc and me."

"Sounds serious," came back Ed.

"I'm going to be doing a lot of sleeping."

"Why will you be sleeping lots?" asked Ed.

"Never mind. If you can think of a way to get rid of Boyd tell me or do it yourself. I may not be up for a while."

"Carol, that nice looking dark haired young woman, tore a strip off of Boyd at dinner," said Ron.

"She blamed Boyd for the death of her father on the Sheldon Expedition. Her father starved to death."

"Should have been bloody Boyd!" said Doug.

"OK," said Ron. "We'll leave you and pop back in the morning."

They left, and looked at each other as they headed back to the lounge.

"I think it's serious," said Ron.

*

The lounge was emptying. It was darker outside than the last few nights. Heavy cloud moved in. It felt like bedtime for many. The hardy types were still keeping Sandy busy. Boyd propped up against the bar was searching his mind for more Antarctic material to keep the diminishing company enthralled. Colin the historian wanted more information on the old Sheldon Expedition. Boyd was not prepared to go there and remained tightlipped. Kim stepped in, and asked Andrei: "What do you do, if you have an accident on Vernadsky?"

"We have a doctor and several men have first aid."

"I heard," said Boyd having found his opening: "that there was a Russian doctor who removed his own appendix. That must have been interesting." Kim regretted her question as Boyd continued with: "And then there was that chap who had to have an eyeball removed. I believe they had to sharpen a spoon to gouge it out."

"The only medical crisis we had," said Frank, "was one of the blokes needed a tooth pulled. We all drank heavily and got as drunk as the patient. Then the fun began. For us, at any rate. We took lots of photos."

The young Australian couple left Jim to his wine. He had listened to Boyd's "bring 'em all" to Pamela, and saw her stomp off to bed. Jim had half listened to the bar flies, and decided to call it a night. On his bunk Martin was blowing bubbles in an alcoholic stupor. Alec was writing in a notebook. His only interest was birds.

Jim said good night and climbed slowly up to his attic accommodation. He felt tired and unsettled. He tried to avoid thoughts of Mandy. And Carol? Was her condemnation of Boyd enough for her? Was her Sheldon side, finished? Would he find out who the killer or killers were? Was Boyd the one or not? And was there anything serious between Carol and himself?

CHAPTER THIRTY-FOUR

Jim, after a loose night on the toilet, showered, left his cabin and met Carol on the aft deck. He stood with her at the railing in a damp mist. She had said little except that she had been up early as the ship moved through cloud between the high cliffs and ice of the Lemaire Channel. A large whale had traveled parallel with the ship. Two travelers heading north. The ship was heading towards Almirante Brown, a disused Argentinean base on the mainland.

"You didn't sleep too much last night." It was a statement rather than a question from Jim. Carol nodded, looked away and continued puffing. The smoke whipped behind them and disappeared into the early morning cloud.

He explained how he had been up several times that night because of food poisoning. Jim still felt shivery. The doctor had confirmed that the half a dozen on board who ate the fish pie had become ill. All the doctor had said was:

"You'll live. Rest up and drink lots. It will go away in a day or so. If not see me later."

Carol said: "Are you going to land?"

"No, I'll stay on board. Some are doing a Zodiac iceberg and glacier tour. I wouldn't have minded looking around Almirante Brown and climbing the hill. But my knees still feel a bit shaky."

"You're not one of those tough outdoor Canadians?"

"Some times."

Carol didn't want to talk any more, especially about her Boyd outburst. Jim decided to have a small breakfast and lie down.

Greg's message from Shackleton: "We have seen God in his splendors, heard the text that Nature renders. We had reached the naked soul of man," did not make Jim feel any better as he tried a small juice but no toast. He lay on his bed. The call for the Zodiac tour passengers came first, and then the land passengers.

After a boring hour, he rose and slowly climbed up to the bridge. The captain motioned him to his cabin and handed Jim some emails on the financial affairs of other passengers.

"I approached another London source. It seems that Boyd Barrington's father backed the Argentineans and lost money after the Falklands War. He started the Antarctic Trust Fund to repair his finances. Boyd inherited though he had nothing to do with the running of the company. He didn't have a head for business. So maybe he wasn't in on the robbery."

Jim put the new sheets inside his Shakespeare play, and walked up to the suite level. The cleaning staff had not started yet. The names of each occupant were tucked neatly into metal holders on the doors. Jim peered down the corridor then popped into Frank's large cabin. It was better designed than his threesome, but there was no obvious sign that Frank was involved in stealing gold. No revealing emails or coins only a large bottle of sleeping pills, the drug of choice, next to the bed.

Arthur and Georgina, Jack and Doreen, Boyd and Rachel's suites were empty of incriminating evidence. He supposed that Jack hopped next door to Rachel's.

Any laptops would have security codes. He was about to sneak into some other cabins when Marissa arrived with new towels. Jim smiled at her and casually walked back to his level.

She called out: "Bye, Sir Jim."

He was a knight now. Jim went down to his cabin. With the dead light over the porthole he normally put on the light. But with light coming in from the corridor he could reach his emails. As he stepped into the darkened cabin a punch landed in his face. He staggered back. The washroom door to the next cabin slammed. Jim got slowly up, put on the light, and stumbled through the washroom, into the next cabin and out into the passageway. There was no one. His face hurt. His pride more so. By his bed the play *As You Like It* was empty. A space took the place of the emails.

*

Boyd thought about what Colin the historian had told the newbies about the Almirante Brown base. Its name was for a nineteenth century Irish-Argentinean admiral. At the base an Argentinean doctor had been informed he *had* to stay on for a second winter. It was too much for him, and he burnt the place down. Fortunately an American ship rescued the men before winter arrived. Later a new base was built but it was no longer used.

The ship anchored. Low cloud and wind swirled across the glaciers. The hill behind the base with its one steep snow slope up to a sharp peak was almost covered by cloud. By the time Boyd got to the top he hoped the cloud would break up and another masterful photograph would be taken. He was on his own. Kim and her sidekick Maisie had taken the coastal tour. Boyd needed some exercise after an eventful night. Kim had been very friendly.

He walked around the remains of the base. The old concrete foundations peeked through the fresh snow. The newer red metal buildings were shut tight. Boyd trudged over to the hill. Some of what he considered the weaker brethren had given up on the ascent. Their expectations were too high. Mist and a bit of rain came in. Who said it never rained in the Antarctic?

Boyd slogged up to the top of the hill through the damp snow. Bob the birder was at the top to stop any one from falling off the edge of the cliff. There was only room for a couple of bodies. Just a few at the top of the food chain. Boyd mused he was getting philosophical again. It must be his mature age. He hunkered down on the snow to see if the weather was going to change. Below the ship looked tiny The Zodiacs had disappeared along the coast.

A cry came from below. Then a female swore. Pamela? There were more calls for help. Bob told him not to move and went down to assist. Boyd stood up, camera at the ready. Someone else arrived. Too well clothed to see who it was. He stepped back to allow some room, and was pushed back. He turned and said: "What the heck are you playing at?" He felt an agonizing blow in his eye and then another to his throat. Boyd bent over retching, and was slammed back to the edge. He yelled" "What the…!"

*

There was a loud splat as Boyd hit the rocks below.

Murder in the Antarctic

*

Neko Harbour was the last Antarctic mainland stop. The ship steamed north through Paradise Harbour, past the Chilean base, Videla, and into Andvord Bay. Kim looked for Boyd. He never missed lunch or any other meal.

On his cabin door there was a "Do Not Disturb" sign. She checked the tag board. Boyd's name was closed so he should be on board. Kim would take him some soup. There was no answer when she knocked. She opened the door saying: "Boyd?" There was no one and the bed was made.

Kim hurried down to the reception center, the heart of the ship. For some travelers it was the first port of call for the day. It was a place to talk to staff and complain if necessary. She garbled her message to Elsa:

"Where's Boyd?"

Elsa spoke to Greg. He in turn spoke to the captain. Crew members searched the ship. No Boyd. There was a second search.

John the geologist said there were no life jackets left at the Almirante Brown landing so Boyd must have come on board. Was he sure? Greg had to have every detail retold. Bob explained about leaving the top to help Pamela and others. He had not seen Boyd after that. Greg told Bob to write down exactly what had happened. Greg turned on Elsa, his second in command, and berated her for letting the situation get out of hand. Elsa shook her head and stomped off.

When the *Polar Adventurer's* course shifted a hundred and eighty degrees, the rumors started. Staff denied knowing what was happening. What about the Neko Harbour landing? There were shrugs. The ship was returning to Almirante Brown. Boyd was missing. Why was it always him?.

The Almirante Brown base buildings were checked. The coastal area below the black vertical cliffs by the base was examined. On the ship passengers leaned over the railings rather like vultures as if this would help the search. John, the staff geologist, and Ricardo, the Chilean birder, climbed to the top of the hill.

From the footprints several people had reached the top. There was some snow slippage at the back of the summit. Roped up to Ricardo, John gingerly slid to the edge on his stomach and peered over. The precipitation turned to stinging snow pellets. He thought he saw a shape below. John radioed back to Greg and asked him to change channels.

At the base of the hill on the north side John and Ricardo cut steps across a large snow wind scoop. They scrambled over large boulders and through snow pockets. Beneath the cliffs on the east side they found Boyd, splayed out on broken rocks and snow, dead. John checked for a pulse and called Greg. The stretcher would be needed again. Before Ricardo covered the body with his jacket, (John thought it was unnecessary, Boyd was dead, wasn't he?), Ricardo pointed to two or three places where sharp rock shards had pieced through Boyd's legs.

"His legs would have been impaled on those rocks, and he wouldn't have been able to move," said Ricardo.

John nodded and stomped around. He was cold.

The passengers and crew looked at the slow procession back to the landing stage, and the transfer of the covered shape to a Zodiac. The boat was hoisted straight up to the Zodiac deck. Kim collapsed with a wail. Maisie for once was speechless and started sobbing. Carol took Kim to her cabin.

The doctor sent Doug back to his cabin, and examined the large but dead remains of Boyd stretched out on a stainless steel table. The second officer, not on duty until the middle of the afternoon, took notes. The body showed a few broken leg bones and gaping holes where projecting rocks had penetrated the flesh of the lower limbs. But the doctor could not see what had killed Boyd. The drop had been comparatively short when he hit bottom. If Boyd had survived the fall he must have died of exposure.

"Worse than sudden death," said Petr Sidorov.

The doctor didn't reply. He examined the body. Having only had one short lecture on pathology, Doctor Bob had to search a few manuals for help. There were several doctors on board, but none were pathologists. Too many doctors could spoil the patient even if he was deceased. Rigor mortis had not set in which was normal for low temperatures.

"The outside temperature this morning?" he asked the officer?

"Zero degrees Celsius and a wet wind."

"His watch told us when he fell, but not when he died." The doctor took the temperature from the rectum. The internal temperature was certainly not the usual thirty- seven degrees, but it had only fallen a few degrees. Looking at Boyd's still warmish body and thinking of the clothes he had on, the doctor said that Boyd had probably died three or four hours after he fell.

"Oh," said the officer.

"He was pear shaped in body, and his death was pear shaped."

Petr Sidorov asked: "Pear shaped?"

"It means something had gone badly wrong. Look here." He pointed to a damaged eye and a small round wound in Boyd's neck. Inside were three deep gashes. "That didn't happen from the fall." There was frozen blood around the neck wound circle. "There's also a ring of blood under the chin. His head must have snapped down on the wound."

"He was struck, and then fell?"

"I think so. We must discuss this with the captain. This is serious. I need to remind you not to talk to anyone else."

"Of course."

Captain Engstrom was informed that he should come to the sick bay. He was shown the circular wound.

"What did this?"

"A walking stick? My question for you is *who* did this?"

The captain sat down on a sick bed. It groaned a little with the weight. The commander of the ship groaned more:

"Why on this voyage? What the hell is going on? Three deaths! That is unheard of!" He gripped the blankets on the bed and then got hold of himself.

"No one must hear of this. I must have time to think and check my legal books. It was a terrible accident. That is all that we can say at the present time."

"But that is not what happened," said the doctor.

"I am aware of that," snapped Captain Engstrom, "but until we get to Ushuaia that will do. The show must go on. Even Greg must not be told. The Argentineans can hold an inquiry. My paperwork will be terrible."

There was little thought of Boyd.

With the second office back on the bridge the *Polar Adventurer* resumed its course. Boyd's body went to the food locker to join Leon among the vanilla, strawberry, chocolate and Neapolitan ice cream.

CHAPTER THIRTY-FIVE

With the captain at his side Greg said: "Boyd slipped off the top of the hill. The Antarctic is always a dangerous place. There should be safety at all times. We will contact Boyd's family. Is anyone in contact with his relatives back home?"

There was silence. There was no mention of Kim.

Greg continued: "The head office will do the necessary."

He repeated himself by saying though beautiful the Antarctic was still dangerous. The cruise would skip Neko Harbour, as they had had to return to Almirante Brown. But otherwise the schedule would remain the same. Boyd would have wanted that. They had all appreciated Boyd's enthusiasm and his story telling.

Jim thought that at times like this there was never an even-handed look at a person's character. The dead were good regardless of who they were. There was no mention of the need to keep the company's business going. The adventure and the money must continue.

When one of the passengers, a professor from San Francisco State University, asked about having an inquiry, Greg said that the ultimate authority lay with Captain Engstrom. Greg continued that there would be another inquiry in Ushuaia, as the accident had happened at an Argentinean base. When the professor persisted, and said that surely there was no juridiction in the Antarctic where visitors of different nationalities were concerned, Greg repeated that the captain was the only authority.

The passengers looked somber and talked quietly. Ed said to Ron that this was getting a bit repetitive.

Three on a trip. Ron nodded. Doug, doped up and relaxed, croaked out:

"There is a God, and ice cream will be served tonight and for many nights. And if you'll excuse the phrase: revenge is best eaten cold."

Ron and Ed looked at each other. Whatever Doug was on it was interesting stuff.

As Captain Engstrom left he looked hard at Jim. Jim had wanted to find Carol. Instead he followed the captain's facial "suggestion" and made his way upstairs.

"This is a bloody business." There was no offer of aquavit by the captain. Only the blunt comment: "I have never had three deaths on one trip. This one is not as we said. Boyd Barrington was pushed over the edge. He died of exposure. Someone killed him."

"How do you …?"

"The doctor found a small bloody circle in his neck. Probably from a walking stick. He was pushed off the cliff by the thrust to his neck and left to die of exposure. The question is who did it and why. We will leave it as an accident with only the doctor, the second officer, and you and I the wiser. Make this murder and the other deaths your main investigation not the robbery even if they are connected."

Jim had failed to deal with the bank robbery, he had been punched, his emails on passenger finances stolen, and he had three murders on his hands. He didn't feel too effective.

"Why was Boyd killed if he wasn't behind the bank heist?" asked Jim.

"That is for you to find out. Keep on observing and do not talk. You may find something. This is turning out to be a death cruise not an Antarctic cruise. And be careful. There is a lot of sea between here and Ushuaia."

Jim thanked the captain for his concern and left. Could Captain Engstrom have got someone to kill Boyd? But if Boyd was not in on the robbery why bother? Was the captain straightforwardly looking after himself and the gold, or was he playing a deeper game and Boyd's death was just a distraction? Things were getting complicated.

He headed to his refuge. There weren't too many people in the library after the accident. There would be even less if they knew there had been a deliberate homicide. Once more Jim was out of his depth, but he was willing to look at what he thought might have happened. The blow to his face rankled, but paled before a murder.

Jim and the captain had seen a few figures outlined on the way up the hill, like Yukon gold diggers on the Chilkoot Pass. They all had the same blue passenger jackets.

The assumption was that the murderer was a man, though you could never tell. It would have been a passenger unless a crewmember had borrowed a passenger's jacket. The jabbing pole could have been one of those retractable walking sticks, hidden under a jacket. It would have long gone.

And the extra life jacket? It was probably carried back to the ship in a knapsack. Boyd's cabin number on the tag board had been closed. Then, the final stroke, "Do Not Disturb" on Boyd's cabin door. If Kim had not been so persistent the ship might have reached Neko

Harbour and then headed north, everyone assuming Boyd was ill in his cabin.

He was on board now but not ill. Jim had no wish to see the body though detectives in novels usually went to the morgue to view the body for more clues. Jim wondered if there would be anything from the attacker on Boyd. What did they call it in forensics: trace evidence? It was unlikely if the murderer was smart. Jim would check with the doctor later. He decided not to write things down. His emails had already been stolen. He would not say anything to Carol.

*

What the hell happened? Boyd didn't have anything to do with the gold, so why was he killed? I felt like doing him many times but it would not have come to that. Those emails showed that McKinnon knows Boyd had no connection to the "job" in Ushuaia. McKinnon will be dealt with.

*

Sandy handed out a few drinks and busied herself cleaning more than necessary. People gathered in groups, talked or just sat. The occasional sotto voce came through with

"Pity about Boyd. He always was a loose cannon."
"True."

Some wrote pensively in their diaries as if not quite sure whether to write about the death. One or two wondered how Kim was getting on. Of Boyd there were few thoughts. He was here and then he was gone. He had been a presence but not the most likeable man. Some thought it was a strange business. Must be a record, three on one trip.

Jim found Carol coming out of Kim's cabin. He could hear Maisie keening inside, making more noise than the bereaved. You would not expect her to comfort Kim. Her own sorrows needed an outlet.

"How's Kim doing?"

"She's distraught. They were getting close. I think she even thought marriage was a possibility. She repeatedly said he had no worries except people bugging him about the bank robbery. He wasn't sure why he was considered to have run it." Carol looked at Jim with an accusing look.

He deflected it with: "How are you doing?"

"OK. It's like a busman's holiday."

"A what?"

"You do your job while on vacation. Mine's nursing."

Jim was silent for a moment and then asked:

"Did you get up the hill?"

"Yes, and I pushed the bastard off as well." Carol gave Jim an angry look. He instantly thought: "Oh, no!" but caught himself, and said:

"I didn't think that at all. I wondered how your trip went."

"Fine." They went for some R and R and watched the glaciated landscape flow past.

Had Carol shoved Boyd off the hill? She didn't have a walking stick, but might have used someone else's. He pushed the thought aside. But she wanted Boyd gone in a way. She could have done it. Nobody knew anybody that well. Jim wasn't sure what to do.

And even less certain what to say. He got little satisfaction in thinking if Carol had pushed Boyd she presumably wasn't in on the gold robbery.

He would listen and see who else had been up on the top of "that hill". There might be someone who would say: "I'm sure I was the last person to see Boyd on the hill, before he died." There would be conflicting times and who actually saw what. But that was normal. Jim would persist.

And the missing gold coins? Jim was aware of a certain lassitude when he thought about them. Who cared anyway? Only Captain Eric Engstrom and who ever was behind the scheme.

The murder of Boyd was the most important subject even if he hadn't liked the man. Jim thought of the "R.I.P" on Carcass Island, (or as some called it: "Roast In Peace"), and the rock that fell close to Boyd at Salisbury Plain.

Boyd, Peter and Leon's deaths could be dangerous for Jim. Who had killed them? He thought of the old saying: "When one was about to be hung it concentrates one's mind". Jim focused on the deaths. Even if he could not see how he was going to get any answers.

CHAPTER THIRTY-SIX

Jim persuaded Carol to have dinner. She might have pushed Boyd off the top of the hill, but he didn't want to believe it. The physical attraction was easy to understand. Why he felt he needed to be with her all the time he didn't know.

And who wanted Boyd dead was another puzzle. He made enemies from all countries. He hadn't discriminated. Age wasn't a factor. The younger set would not have killed him. For them Boyd was a nonentity. A swift face punch would have been their solution, male or female.

Jim sat a table with some English people who were a little younger than Boyd and might have had some connection with him. They turned out to be those who he had questioned at Fortuna Bay. Or rather they had questioned him on why he was interested in the robbery. They asked Jim and Carol to sit with the "odds and sods." They did not belong to any larger group. Jim explained about the fish pie and not wanting to land. One was not supposed to defecate ashore south of sixty. A woman of medium height with a sharp dark look about her, smiled.

"I risked the pie and suffered for it. I took some bismuth and cruised along among the icebergs. Did you go up the hill?" She looked at Carol.

"I did. It was a bit damp."

"I suppose none of us saw that man Boyd on the hill," ventured another woman.

The other two said "no." Carol said nothing. The conversation staggered along. After the vegetable curry Carol quickly excused herself and headed for a smoke.

Jim stayed for fruit salad and ice cream. His poached chicken had been a bit dry.

He gleaned no further ideas from this table. Time was running out. One stop at Deception Island tomorrow, and then home across the Drake Passage to Ushuaia. Three more days? Jim headed to the stern. Carol was fuming and dragging hard on a cigarette. It didn't have a chance.

"That bloody girl friend of yours, Rachel, said I must have been on the hill the same time as Boyd. She implied I had something to do with him falling off. I could kill her!" The wrong word always came out at the wrong time.

"Maybe she was involved with the fall and was trying to pass the blame."

"I didn't see the bloody man. There were others on the hill. Why me?"

"Maybe the conflicts between you and Boyd, and you blaming him for your father's death?"

"You think I killed him, don't you?"

"No. Of course not." His reply sounded a trifle weak.

"He died at a dead Antarctic base. I'm glad he's gone. Don't be a bloody policeman all your life." With this partial Parthian shot Carol tossed the butt over the side and stalked off.

She must be upset, thought Jim, polluting Antarctic waters like that. He wandered back to the lounge, not feeling like the great detective or great lover, and unsure of what to do next.

A dark clothed figure moved along the deck towards Jim. He moved a little quicker towards the lounge, and then saw it was the doctor. Would there have been any fibers on Boyd's gloves, or anywhere else? The doctor said he would check.

Jim headed down to his cabin for another think or was it just to get away from people for a while? Martin was drinking, and Alec was at his usual post on the bridge. Jim was overwhelmed by Boyd's murder, Carol's anger, and the lack of progress on the stolen coins. He wondered who had stolen the emails. They must have assumed he would have been onshore or in a Zodiac.

Below decks his corridor was empty as travelers relaxed upstairs or wandered outside. As Jim turned to his cabin a hand grabbed his shoulder. He turned ready to fight, and looked at a man with ski mask covering his face.

"Stop your questions!"

Jim tried to see who it was. A two-knuckled fist punched him in the throat. He gasped and hunched over. He managed to swivel his body, his right arm blocking another hit, which didn't come. Before Jim could counter attack the man ran down stairs to the crew's quarters saying with a Filipino accent:

"You say anything. Your girl friend gets hurt!"

Jim slowly climbed back to the lounge. His throat hurt. Whose toes was he stomping on? And why hadn't he retaliated? Age or just surprise? "Stop your questions!" Which questions? Why the attack?

When he got to the lounge the two Australian medicos greeted him. James asked:

"How's your questioning?"

Jim touched his throat.

"OK, I guess."

"Keep your questions coming. As my old prof used to say: 'Don't let the sun go down on a strangulated hernia.'" The husband beamed at Jim who wasn't sure what the comment meant.

The room recovered a little of its spirits after dinner, some of it alcoholic. Jim did not hear much that pertained to the morning's main event. He walked slowly through. Maybe someone would let slip a hint of being on the hill. They didn't.

At the bar Arthur took Boyd's place. A few gathered around. He related the times he had met up with Boyd Barrington. Some liked him, others didn't. Arthur sided with him even if he had been a bit bombastic: "There was no harm in him."

Mark on the outer reaches nodded as in agreement.

"And he livened things up," said Georgina.

"True. I guess his death bought up my own near death experience when two of us almost didn't make it."

"So after all these years I get to learn a bit more about you." Georgina looked at Arthur.

"Some topics are hard to tell. Anyway, Neville and I got caught out in a storm on a sledging trip. The tent was torn away. We crouched in a crevasse as the wind screamed over us.

"Neville wanted to check on the dogs. I forced him to tie a rope on. He hadn't thought it was necessary. He disappeared into the swirling snow. He never did reach the dogs. Neville crawled back on his hands and knees, frozen and barely able to find the crevasse.

"If Neville had not been roped up would I have stood at the crevasse edge yelling for him and freezing to death if he didn't return? You forget when you're young how close to death you push yourself." He looked at Georgina.

When Carol entered the lounge there was some slight head turning and the odd comment: "She got what she wanted." "What did Boyd do to her?" She sat with Jim awhile and then made an early exit. A slight touch of his arm by Carol left Jim feeling better.

Georgina headed off to talk to a couple from Australia. She wanted information on Perth where her niece lived. It was time for a family visit. As Arthur sipped his whisky and water Jim asked him about the Sheldon Expedition. Jim would keep away from the bank job. Perhaps there would be something for Carol.

"Why did Dave Bapton, the guy who died, want to go off on a sledging trip with a guy he disliked?" Jim asked.

"I'm not sure," said Arthur. "It could have been a relief just to get away from the cramped hut. It wouldn't have mattered who it was."

"But there were definite clashes between Dave and Boyd?"

"Yes. I did hear from one member of the expedition many years later that Dave might have had some ulterior motive for going off with Boyd. That was just a rumor," said Arthur. He really did need a refill but decided Jim was not the person to fill it.

"What to get back at Boyd?" asked Jim.

"Maybe." Arthur shrugged and wandered off for more whisky.

In his cabin Jim washed and climbed up to his second storey bunk. There had been no offers to swap bunks from the other two. Now it was too late. It was not the bunk of the month.

Ideas crowded into his mind. He kept switching on the light and writing possibilities down. He told himself he wasn't going to write stuff down. Each time he had a new idea he sat up and banged his head on the ceiling. The notes he should tear up and flush down the toilet. He then remembered: "Nothing down the toilets," they clogged too easy. He couldn't be bothered with the correct nautical term: head.

While he tried to relax, Alec entered. Jim asked him how his bird lists were going. Alec said they were going great. Today there were some Antarctic petrels flying along the coast. Maybe a year old. They were not mottled like the cape petrels, but had a distinct dark brown leading edge and head, and white the rest of the body. Jim nodded as if he was interested. He hadn't seen Alec this communicative before. It must have been a special event.

CHAPTER THIRTY-SEVEN

Deception Island was the low mass on the horizon. Under a dark sky squalls of heavy clouds and rain swept across the rolling grey sea. A few black and white cape pigeons flew along with the ship.

Greg gave the morning temperature. The wind was out of the northwest, with the pressure falling, and it was raining if they hadn't noticed. There was no quote of the day. Maybe Boyd's death had cut out some of the usual routines. Jim realized that among the passengers looking into the distance was a murderer of three people.

Greg came on the blower again, and said there would be brief lecture on Deception Island. The lounge rose and fell as the sea rolled along. Only a few attended the historian's talk. Breakfast had been sparse. Once the shelter of the Antarctic Peninsula was left behind the waves heading east took on the ship and the passengers.

The historian, Colin, mentioned the discovery of the South Shetlands by a Captain Smith, early nineteenth century. No one believed him that there was land to the south. Captain Cook had only found ice. However, the lure of fur seal pelts soon had most of the northern part of the Antarctic Peninsula and its islands explored, and its seals decimated.

Deception Island had a safe anchorage. A slide showed a horseshoe shaped island with a small southeast entrance that led inside to a wide natural harbor.

"You could put three nation's navies inside," said Colin. "That is why starting during World War Two and some twenty-five year after there was a British, an Argentinean and a Chilean base inside the island, all year."

"But not now," interrupted Frank.

"Right," said Colin. "Two large eruptions stopped the yearly scientific work. Today two bases, Argentinean and Spanish, only monitor in the summer."

"Volcanic?" asked one passenger.

"Oh, didn't I tell you? Deception Island is dormant volcano. It's had a few rumblings and smoke since the late nineteen sixties, but it is quite safe. The major eruptions are infrequent. There was even a whaling factory inside the island for the first twenty-five years of the twentieth century." Colin didn't mention when the water around the whaling ships boiled or the land at one time dropped several feet. "Any ways it's straight ahead."

There were black volcanic cliffs with thick cloud down to a few hundred feet of the sea The ice and snow covered hills were in cloud.

"A typical Deception summer's day," said Frank cheerfully. "It can be manky for weeks on end. Supposedly the winters are snow white and bright."

The passengers peered through the pelting rain. Around the ship hundreds of chinstrap penguins surged towards the island.

"The outside rookery on Baily Head has over a hundred thousand pairs," said Ricardo, the staff bird expert

"Why on the outside. Wouldn't it be better inside?" someone asked.

"It's too warm inside," said Ricardo. "The warm beaches are heated by volcanic water. You can enjoy a hot bath if you like after we dig a hole in the beach."

Another cruise ship further north in the Shetland Islands had been delayed. They had asked if they could take the morning spot for Whalers Bay. Greg and the captain decided they had time so the *Polar Adventurer* would cruise along the east coast.

And yes, towels would be supplied for those wanting to have a genuine Antarctic afternoon dip in the warm water on the beach. All passengers needed were swimming togs.

Jim asked Carol what she was going to do on the island. She said: "Birds." He was more interested in walking as far as possible, and seeing the remains of the old whaling factory and the British base. He would try and connect with her later. She detached herself from him by photographing chinstrap penguins streaming through the waves.

With a "See you later" he went in search of the doctor. The doctor said he had found no cloth fibers on Boyd's body. There had been no time to grab the pole. Jim was relieved he didn't have to view the body. He thought of all the incidents that had happened on the trip. Jim made sure that he was always with someone during the day. He didn't want to join Leon and Boyd in the frozen food locker.

The ship paused off the massive somber cliffs of Baily Head. Hard volcanic brown rock rose five hundred feet straight out of the waves crashing below. Thousands of black and white chinstrap penguins swarmed in and out of the water at a narrow black beach.

Murder in the Antarctic

The visitors watched the bleak scenery as the rain dripped. A glaciated-backed beach straight as a ruler ran into the distance. Waves raced along its shore. The deputy leader said that landings at the vast penguin rookery were rare. You might land but getting back off the beach could be treacherous. A few photographs were taken through plastic bags. Some viewed the gloomy vista and retreated to the lounge. It was dry and there were hot drinks. The cloud and rain continued. At the north end of Deception Island the ship turned and headed slowly back to make its way into Port Foster.

*

Carol looked at the grey icy coast. Was the trip a waste? She was a surrogate for her mother who had died a few years back, and who had never forgiven her husband for deserting her and her baby, Carol. No one knew what had happened on that sea ice several decades back. Maybe it was not as black and white as Carol thought. Maybe her father had to take some of the blame. She resisted the idea.

Kim had become quiet and stricken. Carol talked to her when she could. Maisie still carried on sniveling. She fed off Kim's grief. She needed a good slap.

On her own at breakfast, if you could be on your own in that crowded dining room, Carol had received some glances from Pamela and some catty comments from Rachel nearby.

Jack asked: "Who was on the hill with Boyd?"

"I wasn't, but *someone* certainly was," said Rachel.

Carol wondered why Pamela was with Rachel, a person she considered rather coarse. Closing ranks. Why would they do that?

As Rachel and her group left the room, she asked Carol:

"Do you love him?"

Carol assumed she was not talking about Boyd. She snapped: "That's none of your business!" Did Rachel want Jim as well as Jack?

Rachel snickered and Pamela smiled condescendingly. Jack looked away. A catfight had nothing to do with him.

Fuming Carol headed back to her spot. What would Jack have called it if she had had words with those two women? A slag match? That would be really nice, Carol Martins.

*

Jim found that most of the ex-BAS types had gone on the Zodiac cruise at Almirante Brown. The weather and the hill climb had cut down on their manly zeal. The rest who had tried the hill were small groups like some of the Manchester four. Certainly no one came up to him, broke down, and confessed. No one seemed to have any strong feelings about Boyd except Carol.

Jim had overheard Doug at lunch talking about the need for more ice cream as Boyd was no longer around. What brought that on? Ron and Ed stuck close to Doug. They brought the conversations back to Adelaide, and what they would do when they got back. It did not seem that Doug or Ron and Ed were involved with the fund.

Neptunes Bellows, a mere five hundred yards wide, was the entrance to the several square miles of Port Foster inside Deception Island. The penny dropped for Jim. Oh, that's why it was called deception. It looks like a normal island on the outside, but it was hollow inside.

The *Polar Adventurer* traveled close to the vertical tuff cliffs, the old layered volcanic ash. Ahead the harbor was still covered with light sea ice. They veered starboard and moved into Whalers Bay. Dark cliffs ran along the right hand side.

In front a mile long black beach stretched itself. Dotted along the dark sand were the rusty remnants of the whaling factory and the weather-beaten wooden British base hut, or what remained of it. The day stayed moist.

Keeping close to other tourists, Jim landed among squabbling white-spotted cape pigeons, feasting on krill cooked in volcanic waters. Steam rose from the low tide beach. Greg had warned them not to put their hands into the sand unless they wanted to be scalded.

Jim followed a formation of Australians. Ron and Ed tagged along. Doug was not with them. They passed tilted rusty brown whale oil tanks, and arrived at the remains of a whalers' cemetery. The staff historian had said only two crosses of the original forty or so survived the massive volcanic mud slide that poured down from the hill above, and swept through the old British hut.

The hut's floor was buried. A large opening gaped through the middle of the wooden building. The east end had collapsed. The building would not last much longer. Jim trailed along with the Aussies to the 1960s aircraft hangar further on, and then headed back to the landing area.

The staff had dug a large hole in the sand so the passengers could have an Antarctic "swim" complete with an authenticated certificate. Squeals from those undressing in the cool damp air were by followed by sighs as they sunk into the volcanic-heated seawater.

Jim, bypassed the pleasure pit, and headed along the beach to Neptunes Window, a cliff notch, and thought on his tasks. He still considered himself on the case or cases, as the case might be.

McKinnon skirted old wooden oil barrel staves, a couple of water boats flooded with ash, and several young fur seals guarding their beach. He attached himself to a British couple. They had not climbed the hill at Almirante Brown, but like him they needed exercise after their sea travel. They had never heard of the gold heist.

Passengers were coming and going from the steep slope that led up to Neptunes Window. John the geologist stood guard at the top. There was an eighty-foot drop behind him straight into the sea below. Carol was perched above the notch photographing Wilson petrel nests. At the edge Jim stood close on one side to give others room.

A small group of crew members huffed up to the top, and stood around, and snapped each other with pocket cameras. One of the female hotel staff who he did not know smiled at Jim, tripped over a stone and pushed into him. He fell sideways, grabbed a protruding rock, and felt his legs slide over the edge as the crumbling volcanic sand slipped into the sea. As he hung there Carol leaped down from her perch above, knocked the young woman aside, and grabbed Jim's shoulders. John rushed over and helped Carol pull Jim back. By the time Jim had sat up and looked around, the crew had headed back down the hill.

"Are you OK?" asked John. The well-being of the passenger always came first.

"Yes. I'm just a bit winded. It's a long way down."

"Well, keep away from the edge. I've got to keep other people from having a hard swim," John said.

Jim ruefully smiled at Carol and said he would head back. She accompanied him. On the way she said she had watched as the young woman tripped into Jim:

"There was no way she stumbled accidentally. There wasn't even a rock there."

Did it happen because he was a threat to someone or was it an accident? He needed something with more proof than an accidental trip, but without being fatal to him. And a masked man had threatened him.

"I think I need to come clean."

"I think you should, Mckinnon. Was the push to do with all these questions you've been asking?"

Jim said: "I'm not sure if it was a push, but if it is it could be connected to that Ushuaia bank robbery." He glanced at Mandy as she smoothly got into a Zodiac.

"Why did you start this questioning?"

Jim admitted that it was at Captain Engstrom's request.

"So he is behind all this questioning that has annoyed passengers. Someone wants to deal with you?"

"It's possible," said Jim.

"So much for a quiet Antarctic cruise among interesting wildlife and great scenery," replied Carol.

Jim followed up with: "Boyd, and this is in strict secrecy, was deliberately pushed off the cliff at Almirante Brown. The doctor found a wound made from a walking stick thrust into his throat." He wondered why he came out with that when Carol could be the chief suspect. Not sexual attraction surely?

"So you don't think it was me."

"I never did."

Carol humphed a little, and said nothing. "And you," asked Jim. "Did you get what you came for?"

Carol was thoughtful for a moment.

"I guess it was good in parts. Like the curate's egg?"

"What?"

"Oh, it's an old Victorian joke about a curate having breakfast with a bishop. He needed a job, so when the bishop asked him how his egg was, which was rotten, the curate said: 'Good, in parts, my lord.' I've enjoyed your company and the photography. And I didn't kill Boyd." She looked seriously at Jim. He believed her.

"I'll see you at dinner."

Jim wasn't going to object. He was not going to ask any more questions about the robbery or the murders. He would just listen. There was a limit to how much more interesting he wanted the voyage to be. Dying at sea was not part of the plan.

Happy Hour though less boisterous than normal had picked up a bit. Several were retelling the heroics of undressing with a freezing cold wind, and the sight of purple bodies stepping into the pool. And how it was even worse getting dressed, with grit, salt and wind whipping around your what's its.

Murder in the Antarctic

Jim noticed that Jacqueline and Richard were no longer isolated at their own table. They talked with Arthur and Georgina for a while. Later they had a few words with Mark. An Antarctic or South American connection? Or were they being more social. But perhaps that was a way of masking what they were really doing. They were still high up on the suspect list, which did not move and seemed to float in the ether, insubstantial and ungraspable.

CHAPTER THIRTY-EIGHT

Sitting with Jim and the two young Australians Shaun and Pam, Carol brought up the accident that had happened at Neptunes Window. Jim tried to be casual.

"Why would anyone want to do that," asked Pam.

"Maybe I asked too many questions about the Ushuaia robbery."

"And why was that?" she asked.

"Just curious, I guess." A partial truth was always an option.

Jim stared at his drink. He wondered why Boyd was murdered. Part of the robbery or something murkier? Who else was on the recording? Was there a third person other than Leon and the second man?

Carol looked at Jim and suggested one last look at the sea.

"And a ciggy?"

She poked him and led the way.

"They look well together," said Pam.

"Though not as good as us."

Under an outside light Carol peered at Jim. He looked a bit haggard and preoccupied.

"Are you going to get any sleep tonight?"

"I hope so." He left it at that. Would there be more "accidents"? Maybe his cabin with the access to another cabin through the washroom was not as safe as he thought. He asked:

"Can you lock your cabin?"

"Of course. It stops all my suitors from getting in."

He looked at Carol. She was very attractive, not shy and said what she thought. He liked that. She smoked, but maybe he could get her off that later. Later? What was he thinking of?

"Hello? Anyone there?" Carol broke into his musings.

"Sorry. I was trying to get a handle on what's happened today."

"To answer your unspoken question. Would you like to stay in my locked cabin tonight? Strictly for your protection rather than mine."

Jim looked into her face and said: "Could I? I won't be up to much."

"And I should hope not." Carol smiled at him, led him up the outside stairs and slipped him into her cabin. It was better decorated than his narrow shared threesome, it had a fresh bunch of grapes on a side table, and the window was a full window not a covered-over porthole. And it had Carol.

*

During the night the push on him, Peter, Leon and Boyd's death, the bank robbery and the missing gold coins coursed through Jim's mind. He was not sure what he should do next. Carol had resisted forcing herself on him during the night. A few pillows between them had helped. He had been tempted to pursue that line of endeavor, but decided that he would keep the relationship neutral until there was some resolution or Ushuaia arrived.

Early he headed up to the gym. The French guy Pierre was trotting away on the treadmill. His sideways motion was interesting. Jim decided to wait until he was on the firm surface of South America. He was still young.

The waves rolled out of the west against the *Polar Adventurer*. The sideways lurching put some including Carol off their breakfast. Jim sat with some Australians. Mark joined them. He smiled lightly at Jim and slowly ate his modest breakfast. Jim needed bolstering so he indulged in a full English and a full continental breakfast. He had lots of time to get fit. Jim thought about the captain's warning. He would keep inside most of the day.

"How is your day going?" asked Mark.

Jim tried for some Canadian politeness: "It's going well."

"And your questions?"

"They're proceeding."

The Australians talked back and forth, and ignored the other two. Jim deliberately slowed down as he ate methodically through his spread. Mark had said little to help the investigation. He talked about changes in Antarctica: such as more visitors, changes in seasonal icepack and the breakup of old ice shelves.

Jim noticed that Arthur, Georgina and Frank stayed away from his end of the dining room. Was he a pariah to some people? And did any of this have any bearing on his questions? The three deaths and the Deception Island push on him made things murkier. Why push Peter? He hadn't dealt with the robbery as far as Jim knew. Neither had Boyd.

And the stumble or push on him? Yes, he had been asking awkward questions. He could have had a final Antarctic resting place though with no name on a map if Carol hadn't rushed down and grabbed him. As

Mark burbled on Jim mentally shuddered at the eighty-foot fall into the crashing waves below Neptunes Window.

"What will you are doing after we arrive back at Ushuaia?" Mark broke in on his thoughts.

"Going back to work I guess, teaching that is," he added quickly. He had no idea. The trip had not been a restful holiday. There had been impositions and accidents. And there was Carol. Was she up? Jim would hang around with her for the next two days, and see what developed.

The morning's lecture was a recap by Greg the expedition leader of all the places they had been to in the last two weeks. The staff photographer displayed photographs of each site. All were for sale. There was no mention of any deaths.

Greg told the passengers: "Today is the last day to get any laundry done. Daniel and Elsa will be looking after the bar reckonings."

Elsa stood up and said that if anyone wanted to have other people's email addresses the reception center would have a sheet of names and emails. Just sign up, and, of course, no commercial transactions. Jim did not have Carol's address. He should be able to get it.

Later a pale Carol appeared. She propped herself at the aft end of the ship and gently puffed on a B and H. A short smile showed that Jim was still to the good. They said little and watched black-browed albatrosses waft past. The ship rolled a little but the weather stayed reasonable. Jim was comfortable, but the deaths and everything else connected with this ship preyed on him. He grunted.

"Is that the start of brilliant conversation?"

Carol's comment irked, but Jim started slowly talking about the captain's original request.

"I'm to be trusted now is that it?"

Jim wasn't sure whether it was her smoking or her forthrightness that bugged him the most. He looked at Carol:

"I wanted to include you but Captain Engstrom was rather adamant that I limit my contacts."

"So, it was the captain's fault not yours?"

Jim muttered: "I suppose so."

She let him suffer a while and then said: "So, what's next?"

Jim wasn't certain. The captain was doing his own judicial moves as far as his authority went. But the threats to Jim and the other concerns were still floating around out there as was the second man on the recording. Jim looked vaguely out at the grey ocean.

"Well, if we keep you safe that will be one good thing."

Jim turned to Carol and said: "Thanks."

"I may even give you my email address."

"I would like that."

"Why?"

"I like you."

"Despite my faults?"

"We all have them."

"A bit of philosophy from Jim McKinnon!"

"No, no. I think we could do well together."

"That's not a proposal, is it?"

"Well, no... not exactly." Jim felt the waters rising.

"You think I would be better off with you than on my own? You know that single women live as long as married women."

"But are they happier?"
"That depends on the couple."
The conversation stopped. It rested, waiting for an event or word to revive it.

Slowly from the back of the lounge Ron, Ed and Doug moved out on to the deck. Doug irritably turned and went back inside. The other two turned with him like guards with a prisoner. Carol looked at them.

"Doug is a very sick man. He reminds me of a Mrs. Symons at my hospital who had terminal cancer. She lasted a month. She had symptoms long before she came to us."

"You can tell?"

"Doug has that look about him. What ever it is the ship's doctor can't treat it. He's getting worse, and he's on heavy painkillers. He's probably left it too late. Men!"

Carol looked at Jim as if he would go the same way. He changed the subject by asking her if she would like some lunch.

They loaded up their plates, at least Jim did, and scanned tables for a space. Before they could decide Mark came up to them and said his table had bought some wine. Would they like to join them? Mark swiftly poured wine for Jim and Carol, and chatted about the reasonable crossing they were having. Why he could remember times when no one could get out on deck for the two days crossing the Drake Passage.

"How about you Arthur?" he said, "You must have had some rough passages."

Arthur grunted: "Some."

Pamela ignored Carol and Jim and talked to Georgina. Mark continued to talk to the pair about how fine the cruise had been and to top up their glasses.

CHAPTER THIRTY-NINE

As the *Polar Adventurer* headed north through the Drake Passage Mike the sea mammal guy and Bob the birdman started the afternoon with reading out questions asked by passengers on past trips, but certainly not from *this* trip. What happens to an iceberg when it *melts*? What is a *female* sperm whale called? Why are those islands called the *Seven* Islands? If it's January at the North Pole what month is it at the *South* Pole? There was a lot of laughter until Mike said it was their turn. Did they have any questions for the expeditionary staff?

"Remember there are no stupid questions. Though you may get some stupid answers."

James the Australian doctor asked: "What's the life expectancy of an iceberg?"

"It depended on the size of the iceberg, and where it lands up. Most can survive for several years traveling around the coasts of the Antarctic," was the reply from John, the rock and iceman.

Pierre asked about the long nose holes of albatrosses.

Ricardo, the staff birder said: "That's how the birds get rid of salt from their bodies as they skim over the sea."

("I'm sure the birders covered that in their presentations," Carol whispered to Jim.)

"What was the biggest storm encountered by the *Polar Adventurer*?" Rachel was still after the thrill of danger, any danger, to the ship.

Greg answered: "The captain said that at one time waves pounded over the top of the bridge. Some ships have lost all their electronic controls when a large wave smashed into the bridge. Not that that would happen to this ship."

Mike the sea mammal guy came up with a hard question for the audience: "What's the largest Antarctic land animal?"

"Elephant seals, surely."

"Do they go to the Antarctic?" someone asked.

"Rarely," replied Mike.

Leopard or fur seals were suggested. Each suggestion was knocked down.

"The answer," said Mike "is a flightless midge about half an inch in size. All the other animals come from the sea."

"I knew that," Jim told Carol, "Alec mentioned it once in our cabin."

Bob the birder stepped forward and said that while every one was here he would talk a little on the yearly decline of albatrosses. He described long line fishing where thousands of baited hooks attached to a mile of so of cable were strung out across the ocean. Albatrosses feeding on the bail were drowned. Their numbers were going down by three to five percent a year.

Many legal fishing boats were bringing in measures such as fishing at night to lessen the killing of birds. But there was still illegal fishing going on, and thousands of albatrosses died every year. And each albatross chick rather like most kids needed two parents to look after them.

"That makes sense," said a woman passenger.

Bob continued: "We would like to auction a variety of beautiful gifts tomorrow afternoon to raise money for saving the albatrosses of the world."

As the travelers headed off to Happy Hour Carol grabbed Jim by the arm. I am the one he thought. Carol looked at him and said that she felt queasy. The waves had risen and the ship was rolling more. She would head to her cabin for a while. Hopefully she would appear at dinner.

Jim escorted her to her cabin. Carol bleakly smiled at him and closed the door. Jim clattered down the stairs making a comforting noise for himself. He needed people around him.

Jim joined Shaun and Pam. They discussed the organizing of the thousands of unforgettable shots they had taken over the last two weeks.

"We need another holiday to get a handle on them," said Pam.

"As long as it doesn't involve any more accidental deaths," countered Shaun. Jim did not say anything.

The Drake Lake gradually became the Drake Shake. Carol took on some soup at dinner, told Jim he knew where her cabin was, and she would see him later. Jim tried to be with Shaun and Pam at dinner, but left it too late. A large group of Australians crowded their table.

Mark waved him over: "Where's Carol?"

"She's a bit under the weather," Jim said.

Mark added: "The weather's going under in the next twenty-four hours as well."

Some passengers headed for their cabins. Mounting waves outside brought plate crashes from the kitchen.

The few hardy types struggled to the ship's watering hole where Sandy put out a few glasses at a time as a the orders came in. Jim sat with the Australian trio for a while. Doug, pale and sallow, morosely clutched a soda and was silent. Ron talked to Jim and Ed.

Jim then moved to the edge of the bar area, close to Sandy, but without intruding on the old Antarctic types. Rachel linked to Jack slid into a nearby seat.

"So, where's your girlfriend?"

Jim shrugged. It was late; the voyage was near its end. There was no percentage in crossing swords with someone as self-centered as Mrs. Weinberger. The robbery did not seem to interest her. They would leave at Ushuaia and never see each other again. Fortunately.

As for Jack he would bully his way through life with or with out Doreen. Whether Rachel would be part of the equation Jim didn't care. Maybe she didn't care either. Jim had crossed Jack off his suspect list. Not enough what his father called nous: practical intelligence.

Jim had looked at the diaries on the Internet of other first-time Antarctic travelers. They all seemed to have enjoyed the experience. Jim supposed they had not had three deaths on their voyage. Hopefully for Antarctic tourism there would not be any more trips like this one.

Mark came up to him and suggested that he shouldn't be in such a contemplative mood. The trip must have been a great experience for a first timer, like Jim. Hadn't he enjoyed himself? Jim agreed, but refused to have more drinks. He said he felt tired and would have an early night in his cabin.

Jim headed down to his level and then reversed direction and took the stairs up to the bow end. By a roundabout route he reached Carol's cabin and knocked. There was no answer. Had she taken too many seasick pills and knocked herself out? He knocked louder and called: "Carol!" No welcoming arm dragged him in.

Jim clattered down several levels to his cabin, grabbed his camera and *As You Like It*, and headed breathlessly back to the lounge. At least it made him look as if he was busy and not vulnerable.

He braced himself in a chair as the waves continued to pound the ship. Jim looked around at the few people left. The usual group was around the bar, and the Manchester four at the end were arguing about something.

One Australian tour group was tasting Argentinean wine. "Not as good as ours," was reiterated a few times. This did not stop them from having several fill-ups. Jim wondered what some bar bills would look like.

As Martin headed out, Jim hurried after him. Could he be the murderer? How convenient for Martin if Jim stayed in his cabin tonight. A slight accident and… Jim retraced his steps and landed once more out side Carol's cabin. All the other cabins were shut tight. He banged again and waited. He heard a slow shuffling movement on the other side of the door. A "Who is it?" and his reply got Jim into Carol's room. She locked the door, and hanging onto the bed smiled at him.

"Sorry, I was bit out of it earlier."
"You're better?"
"Yes."

The glittering conversation halted. Jim sat on the edge of the bed and looked at a ruffled but good looking Carol. Her deep red nightgown flowed around her body.

"You look great."

"Weak compliments will get you everywhere."

"Such as this?" He held her face in his hands and kissed her open lips. Carol wrapped her arms around his neck and clung to him. She smiled as she let go of him and slid between the sheets.

"I think that light needs to be out."

Jim stood up aroused. He flicked off the light, and found Carol with no difficulty. She slowly undressed him. Her softness excited him as she ran her fingers along his body. He slid one leg over her. They slipped together as the ship moved through the rolling night sea.

CHAPTER FORTY

The ship reared and plunged like a tiny sailboat heading back from a fur seal hunt two hundred years earlier. Later than usual Greg gave out his last quote of the voyage, one from Nansen, not an Antarctic explorer, but as Greg explained he had helped explorers like Amundsen: "Strange. There is always sadness on departure. It is as if one cannot after all bear to leave this bleak waste of ice, glaciers, cold and toil…"

Greg gave a few cursory comments on the weather, told everyone to stay inside if possible and to hang on to the railings. The weather would be rough for the next twelve hours. The trip was ending on a somber note.

As Carol slept, protected against the rolling of the *Polar Adventurer* by more anti-seasick pills, Jim ate some breakfast. There were few up for it. He admitted to himself that he had not been thinking like a detective. Gold coins, murder? What coins, what deaths? Sex will out every time.

Jim hurried up to the lounge where there were at least a few people sitting around. He no longer felt that the captain was behind any of the deaths, unless he was an extraordinary good actor. Besides he had agreed to a certain demonstration at dinnertime.

As Jim sat down he felt the atmosphere was like being at a family funeral where everyone looked around wondering who would be next to die. Or was that just his vivid imagination? Was the murderer relaxing here in the lounge, a coffee in hand? Jim thought about the robbery, the gold coins, (where were most of them?), the death of Peter, Boyd, and of Leon because of Rita's confession.

Rita had brought down Leon if that was the phrase. Did she know more? She didn't know who the second man was on the recording. Rita had been friendly, except for a few days ago when she looked harried and upset. Boy friend trouble, work related or something else? She had never been "down" before. This evening when she was off duty he would approach her and ask who else was linked with Leon. He hoped she would give him some clues.

The ship rocked along. A 1920s black and white film on rounding the stormy Cape Horn in a merchant sailing ship was watched, but with little attention. Three modern deaths outscored the sailing ship movie. Jim sat on the edge of the group, his back to a wall, and half watching as the screen moved up and down.

Before the end he left and headed up to the safety of the bridge, his arms stretched sideways like a penguin for balance. He followed a younger couple, balancing the same way. There was no sign of Captain Engstrom. Alec and Bob maintained their watch on the bird life as the waves raced along. Water crashed over the dipping bow.

As the morning moved along a few more passengers came onto the bridge. Only the rare wind-blown one stood outside to view the surging waves and the birds flung over the waters.

Closely monitored by Ron and Ed, Doug entered. He moved slowly up to a wooden railing and clung to it. He looked as if he was taking everything in but it wasn't registering. The other two tried for the last wave-crashing shots through the forward window. Ron nudged Doug, who shuffled sideways to where Jim clung to his own bit of rail. A slight cough made Jim look at the pale yellow face and the blood-shot eyes.

"I'm not my best today. I may never be, but I want to…" Doug coughed some more from a raw throat. "I want to say that I don't believe Boyd was behind that effing Antarctic fund I lost money on. I thought he was, and I was glad when he died. Now I'm not sure. That's a big admission from one who's never wrong." He gave a wry smile in Jim's direction.

Jim said: "You could be right."

They nodded as if all the world's problems had been solved. Doug turned to Ron, who led him downstairs. Ed tore himself away from the window, and followed. It seemed to Jim as if Boyd's death had left a void in Doug's life. Was Doug coming to the end of his?

Near lunch Jim headed back to the lounge, satisfied that there was no one behind him or lurking in the corridors. Some fellow travelers were putting the finishing touches to their journals or trying to finish the library book they had never got around to reading. Jim assumed others were packing. He had to get around to it sometime. Possibly after dinner. He didn't really care.

Lunch saw a repeatable pizza with few toppings and a guarantee to repeat on oneself. A revived Carol looked at him with a smile and ate a little. "Are you still vulnerable?"

"Yes, though that's not the only reason I'm glad to see you."

"Have club, will travel. Protecting the weak, special price."

They looked at each over the bits of chewed pizza. Jim felt better.

They headed up to the bridge. There were ship's crew up there, other passengers, and Carol could keep on noting her bird sightings. Jim enjoyed being with her.

*

The afternoon found Elsa and Daniel ensconced at a lounge table. They called people up by their cabin numbers to pay their final bills.

Elsa said: "All drinks from now on will be cash only."

Ron remarked: "There will be no moaning at the bar," as each person went up to pay their account. "I reckon if he had been around, Boyd's bar bill would have been well over a thousand dollars."

Doug looked at him but made no comment.

Ed wondered how much he owed. Those long sea sections meant big bar bills. He hoped his credit card was good for it. "Well yours won't be too bad," Ed said to Doug.

"Thanks for those kind words."

Georgina joined Pamela further down the lounge. After the initial comments the conversation dried up. Their contacts were through Antarctic men or more distant home acquaintances.

"I still believe the less those others travel to the Antarctic the better."

Georgina shook her head as Pamela stared around at those others.

CHAPTER FORTY-ONE

At three o'clock Bob announced the start of the albatross auction.

"But we are not selling albatrosses. Only gifts to raise money to preserve albatrosses. And they're fabulous. The gifts that is though albatrosses are as well. Bring your checkbooks and credit cards. We will even take cash. Any currency gladly accepted."

The lounge was less than half full. The ship twisted, gripped by the waves. There was reluctance for some to leave their bunks.

Smiling and with a continuous patter Bob and John ran the price up for each auctioned item. One picture of the Lemaire Channel hand painted by one of the passengers went for two hundred and fifty dollars. The rest, of the gifts, small penguin toys, a few items from the store, went for less.

Only a pair of Elsa's waterproof pants, on which she signed her name and parted with a few fake tears, led to some competition from the males. James the Australian doctor outbid everyone else. His wife was only slightly amused.

The item that reached the highest was the itinerary of the voyage carefully inked onto a chart, and signed by the captain and Greg. As Elsa said to the staffer, Jill:

"Those signed charts of the trip usually go for a thousand dollars. This one only went for five hundred."

Jill said it was probably the weather and what had happened on the trip.

At the end Frank raised himself up and gave a few words praising Boyd Barrington's enthusiasm for life and the Antarctic. There were a few "Hear, hears." Carol looked pensive. Her lips tightened.

Jim noticed there was no mention of Peter or Leon. Were they a separate issue? He was still no closer to knowing what had gone on or was going on. And where were those coins?

Arthur mentioned he had been in the ice over forty years ago, and he had never forgotten his first experience. He was sure they too would not forget the frozen south. The Antarctic casts its spell.

"As someone once said everyone has their own Antarctic. My question to you is what's yours?"

Arthur sat down to a round of applause. Jim was left wondering whether he was playing clever. There was still Pamela with her South American connections, Mark, who knew a lot about the Antarctic but said little, one of the other Antarctic men, Jacqueline and Richard, or someone completely out of left field? Jim had no further information on the robbery, but it must be important enough to murder three people.

Arthur motioned to Carol to come over and sit with him. He said quietly:

"I want to tell you something about the Sheldon Expedition." Before Carol could ask what, Arthur said: "After your father died, we helped Boyd's Antarctic career, by keeping quiet about the accident. I looked after the home end of things. Eric Sheldon needed money from Boyd's father so we moved Boyd on to other projects."

"That was nice for Boyd. And what about my father?"

"Your father's death was unfortunate though I don't think Boyd was entirely to blame. I never believed those rumors that Boyd killed Dave because he objected to Argentinean money being used for the expedition. Boyd was not to blame."

"Based on what?" Carol blurted out.

Arthur carried on smoothly: "The research needed money to continue. We couldn't help one young man, but we could help the other."

"That's it? How convenient for you to rely on the word of the person who survived." Carol bristled. Her father had been killed by Boyd, and others had looked after Boyd.

"Well these events are always nebulous. Your mother was helped financially. Money, support, and so on. I believe your nursing studies were paid for by one of your father's friends.

"With the whole unfortunate matter we needed to move on so we did." Arthur looked suitably solemn, repeated how sorry he was, and waved his right hand slightly. What was done was done.

Carol looked at the older man in anger. His bushy white eyebrows looked pathetic, as did he. She shook her head. For her there was no closure. But was there ever? You could not rerun the past. The dead man whom she never knew would not return. Nothing seemed fair.

She slowly got up, turned away from the old man and went back to Jim. She nudged him and said she wanted more bridge time. Jim said he would stay and be close to others.

"Not too close." Carol slowly left the lounge.

*

Carol still queasy from the rolling sea hauled herself up to the bridge. Her father was no more, would never return and the instigator was dead. She had to let go. And she needed to think about Jim. She was still hesitant as to whether this was a shipboard romance, or whether they had a relationship. How could you tell? And certainly once they got home with a continent and an ocean separating them email endearments wouldn't cut it for her.

She gazed at a flock of dark shearwaters tipping over the breaking waves, and did a mental check on the man in question. He was average height and weight, with a slight balding spot, (that always worried them!), kind, considerate, not wealthy, but enjoyed her company even with her occasional outbursts and the smoking.

The latter she would try and deal with. Hypnosis and patches had failed. It was probably the job. A large number of nurses despite being health professionals smoked. Long hours, shift work, and broken meal times made cigarettes a lifeline. A change of occupation might be the only way to quit the habit. But would she put on weight?

Bob, Alec and Ricardo suddenly synchronized their binoculars. A large white albatross languidly glided over the waves past the ship and headed out. A slow turn brought the bird back into focus.

"It's an old royal!" said Ricardo.

Carol asked how he knew. "Didn't they live around New Zealand?"

Murder in the Antarctic

"There're similar in size to the wandering albatross, but they have a pure white tail," said Bob, before Ricardo could do the honors. The bridge denizens watched the large white albatross swoop over the water before heading further out to other seas. Carol's bird list like the voyage was almost at an end. It would have to do.

*

The final dinner was a subdued affair. A few people dressed up. It was their last chance to do so on this cruise. There had been a small spark of interest at seeing the distant Cape Horn before dinner. Greg said it was the little whitish projection in front of the large headland. A few photographs were taken through rain and wind. The *Polar Adventurer* turned away to the east.

As Colin the historian remarked to John the geologist the last major meal of the trip was generally boisterous, and filled with wine and speeches both from the staff and grateful passengers. The usual lightness was absent at this meal though the captain made a slight stir when he showed selected passengers some coins.

At the end Greg made a short speech thanking everyone for coming on their voyage of discovery, (a rather unfortunate phrase thought Jim), and hoped they would return for further explorations. No passenger rose to give thanks for the staff's support or the amazing sights they had all seen. The three deaths, however accidental, were three too many.

As Jim's thoughts ran round and got nowhere he knew it wasn't just the rolling sea affecting people. Most passengers were at dinner. They wanted to get to Ushuaia and get home. He wondered about the Argentinean authorities, and what would happen to the passengers. Bailed or imprisoned? Well at least they would be on terra firma. Even with his constitution the sea was getting to him.

Carol looked if she had enough sea though she burbled on about some sort of white albatross and her long bird list.

Then said: "I'm going to do some packing and check my emails." She left.

As Jim finished his coffee Mark came over, sat down. He turned to Jim and said:

"Would you meet me at the Zodiac deck below the aft deck? I have some papers that relate to that bank affair in Ushuaia. They seem to implicate one of our old Antarctic friends. Shall we say later, around nine?"

"What's in those papers?" asked Jim. Would the Antarctic man be Arthur?

"They're are highly confidential. I'm sticking my neck out to show them to you. There's also a connection with the Sheldon Expedition and Carol's father."

"Wasn't the Zodiac deck only for staff and crew?" Jim asked.

"True, but on the last night it won't matter. These papers expose certain people. It is better that we keep the matter hush-hush."

Mark gave a short smile and hurried away. Jim thought maybe the investigation would at last become clear. After his meeting with Mark he would get more out of Rita.

*

In her cabin Carol sat on her suitcase. There was still room for the odd South American souvenir from Ushuaia. She checked her emails on the ship's computer. Some were from friends congratulating her on surviving the rigors of the South Pole.

She lay on her bunk. The cabin was still moving up and down. She had not gone with the doctor's injection for seasickness, but she felt well drugged on the heavy-duty stuff she had bought along. Supposedly it was good for twenty-four hours. She dosed.

CHAPTER FORTY-TWO

The bar crowd relaxed. The voyage was at an end, the unfortunate incidents would be behind them, and life would carry on as before. The Antarctic voyage would be a small but memorable occasion.

Jack his arm firmly around Rachel's slim waist was knocking back the whisky. Rachel giggled happily and sipped her gin and lime. Doreen half way down the lounge took notes. She seemed to be picking up statements from one or two British travelers. Was there to be a legal surprise for Jack back home?

Propping up the bar Frank gripped his rum and coke. Arthur sat with his wife deep in thought. Maisie sitting with Kim blurted out that the time felt dead and then apologized. Shaun and Pam talked with Pierre the French man about hiking around South America especially the Torres del Paine, area, where granite spires, a rock climber's dream, rose vertically for thousands of feet.

Jim sat on the edge of this group. Hopefully everything would become clear with Mark's papers, and then he could deal with the more important issue, Carol. She had not appeared. Must have lots to pack. Would he be acceptable in her suite tonight, or would he be back with Alec and Martin? He had a strong preference, but it took two to make the decision.

The wind picked up. There was a movement of passengers to call it a night. They had said all they could say to like-minded strangers over the past two weeks or so. Most would have two days of traveling, before they could relax at home. The ship was comfortable enough but their own beds were better.

Sandy accepted the few used glasses offered her and started putting the bar to bed. She and Daniel would tot up the liquor sold, and the liquor needed for the next trip.

Jim left it till well past nine before heading to the back end of the boat. No more nautical terms for him. The deck was quiet. A few giant petrels floated along behind in the dark. The waves reared up but for him the sea was manageable. The deck light was dead. No doubt the crew would replace it when they reached port. There was a stern light to indicate where the gangway descended to the Zodiac deck.

The lower deck, loaded with black piled-up nylon boats, was murky. A few outboard motors hung on brackets. It was difficult to see. A cable banged against the side of the ship as the ship rose and fell. Jim waited. It was dark. He wondered if he should have told some one where he was.

Ten minutes later there was still no Mark. Jim turned to head back up when he heard soft steps coming down.

"Sorry, old chap. Had to wait until the coast was clear."

Well, I can't see any coast out there, thought Jim. "So what have you got to show me?"

Mark pulled a small flashlight out of his pocket and produced an envelope.

"You won't tell anyone I've shown you this? It's for your eyes only."

Jim nodded.

"I hope that's a yes."

Jim stepped towards Mark who leaned on a railing and pulled out some papers. Jim could see a smile on

Mark's face and a faint gleam in his eyes from the flashlight.

"Do these papers have to do with those who died?"

Mark looked at him steadily. He reminded Jim of a rancher back home who had an open face, but was competent in gelding and putting animals down. Jim turned slightly to the gangway.

"You should see what else I have here."

Jim turned back as Mark emptied the envelope. There were metallic clinks and flashes of light.

"Here let me shine the flashlight on them."

Mark moved several gold coins from hand to hand

"The cause of Peter, Leon and Boyd's death?"

"I know nothing of Boyd's death. The other two got in the way. Tielmann had to be finished off and Leon had to go. Most of the gold is mine. That slut Rita put you on to Leon and then me?"

"Rita helped as did your lack of excitement when the captain displayed *his* gold coins at dinner."

Mark suddenly pushed Jim against a metal rail gate. It broke away and plunged into the sea followed by Jim. He grabbed the side rail with his left hand as he went over. He hung by one hand. His body rose and banged against the wet slippery hull. Seawater slopped up his legs. The left hand slipped on the wet metal. Up above Mark hammered with his fists on the hand that stopped Jim from plunging into the sea. The strain was telling on the older man. He gasped: "Go, damn you!"

Jim failed to get his right hand on the rail. He grasped his left hand with his right, and hung there. He couldn't do a one-hand pull up. He never could.

A harsh scream broke above. Jim's hand slipped. But it was no longer being battered. He peered up in to the gloom. A long object was repeatedly rammed into Mark's face. Mark put his hands over his crushed nose, and gasped: "Stop!" As he staggered back he slipped through the wet opening and fell past Jim into the sea.

A hand clasped Jim's left wrist.

"I can't pull you up. I'll tie your hand to the rail and get help." Carol's voice was hard. She put a loop around Jim's hand and secured it to the rail. "Don't go anywhere."

Jim with one hand tied, and the rest of him sliding up and down the wet side of the ship, couldn't see any reason for doing that. He hung on until a few passengers pulled him up, untied his hand and placed him on the deck. Jim, soaked, crouched there rubbing his wrist.

"You *are* a tough Canadian," said Carol.

Greg looked at him closely. "I suppose I'll find out what's been happening. I seem to be in the dark about a lot of things."

Jim mumbled: "Mark?"

The procession of Bernard, the first officer, on one side, Greg on the other, and Carol and the few passengers behind herded Jim along the deck to meet the captain. A few faces peered out of the lounge windows as the group moved by. Another unexplained happening on this voyage of discovery?

With only Bernard and Carol allowed in, (Greg felt put upon as expedition leader that he was excluded), Jim sat down. He enjoyed the aquavit. Carol and Bernard did not refuse theirs. The captain had already told the bridge to circle back in case Mark Stringer surfaced. He didn't.

Jim explained about the secret meeting with Mark. He apologized that he had not been more sensible. The captain grunted. Jim told of the coins in Mark's hands, his comments and Mark's push on him against the gate.

"It wasn't fastened," Jim said.

The first officer said the bolts had been removed.

"You were not supposed to get to Ushuaia," said the captain dryly.

Jim said that Mark slipped over the edge.

Carol, her eyes shining with excitement and liquor, supported Jim's statement.

"So, why were *you* there?" Bernard turned to Carol.

Carol explained she had dozed and then got up to find Jim. Martin had said he had seen Jim head to the stern, followed after a while by Mark. She had heard sounds on the lower deck, and saw Mark trying to push Jim into the sea. Using her only weapon, her three hundred millimeter lens, she hit Mark. He slipped into the sea.

"The strap came in handy as well. I couldn't pull Jim up so I tied his wrist to the railing. See how useful good camera equipment is?" Carol looked pointedly at Jim. "But it's going to cost you." He received a smile.

Jim gave one in return. He felt like one of the heroes in the thrillers he read, but he also felt rather tired.

" I suppose he had most of the gold?" The captain's question was answered with a slow nod.

" Three deaths for those coins." he added.

"Mark said he was not responsible for Boyd's death," answered Jim, "but he admitted to Peter and Leon's."

Murder in the Antarctic

The captain said: "I will get more from you tomorrow before we reach port. See me early. I have a lot of paperwork to deal with. A report will have to go to the Argentinean authorities, but at least we will not have passengers out on bail screaming law suits. I assume everyone can go home."

Carol and Jim headed to her cabin.

"Care to relax here?" she asked.

"Do I have a choice?"

Carol didn't answer, but said: "I knew I had to keep an eye on you. Will you need more rescuing soon?"

"If it's you I will like that."

They looked at each other for some time.

"We don't have to do any dramas." Carol slowly undressed. Jim felt better, for some reason.

"Dramas?" he asked.

"Plays, you know, four plays, fore…" She said nothing else and naked got in between the sheets. A bare shoulder and one rounded breast looked at Jim.

"I wonder if I should retire to my own cabin." Jim felt he needed to take charge of what was going on.

"If I say please would that help?"

"I can never say no to a damsel in distress."

Jim locked the door, slapped the light off, threw his clothes on the floor and joined Carol under the sheets.

CHAPTER FORTY-THREE

The *Polar Adventurer* moved briskly along the Beagle Channel. At Ushuaia it would unload one lot of passengers before taking on more for the next trip south. Green hills bordered the waterway. The sun rose behind the ship. A few gulls followed the early morning journey.

Jim got up from Carol's bed, grinned at the dark tousled sleeping head, and headed down to his washroom. He knew that there would be a rush for the shower on the last morning. Jim had some packing and a few bits of information for Captain Engstrom. Martin noted his reappearance and said:

"You'll going have to make a more permanent arrangement with that lady of yours. Mind you, you'll be doing doubles."

Jim gave him a quizzical look.

"Two countries, two jobs, two cars and two kids."

Jim smiled and quickly threw his clothes into his bag. He had still not read *As You Like It*. The book held emails, and then they were gone. They must have been stolen by a crewmember, a friend of Mark's. Jim met the captain, as the hills became dark-pointed mountains near Ushuaia.

Captain Engstrom sagged at his desk. He looked as he had been there all night. "I should hire you to do some of this paper work."

Jim thanked him and said he had had done enough already.

"It was tough questioning people who didn't want to give answers to the robbery and the murders."

Murder in the Antarctic

"We now have all the four gold stashes. One was in a storage locker. The final one, Mark Stringer's I think, was hidden behind an access door on top of the luggage lift. The bank is pleased. You and I will be sharing a finder's fee.

"And maybe the company will give you a free trip as compensation" added Captain Engstrom.

Jim said he would think about it. He realized he had never had a chance to show his Arctic slides. Oh, well, the passengers could just sign up for an Arctic cruise and get their own.

On the main deck passengers stood in small groups with little to say to each other. They had become strangers again. Email addresses had been swapped for those who wanted them. After the recent death the list was rather tentative.

The mountains still overlooked the spread out city of Ushuaia. The ship nosed home towards the pier. Bow thrusters moved the vessel sideways. Hawsers were dropped to the men below. Along both sides of the pier other vessels were ready to head south to the Antarctic. The pilot went down the gangway. Several custom officials and local agents went up.

Passengers clutching their passports stood around watching the activities as the city woke to another day. Groups of luggage lay around, each piece color coded with ribbon. Red for those immediately departing Ushuaia, blue for later flights, and yellow for those making their own way home via the Galapagos Island, Easter Island or where ever.

The smiling staff checked that the passengers had everything, and made small talk. There was relief that this trip was over. By four o'clock another trip would be on its way. Staff members had a few hours ashore before welcoming more travelers. Greg and Elsa had maybe an hour before being back on board to dish out more hospitality. Greg hoped that the next trip was normal. This trip had been anything but.

Most of the staff, looked upon by some as firm friends, stood on the pier as the passengers descended to their buses. Along the line of staff some passengers hugged their favorites, others shook hands, and a couple of the Dutch women gave continental kisses on both cheeks. Pamela gave a gracious nod. Doug tailed by Ron and Ed edged towards a bus. He did not look at anyone.

The future looked more promising for Jim. He had a finder's fee, another possible trip and best of all, Carol. Where would they live? Canada or England? He felt happy with her. Would he make the same mistake as with Janet? Unlikes not getting along for the long term? But wasn't it always the case with men and women? There was no certainty in relationships or in anything else for that matter.

To heck with it he thought just take the plunge. As Martin suggested: permanency. What did Paul Pléneau say when asked by the old Antarctic explorer Charcot to come traveling with him: "Where you like. When you like. For as long as you like." What ever happened to Jim he was certain it would not be as bad as what was going to happen to Jack when Doreen's lawyers got to him. Jim thought he should see Elsa about changing the ribbon color for their luggage. A change of destination was in the offing.

Elsa came up to Jim with a letter. She turned and moved quietly away.

Murder in the Antarctic

Jim opened the letter:

Jim,
I enjoyed quite a bit of our trip. But there was no closure for me over my father's death. Maybe there never will be. Arthur's comments about looking after Boyd and the research, but not my father, not even in memory, grated. As Arthur said they needed to move on and they did.
I cannot.
If we had got together permanently I would have had to admit something to you. I can't. I wouldn't have expected you to stay with me if you knew what I had done.
You must move on with your life. You are still young. I don't feel young.
Thanks for the little help you gave.
Carol

Jim stood looking at the passengers heading to their buses, the bustle of the port and the giant petrels arguing in the water. He clutched the letter and felt empty. Near the end of the pier he saw a dark haired woman moving quickly into the town. She did not look back.

Acknowledgements:

Thanks to Alan Buswell, Marion and Gerry Hofmann, Valmar Kurol, Peter and Dianne MacLaurin, and, of course, Norma and Julie.

Murder in the Antarctic

CPSIA information can be obtained at www.ICGtesting.com
Printed in the USA
LVOW12s1048020114

367467LV00005B/2/P